sunglasses after dark

10TH ANNIVERSARY EDITION

NANCY A. COLLINS

WHITE WOLF INC.

Sunglasses After Dark
A White Wolf, Inc. Publication

Edited by: Susan Barrows, Robert Hatch and Liz Tornabene
Cover Art: Thom Ang
Interior Art: Thom Ang, Jeff Pittarelli, Stan Shaw, Hal Robins, Paul Mavrides, Kelly Jones, Matt Howarth, Dan Henderson.
Cover Design: Talon Dunning

Published by:
White Wolf Inc.
735 Park North Boulevard, Suite 128
Clarkston, GA 30021
http://www.white-wolf.com

INTRODUCTION

a Word from the author

Welcome, gentle readers. You hold in your hands the special tenth anniversary edition of my first novel, Sunglasses After Dark. Whoa! Has it been ten years already? It still feels weird to refer to things a decade past and realize I was thirty at the time, not in third grade. When Sunglasses After Dark first hit the bookstores, George Bush was still in office; the Gulf War had yet to happen; Sinatra, Phil Hartman, Jimmy Stewart, Dr. Seuss, Princess Diana, Robert Bloch and Karl Edward Wagner, amongst a host of others, were still amongst the living; O.J. Simpson, Michael Jackson and Pee-Wee Herman were untainted by scandal; no one had ever heard of the Spice Girls, the Back Street Boys, Pokemon, Beanie Babies, JonBenet Ramsey, Monica Lewinsky, or The X-Files. Oh, yeah, and horror fiction was hotter than a worm on a summer sidewalk. What a difference 3,650 days make, eh?

On a more personal level, the ten years since Sonja Blue was introduced into the pop culture roller derby have been the most eventful of my life. I was exceptionally lucky in that my first foray into novel-length fiction enjoyed favorable reviews and sales, enough so to make it a bestseller within a year of its release. Since then its garnered a couple of awards and become an "cult classic". Of course, freshman success can be both a blessing and a curse, but I will wait until I'm on my deathbed to decide how much of the sweet or the shitty end of the stick I've had to endure as a writer. Although the jury may still be out on the blessing/curse issue, I can definitely say that the character of Sonja Blue has assumed a life of her own. Since its initial publication, *Sunglasses After Dark* has been reprinted in nine languages, there have been three sequels (with a fourth on the way), a comic book adaptation, and a couple of licensed T-shirts and prints featuring Sonja in all her undead glory. I have also had the dubious honor of seeing altered-enough-to-avoid-litigation rip-offs of my characters and ideas exploited in various popular entertainment. As my friend Howard Kaylan of The Turtles/Mothers of Invention fame once told me: "Thievery is the sincerest form of flattery." I am also reminded by the wisdom of another icon of the 1960's: "You knew the job was dangerous when you took it, Fred."

I am very excited and pleased with this special edition of Sunglasses. For one, I handpicked the artists whose very individual (and demented) visions of Sonja, Claude, Lord Morgan and the Real World of the Pretenders grace these pages. I believe they have done a superlative job in translating not just the words on the page into pictures, but also the psychology behind the text. I've also used this special edition to return a couple of quotes that were removed from the first printing by NAL's editorial department because they were uncertain of the copyright laws and decided to play things safe by excluding them from the text. It was hardly a Deal Breaker, as far as I was concerned, but it always bugged me. So if you're curious, you can flip to the section breaks for The Danger Ward and The Real World to check out the previously expunged quotes. In closing, I wish to extend my appreciation to all of you out there who have followed the adventures of Sonja Blue over the last decade, and have been so supportive of my work and career.

And for those of you out there who are just now reading *Sunglasses After Dark* for the first time, please keep your arms and legs within the ride at all times.

Nancy A. Collins
Atlanta, Georgia
October 21, 1999

PROLOGUE

Its horror and beauty are divine upon its lips and eyelids seem to lie loveliness like a shadow, from which shine fiery and lurid, struggling underneath, the agonies of anguish and of death.

--Shelley, *The Beauty Of The Medusea.*

Moon.

Big white moon.

White as milk moon.

You're all I can see from my window, here in the dark. Your light falls silver and white across the walls of my cell. The night-tide surges strong in me. So strong I can feel the grip of their drugs loosen. They fancy themselves high priests. Their gods have names like Thorazine and Lithium and Shock Therapy. But their gods are new and weak and cannot hope to contain me much longer. For I am the handiwork of far more powerful, far more ancient deities. Very soon my blood will learn the secret of the inhibiting factors the white-coated shamans pump into my veins. And then things will be very different, my beautiful moon.

My big moon.

White as milk moon.

Red as blood moon.

DANGER WARD

"We all go a little mad sometimes."
--Norman Bates

Claude Hagerty's watch played "The Yellow Rose of Texas." Grumbling to himself, he stuck the dog-eared Louis L'Amour paperback in the top drawer of the desk and produced the keys to the Danger Ward from the depths of his orderly's whites. Three o'clock in the morning. Time for his rounds.

Claude had been an orderly for most of his adult life. He'd originally intended to go into pro football, but a bad knee injury in high school put an end to that career before it had the chance to begin. He later discovered that standing 6'3" and tipping the scales at 280 pounds had its distinct advantages in the healthcare field. However, even at the age of thirty-eight, with high school twenty years gone and his midsection devolved into flab, Claude Hagerty was still an impressive specimen.

He started work at Elysian Fields seven years ago, and as funny farms go, it was an okay job. It sure beat the hell out of the state hospital. Elysian Fields didn't waste time on charity cases. The hospital's clients were the sons and daughters, mothers and fathers of prestigious families. The sanitarium specialized in "dependency problems," but for those with relatives whose difficulties tended to be far more serious than a fondness for tranquilizers and vodka, there was the Danger Ward.

The reinforced steel door, painted a festive pastel for the benefit of the visitors, separated the nursing station from the rest of the ward. Claude rolled the barrier back enough to squeeze through. He remembered an old cartoon from his childhood, where a mouse ran in and out of the jaws of a sleeping cat. Funny how he always thought of that when he did his rounds.

He walked past the dayroom, where the better-behaved inmates were allowed to watch television and play Ping-Pong during the afternoon. Most were so heavily medicated all they could do was sit and stare at the tube or out the windows. There was no attempt at rehabilitation in the Danger Ward, although no one came right out and said it. Just as no one mentioned the exact reasons why these people were locked up. That was what you paid for. All in all, Elysian Fields wasn't any different from any other private asylum. Except for her.

He grimaced involuntarily. Hell, this used to be an easy shift. Except for a patient having the odd nightmare now and then, there wasn't much for him to worry about. He could catch up on his reading, watch TV, even nap if he felt like it, without worrying about being disturbed.

That was before they dragged her in, six months ago. It had been during his shift; she was bound in a straitjacket and, God as his witness, a length of chain, with four strong men handling her. And still she lashed about, yowling like a wild thing. For a minute it looked as if she would get loose. Claude could still hear the sharp snap of the chain breaking. Then Dr. Wexler was there, syringe in hand, jabbing the needle through the canvas into the woman beneath. She collapsed immediately, motor nerves severed. Judging from the size of the dosage, she should have died. Claude was ordered to carry her into Room 7. That was the first time he touched her. It was enough.

That's when his job got tough. Since that night, his shift had yet to go by without one of the inmates waking up with the night horrors. They all claimed the woman in Room 7 walked into their dreams. They couldn't—or wouldn't—elaborate on the details. Claude described the dreams to Dr. Morial, the ward's on-call psychiatrist. Morial asked him if he liked his job. Claude let it drop.

Life was complicated enough without trying to figure out why a bunch of loonies should fixate on a fellow inmate they had never seen. Or how they could describe her so well. He wondered if the patients were as restless during the day. He didn't think so. *She* wasn't active during the day.

I hear the warder's heavy tread as he checks his charges one by one. It is night and the doctors have fled, leaving the patients alone with their dreams. It's been too long since I could think this clearly. It took me two months to crawl out of madness. Another three passed before my biosystem began to break down the narcotic cocktails they pump into me every day. Their drugs won't do them any good; with every night that passes my immunity grows stronger. My mind is my own again. It's been so long. Perhaps too long.

I fear irreparable damage was done while I was away. The Other has been doing . . . things. I'm not sure what, but I can feel the changes deep inside me. The Other has been free to move unchecked. I have to get out of here before something horrible occurs. I may have already done something. Possibly hurt someone. I can't remember, and I do not want to scan the Other's memory for clues. I'm still weak and could easily become lost in its personality. I cannot risk that. Not now.

The Other's been dream-walking, of that I'm certain. It hasn't gone unnoticed, although I should feel lucky they're only lunatics. No one believes them. No one wants to believe them. I've got to get out of here before I lose control. I haven't fought the Other this long in order to surrender in a madhouse. But I'm so tired. Too receptive. I can feel their dreams pressing in on me, like some great unseen weight. I've become a magnet for their nightmares. That worries me. I've never been able to do this before. What other changes have occurred during my lapse?

The guard is nearing the end of his rounds. I can hear his footsteps echoing in the hall and his ragged breathing. He's a big man. I can smell his sweat. I can taste his fear. He's checking on the inmate next door. It'll be my turn next. He always saves me for last. I guess it's because he's scared of me. I don't blame him. I'm scared of me, too.

Claude's frown deepened as he watched Malcolm whimper in his sleep. Even without medication, Malcolm usually enjoyed the slumber of a child. Now he writhed under the bedclothes, his face blanched and perspiring. His lips moved in feeble protest to some unknown command. He'd be waking up in a few minutes, screaming his lungs out, but Claude knew better than to try to shake the boy awake; the last time he'd tried it he'd damned near lost a finger. Malcolm liked to bite.

Locked in his dream, Malcolm moaned and knotted the sheets with blind fingers. The muscles in his clenched jaw jumped as his teeth ground together. Claude shook his head and shut the observation plate set into the face of the metal door.

There was only one patient left to check. The one in Room 7. Claude wasn't even sure of her name. The charts and medication logs simply read "Blue, S." She was the last one on his rounds every night, simply because it took him that long to work up the nerve to look at her. Maybe it was different during the day. Perhaps in the sanity of daylight she was just another loony, but he doubted it.

The door to Room 7 was the same as the others, a cheerily painted piece of metal strong enough to withstand a two-ton battering ram. An observation silt, covered with heavy-gauge wire mesh and protected by a sliding metal plate, was set into the door at eye level, although Claude had to stoop a bit to look through it. The interior of Room 7 was radically different from the others on the ward. The other inmates had rooms that— except for the heavy padding on the walls, the narrow high-set windows, and the naked light bulbs locked in impenetrable cages of wire—could be mistaken for suites found in a typical Holiday Inn. Elysian Fields furnished the rooms with unbreakable fixtures and beds with matching designer sheets and restraining gear.

Room 7 was bare of everything but its occupant. There wasn't even a bed. She slept curled up on the padded floor, tucked into the far corner, where the shadows were deepest, like a hibernating animal. At least that's how Claude imagined it. He'd never seen her asleep. Taking a deep breath, he flicked back the latch on the observation plate and slid it open. Yep, there she was.

Blue crouched in the middle of her cell, her face angled toward the high, narrow window set ten feet from the floor. She was naked except for the straitjacket, her bare legs folded under her as if she were at prayer.

It was hard to tell how old she was, but Claude guessed she couldn't be more than twenty-three. Her filthy hair hung about her face in rattails. None of the nurses wanted to touch her after what happened to Kalish. Not that Claude blamed them.

She knew he was watching, just as he'd known she'd be there, crouching like a spider in the middle of its web. He waited silently for her to acknowledge him, yet dreading it at the same time. It had become a ritual between them.

She turned her head in his direction. Claude's stomach tightened and there was a thundering in his ears. He felt as if he was barreling down a steep hill in a car without brakes. Her eyes locked on him with a predator's guile. She inclined her chin a fraction of an inch, signaling her awareness of his presence. Claude felt himself respond in kind, like a puppet on a string, and then he was hurrying back down the corridor.

In the darkness, Malcolm woke up screaming.

The scene opens on a vast auditorium, its floor jammed with row upon row of metal folding chairs. Wheelchairs clutter the aisles. Behind the raised stage hangs a mammoth banner bearing the likeness of a smiling man. His nose is strong and straight, the cheekbones high, and his wide, toothy grin does not extend to the hawklike eyes nestled beneath the bushy white eyebrows. His silvery mane would be the envy of an Old Testament patriarch.

The eternally smiling man is Zebulon "Zeb" Wheele: Man of God, Healer of the Sick, Speaker of Prophecy, and founder of the Wheeles of God Ministry. The superimposed electronic graphics explain, for those viewing at home, that this "healing event" has taken place in Dallas, Texas, three months previous.

The audience, most of whom are encumbered by canes and walkers, clap and sing hymns while awaiting their chance to be touched by the divine. Many study the huge portrait tapestry, comparing it to the reduced likenesses printed on the back of their programs. The air is heavy with sweat, hope, and anxiety.

Suddenly, the lights go down and a spotlight hits the stage. The organ music swells and a figure strides from the wings. It is a woman in a gold lamé pantsuit, her hair shellacked into a Gordian knot. The applause is thunderous.

The woman is Sister Catherine, widow of the late Zebulon Wheele. It is she they have come to see.

Catherine Wheele accepts the welcome, smiling broadly and throwing kisses to the crowd. She takes the microphone from the podium and addresses the faithful.

"Hallelujah, brothers and sisters! Hallelujah! It gladdens my heart to know that the words and deeds of my late husband, the Reverend Zebulon Wheele, are still manifest in the healed flesh and joyful spirits of those who felt the power of Our Lord Jesus Christ through his loving hands! Every day I receive hundreds of letters from y'all out there, telling me how Zebulon changed your lives. The sick made well! The deaf to hear! The blind to see!

"But I also hear from those who say they are forlorn. They are afraid they'll never know the miracle of Jesus' divine mercy, that they'll never see salvation, because Zebulon was"—she struggles to suppress the hitch in her voice—"called to God. Are these poor souls doomed to live their lives in pain and torment, never to know the grace and forgiveness of Our Lord? Say no!"

"No!" Only a few voices respond.

"Is it? Say no!" Her voice becomes harsh and demanding.

"No," the coliseum answers.

"Is it? Say no!"

"*No!*" Two thousand voices—shrill and pure, baritone and falsetto, weak and strong—join together.

Catherine Wheele smiles. She is pleased. Once more she is a pleasant Sunday-school teacher.

"Do not fear, brothers and sisters! While it is true Brother Zebulon is no longer among you, Sister Catherine is here! As Elijah's mantle fell upon Elishah, so was Zebulon's gift passed on to me. At the time of my darling Zeb's tragic death, I received a vision! I saw Zebulon standing between two angels so beautiful it hurt to look at them. Zebulon said, 'Honey, I have to go now, but promise me you'll carry on my work. Promise me that.'

"I said, 'Zeb, I can't do the things you do. No one can!'

"But Zeb just smiled and said, 'As I leave all my earthly things to you, so do I bequeath my gifts! Have faith and the Lord shall see you through!' Can I get an amen on that?"

"Amen!"

"As it was written in First Corinthians, Chapter Twelve, I found myself blessed with the gifts of knowledge and healing! 'To one is given utterance of knowledge according to the same Spirit, to another gifts of healing!' I was overcome by the glory of Christ and I fell to the floor and stayed there all night, crying and praying and blessing my sweet savior. Now I am able to continue my husband's good works, and that's what y'all are here for, isn't it, brothers and sisters? Say yes!"

"*Yes.*"

"I shall not disappoint you, friends. I have mighty big shoes to fill"—she gestures to the banner draped behind her and its lesser brothers hanging from the coliseum's I-beams—"and for me to let you down would be the greatest sin I have ever committed."

The "healing event" then proceeds according to its own peculiar rituals and traditions. The choir sings. Sister Catherine exhorts the crowd to give generously to her crusade to build a Zebulon Wheele Memorial Chapel in his Arkansas hometown. Strapping young men work the crowd, carrying large plastic trashcans in place of offering plates. A thirty-nine-year-old woman with "sugar diabetes" is brought from the audience and told to throw down her insulin. She obeys and Sister Catherine grinds the ampules into the floorboards with one deft twist of her high heel. The crowd roars amens. Sister Catherine reminds the congregation to give generously to the Zebulon Wheele Memorial Home for Unwed Mothers. An elderly man suffering from a heart condition is wheeled on stage. Sister Catherine places her hand inches from the man's forehead, then strikes him with the flat of her palm. The man begins to shriek and howl in ecstasy, his arms spinning like pinwheels. Sister Catherine grabs hold of the supplicant and pulls him to his feet. To the amusement of the crowd, the euphoric old man pushes her across the stage in the wheelchair. By the time they reach the speaker's podium, the old man's face is beet-red. Two young men in dark suits with narrow ties and narrower lapels emerge from the wings and hastily escort him into the darkness beyond the lights.

The congregation is well-pleased. They clap and shout and stamp their feet. "Hallelujah! Amen! Praise the Lord!" rebounds from the walls. Sister Catherine accepts their veneration, not a hair out of place, her hands held high. Her gold lamé pantsuit shimmers in the lights from the cameras. Tears of humility smear her makeup, leaving dark trails on her cheeks.

"His will be done! His will be done, brothers and sisters! As it was said in Matthew, Chapter Fifteen: 'Great crowds came to him, bringing with them the lame, the maimed, the blind, and the dumb, and he healed them so that they marveled when the dumb spoke, the maimed became whole, the lame walked, and the blind saw!' Praise God! Praise . . ." Sister Catherine falls abruptly silent, her eyes sweeping the auditorium. "Someone here is in dire need of healing. I can feel that need, calling out to God to ease the pain. I have healed others tonight, but this need is greater than all of those combined. Tell me, Lord. Tell me the name of this afflicted soul, so I might minister to his needs." Sister Catherine lowers her head, seeking divine counsel as she prays into the microphone.

The camera slowly pans the audience as they wait for God to speak to Catherine Wheele. Who will it be? Who will be called out to be healed? There are many worthy of attention. The ushers made sure they were seated in the front rows, where the camera could see them. The cameramen linger on particularly pathetic cases: an elderly woman so twisted by osteoporosis she sees nothing but her feet, a drooling microcephalic supported on either side by his parents, a once-pretty girl who fell from her boyfriend's motorcycle and slid twenty feet across an asphalt road facedown. The camera studies these deformities of accident and nature with the eye of a connoisseur.

Catherine Wheele's head snaps up. Her voice is tight with excitement. "Is there a George Belwether here tonight? George Belwether of 1005 Hawthorne?"

The crowd murmurs among itself as everyone turns in their seats to see who will rise and go to be healed. No one doubts there is a body to go along with the name and address. She always knows.

A fragile-looking man seated near the front stands up. The same young men who helped the old man with the heart condition, or their twins, move from the base of the pulpit and into the congregation. Flashes of gold at their wrists leave smears of light on the camera's retina. Their eyes are shielded from the klieg lights' glare by expensive designer sunglasses.

The man they escort from the audience is dying of cancer. He stands between the healthy young men, his flesh the color of bad meat. Chemotherapy has robbed him of his hair and most of his teeth; it is impossible to say if he is young or old. By the time they reach the podium, the man is visibly exhausted.

Sister Catherine rests one hand on his shoulder. Her manicured fingernails, lacquered until they shine like fresh blood, grip the man's ill-fitting suit.

"Brother, how long has the cancer afflicted you?" She thrusts the microphone into his face.

Belwether forces his eyes from the mammoth visage of Zebulon Wheele hanging from the ceiling. "Five years, Sister Catherine."

"And what did your doctors say?"

"It's inoperable. I only have a few months, maybe weeks . . ."

The crowd moans in sympathy, like the prompted gasps of surprise and envy heard on game shows.

"Have you tried everything, Brother George?"

Belwether's balding head bobs up and down. "Chemotherapy, laetrile, crystals, fire-walking, channeling . . ."

"But have you tried God, brother?" Her voice develops an admonishing edge. Once more the microphone is thrust into his trembling face.

"No, not until now . . . not until tonight!" Tears stream down the dying man's face. The camera moves in closer; his pallid features fill the screen. "Help me, Sister Catherine! I don't want to die . . . Please . . ." His hands, as thin and flaccid as an old woman's, clasp hers. His sobs threaten to knock him to the floor.

"Do you believe in the Lord God Jesus Christ's power to bring the dead to life, to make the blind see, the deaf hear, and the lame well again?"

Belwether presses his cheek against her fingers, his eyes welded shut by tears. "IbelieveIbelieveIbelieve."

"And are you prepared, Brother George, to accept the Ultimate Healing?"

He nods, overcome by emotion. The congregation mutters knowingly.

Catherine Wheele motions for one of the stagehands to take charge of the microphone and her gold lamé jacket. The camera pulls back to get a better view of the miracle. She grasps the dying man's shoulders, forcing him to kneel before her, his back to the audience. The congregation holds its collective breath; the Ultimate Healing is the reason they attend services. Even in his heyday, Zebulon Wheele never attempted anything so grandiose and controversial.

After rolling back her sleeves, she raises her right hand above her head, splaying the fingers and rotating the palm so everyone can see it is empty. Her hand remains suspended, the muscles in the forearm twitching and jumping like live wires. Then her hand plunges downward, like an eagle diving to snatch its prey, and disappears into George Belwether.

The supplicant's mouth opens so wide the skin threatens to split and reveal the skull beneath. There is no sound. His head snaps backward until the crown nearly touches his spine. His eyes roll in their sockets and his tongue jerks uncontrollably. The audience cries out in horror.

It is impossible to tell if George Belwether is being eviscerated or having a powerful orgasm. The front of his torso is hidden from the lens of the camera, but it looks as if she is rummaging around in an empty gunnysack.

With a yell of triumph, Catherine Wheele removes her arm from the dying man's stomach. Her bare arm is slick with blood and bowel juices. The congregation comes to its feet, roaring their approval and shouting her name over and over. The thing she holds aloft is a grayish-black lump the size of a child's softball. It pulses and twitches in her grip. Belwether lies at her feet, showing no sign of movement. The young men reappear and drag him off stage. The rubber tips of his shoes leave skid marks on the stage's waxed surface.

A stagehand hurries on camera with a silver washbasin and a white towel. Another stagehand pins a lapel mike onto her vest so she can speak as she cleanses herself.

"See, brothers and sisters? See what belief in the Word of God can do for you? See what the power of Jesus Christ Our Lord is capable of if only you open up your hearts and accept His divine glory? Thus sayeth the Lord: 'He who Believeth in me shall not perish, but shall have Everlasting life!' and if y'all don't want to perish, brothers and sisters at home, send me your love offering and I shall protect you from the diseases of sin and Satan, just as my husband did before me. Send us your seed gifts, and remember, that which you give to the Lord shall be returned to you tenfold! So send us twenty dollars, or ten dollars, or whatever you can, brothers and sisters! Don't let doubt enter your mind. Act today! If you doubt, then you are lost to Jesus! Pick up your phone and give ol' Sister Catherine a call!"

An electronic superimposure comes on the screen, explaining how the check and money orders should be made out and what major credit cards are accepted, should the audience at home wish to call the toll-free Love Offering Hotline. Operators standing by.

"Jesus Christ," muttered Hagerty, thumbing the off button on the TV set. Sister Catherine and her congregation became the dwindling white dot in the middle of a cathode tube.

Hagerty wondered, not for the first time, what the hell was wrong with him. Here he was, spending his waking hours among psychotics, paranoid-schizophrenics, neurotics, and compulsive personalities of every possible persuasion, so why waste his time watching a bunch of religious kooks who'd escaped diagnosis and bought themselves a TV studio?

Claude massaged his eyes. Deep down part of him was fascinated by the sleazy geek-show theatrics and cheap tricks. In a lot of ways it was not unlike watching wrestling. But the truth was that he was watching in order to keep from falling asleep.

Moving from behind the nursing station, Hagerty unplugged the little portable black-and-white set and carried it back into the staff lounge. He hated watching television in the lounge—especially alone at night. The damned vending machines hummed and clicked constantly. Claude always had the feeling they were conspiring among themselves.

There was a long, well-padded sofa located just inside the door. How nice it'd be to take a nap. He shook his head to clear it. No way! He stuck a quarter in the coffee dispenser and selected black, straight up. As if to give credence to his suspicions concerning vending-machine malice, the paper cup dropped through the chute at an angle, and before he could act to correct it, the hot coffee sluiced out, splashing his crotch, the legs of his trousers, and the floor.

"Great! Just fuckin' great!"

After mopping up the spilled coffee and dabbing halfheartedly at his pants with a wad of wet toilet paper, Claude returned to his post. He was still sleepy.

Hagerty wasn't afraid of being discovered asleep on the job. He'd spent many shifts sacked out, his feet propped in an open drawer, but that was before the nightmares. That was the real problem.

He would be on the verge of drifting into deep sleep, where the senses ignore the outside world and react to signals generated by the mind. It always started there, for some reason. Hagerty's conscious mind, still striving for control, would realize he was starting to dream. Suddenly, he wasn't alone anymore. He couldn't see what it was that was sharing his dreams; it moved too fast, a hint of movement at the corner of his mind's eye, made of shadow and chaos. He could see its eyes, though, reflecting light like those of a cat caught in the headlights of a car. He wanted to tell it to leave, but he was too far into dreamtime to make a sound.

The shadow thing scurried through his brain, digging with the frantic energy of a burrowing rodent. When it finished ransacking his mind, it became very still, as if sensing Hagerty's awareness for the first time. And then it would smile.

Claude always woke up at that point, his limbs tingling as if from a mild electric shock.

Maybe he was going insane. All those years being exposed to crazy people were bound to have an effect, like water dripping on a stone, gradually eroding it away. His brain probably looked like the Grand Canyon.

He didn't feel insane, but that's how it starts; you're perfectly normal except for one little obsession, then—whammo!—you're wearing hats made out of aluminum foil so the men from Planet X can't see into your head and read your thoughts.

But he knew he wasn't crazy. There was something wrong with Blue, S. Something no one wanted to acknowledge, much less talk about. Kalish was proof of that.

Hagerty didn't like thinking about the last time he saw Kalish. And without meaning to, he began to doze.

He was at work. He wasn't supposed to be there. It was his night off. He'd been bowling with some friends. Out late. Left something at work. Couldn't remember what. Decided to stop by and check his locker. It was after midnight when he got to Elysian Fields.

Went to the locker room. Surprised to see Red Franklin going off-shift. Red was supposed to be filling in for him. Red said there'd been a change in the schedule. Archie Kalish ended up pulling Claude's shift.

The dream memory begins to speed up and slow down at the same time. Kalish. The damned fools put Kalish in charge! His heart began pumping faster. He didn't want to go to the Danger Ward. He knew what he'd find there. But his dream pulled him down the corridor of memory. Maybe if he was faster, this time things would be different. His movements were slow and clumsy, as if he were moving underwater. The elevator took an eternity to arrive, the doors opening in slow motion. Hagerty wanted to scream at it to hurry up.

He shoved his hand into his trouser pocket, searching for the key ring that would give him access to the Danger Ward. His arm went in up to the elbow. His pocket had been replaced by a black hole. He reached farther down until his shoulder was level with his hip. His fingertips brushed cold metal and he withdrew the keys. His fingers were numb from being in the black hole and he had to struggle to keep from dropping the keys. Fumbling, he finally located the circular key that fit into the recessed override lock that would take him to the Danger Ward.

The elevator groaned and began its sluggish movement upward. Hagerty cursed and pounded his fists against the walls, trying to hurry the damn thing along.

Kalish! The idiots left Kalish up there. Alone. Unsupervised. Hagerty had no love for the bastard. It was rumored he abused patients, like poor Mrs. Goldman. And the brain-dead teenager in Ward C. The one who'd smacked her head into a dashboard at 80 mph. The one who turned up pregnant.

The doors of the elevator opened like a wound. The Danger Ward was dark, the only light coming from the empty nursing station. Claude moved forward, his feet adhering to the floor with every step. His muscles strained until he thought they'd tear from their moorings. His clothes were plastered to his skin.

The gate was unlocked, but had somehow trebled its weight. Dozens of voices were raised in mindless sound. As he continued down the hall, he separated individual words and occasional sentences from the verbal chaos.

"Mamamamama..."

"Blood ... see blood ... on the walls ... the halls full ... flood of blood ..."

"They're here! I can feel them! Make them stop, please ...

"Go away, go away, I don't want you here, go away ..."

"Get her out of me! Get her out!"

Time expanded. Every heartbeat was an hour. Every breath a week. He could see his arm stretching out, his hand reaching for the door handle of Room 7. It took a year for his fingers to lock around the knob. Two years for it to turn in his grip. It was unlocked. Of course.

The door swung open and Hagerty saw he was too late. He would always be too late.

It was dark in Room 7. Unfortunately, there was still enough light for him to see what was going on.

Kalish was sprawled on his back, arms and legs akimbo. His pants and underwear were snarled around his ankles. He still had his shoes on. His legs were pale and skinny. Kalish's penis lay cold and wet against his thigh like an albino slug. Hagerty couldn't see Kalish's face because the room's tenant was kneeling over the body, her head tucked between its right shoulder blade and neck.

Time snapped and Hagerty found himself speeding toward the woman in the straitjacket. Grabbing her by the shoulders, he pulled her off the corpse and held her at arm's length. He caught a glimpse of Kalish's face and the shredded mess where his throat should have been.

Claude pinned the struggling madwoman against a wall, making sure her feet cleared the floor. Her screams, twisted by memory and dreamtime, began to echo inside his head.

When he was a kid he used to spend his summers on his grandparents' farm in Mississippi. During one of his vacations a swamp cat went rogue and terrorized the community, killing chickens and neighborhood pets. When an itinerant field-worker was found badly mauled in a ditch outside of town, the farmers formed a hunting party and chased the panther into a canebrake. Rather than risk their prize coon dogs by sending them after the big cat, they decided to set the field ablaze. The panther was roasted alive, screaming its rage and pain like a demon in hell.

The crazy woman opened her mouth, and the burning panther's yell came out.

All he could see of her face, hidden by a filthy tangle of hair, were eyes that resembled twin bullet holes. His throat burned with bile, but he managed to keep his grip on her.

What now? He couldn't hold her until the day shift showed up. And if he let go, she'd be on him before he could make it to the door. His arms ached as if skewers pierced his biceps.

A white-sleeved arm snaked around his left shoulder. Light glittered off glass and sterile steel as the syringe punctured the straitjacket and the flesh underneath. The woman shrieked, then went limp. Claude stepped away and allowed her to drop to the floor. She looked like a mistreated rag doll.

Dr. Wexler pushed Hagerty aside, kneeling beside the straitjacketed patient. Her head lolled back and for one brief moment Claude found himself looking into the eyes of an animal with its leg in a trap. Then he saw the blood on her mouth. As he watched, her tongue wriggled between her bloodied lips and licked them clean, like a cat grooming itself after the hunt.

Wexler glanced up at him. "Good job . . . Hagerty, isn't it? Good job." As he stood, Wexler wiped the palms of his hands against his pant legs. "Of course, none of this happened."

Wexler wasn't really looking at him. Claude turned to see two young men in dark suits and sunglasses dragging Kalish's body from the room by its ankles.

Wexler cursed out loud. He was staring at the drugged madwoman in undisguised disbelief. "She's coming to."

A high-pitched whine came from the woman in the straitjacket. Rocking from side to side, she rolled onto her stomach. Using her head for a prop, she inched her knees forward, looking like a Muslim at prayers. She turned her face toward Wexler and growled. Her upside-down grin was enough to make Claude back away.

The heavy door slammed behind Hagerty. He felt very cold, despite the sweat running down his back. Something thudded against the door from the other side.

Time melted and he was sitting in an all-hours joint near his house, trying to blot out sounds and sights. An old man hawking newspapers moved from table to table, selling the morning edition. Hagerty bought one and read about Kalish's second, official death: Local Man Found Burned To Death In Car

I am drowning in the dreams of madmen.

I can feel them pressing against my brain, a dozen insistent ghosts with empty eyes and prying fingers. For the first time since I've reclaimed my flesh, I realize the extent of the Other's evolution. If I had remained doped any longer it would have been too late. I would never have found my way back and everything would be lost. Now I have the ability to shape nightmares. It is a power I do not want or relish, but the Other loves it.

I do not have the strength or the knowledge to block their dreams. The Other knows I can't—I won't—let it surface long enough to control the problem. I'm being pulled down by the undertow.

A smiling young man with the face of a bible student and the eyes of a reptile puts out a cigarette on the naked crotch of a four-year-old boy whose screams are warped and swallowed by the vacuum of dreamtime . . . I am surrounded by twisted mountains and weirdly sculpted buttes; the earth is a cracked spiderweb of baked red clay, where animals and people are staked out on the desert's floor. Horses, pregnant women, men in business suits, dogs, old ladies—they're all doused in kerosene; a man stands in the middle and laughs as he clicks his Zippo over and over and over . . . Walking through an empty house, where the doors are ajar I can see things crouching in the dimness, waiting for me to make the mistake of entering, but I'm afraid to stay in the corridors because I know something will jump out and grab me if I don't hide . . . Tied to an iron bedstead, hands manacled above my head, there is a figure made of leather standing at the foot of the bed; the leather demon is covered with zippers and spikes. As it lifts a hand to caress my face, I see the scalpels growing from its knuckles . And I start to laugh because I know I'm in a dream, but it's not me who is laughing; it's the Other. I try to run away because the Other is coming and I need to escape the dreamtime before it gains full control, but I get lost . . . Explosions of lava . . . animals that speak . . . letters in wax melt into walls of blood . . . the sound of the Second Angel crying like a hungry child . . . cadavers smeared with quicklime and cinders . . . burning dogs hanging from lamp posts . . . I'm standing in a barren room, staring at a tall, thin man dressed in institutional pajamas. He looks pissed.

"Get out of my head, bitch."

I've got to get out of here. The Other is free.

How pathetic. Minor-league monsters strutting and performing in their private Grand Guignols. How fucking lame. You want fear? You want terror? You want to see what it's *really* like?

You used to know, before they caught you and threw you in this playpen. Now you have to dream about blood and pain instead of living it out. You're no longer free to actualize the perfection of your private hells on the flesh of your victims. But that's the way life is. Once you're caught, assholes, you're at the mercy of others. Welcome to your nightmares.

The leather demon moved to strike the woman manacled to the bedframe. Laughing was not allowed. Screaming and begging for mercy, yes, but laughing was strictly forbidden. It raised its bristling fist in anticipation of slicing through unresisting flesh. The woman shrugged, indifferent to the threat, and the manacles fell away like cheap plastic toys. The leather demon faltered, realizing for the first time that the course of the dream had been altered. The woman was on her feet, and her hands attacked the demon's shiny black leather shell.

The face mask was a mass of fetish zippers. She ignored them, digging her fingers into the top of its skull and pulling downward with the ease of a woman peeling an orange. The leather demon started to struggle as its head split open, the husk parting to reveal empty air. There was no blood, no flesh. It raised a groping hand to where its head should have been. The scalpels and bits of jagged metal grafted to its knuckles began to rust away, turning into oxidized flakes of corrosion. Its body jerked crazily as the dream thing died, spurting invisible blood.

The Other strolled into the next dreamscape. At first there was only fire, then the inferno lessened and she could see the things that were burning.

A wino dressed in rags and doused in kerosene rolled on the ground, clawing at the flames that ate his hair and skin. His face was a riot of heat blisters and broken capillaries. A dog, its tail alight, raced madly from place to place, howling in dumb, uncomprehending pain. A curtain of flame parted to reveal a family of Puerto Ricans crouching against the red earth. The parents had the children clustered around them, and although their mouths never opened, the Other could hear the wailing of frightened infants and violent coughing.

The Other found the dreamer squatting in the heart of the fire. He was dressed in white and there wasn't a drop of sweat marring his linen suit.

The Other smiled at him and laughed even louder when he recoiled. He tried to squirm away by shifting dreams, but the Other was too fast for him to escape her so easily. She clamped her hands around his wrists, pulling him to his feet. She felt him shiver in revulsion as she pressed her mouth to his.

The dreamer began to sweat. The first beads broke out on his forehead and upper lip. Within seconds he was soaked in perspiration, his lips cracking from dehydration. A wisp of smoke rose from his collar. His pant leg ignited with a polite cough. He struggled desperately to free himself. The Other shook her head as if admonishing an unruly child. His hair ignited with a dry crackle and blisters rose on his face with the speed of time-lapse photography.

By the time his eyes boiled in their sockets, the Other had grown bored and was looking for fresher game.

She walked into Malcolm's dream, trailing shreds of black leather and the acrid odor of smoke in her wake. She knew what she'd find Malcolm doing. He'd become her favorite over the past few weeks. Malcolm possessed a surprising wealth of fear and evil. More than enough to go around.

Malcolm was putting alligator clips on a nine-year-old girl's nipples. She was sitting upright, her girl-scout uniform hanging in tatters about her waist. He'd bound her hands behind her back with the badge sash and stuffed the beret in her mouth. Her face was made up like a *Vogue* model's.

The Other placed a hand on Malcolm's shoulder, easing herself into the rhythm of his dream.

Malcolm began to dwindle. He whimpered, trying to shield himself, and prayed he would wake up soon. The Other's laughter grew deeper as her features flowed into coarser, far more familiar contours. The Other towered over him like a mountain; its voice was thunder, shaking him to the marrow.

"Come on, Malcolm. Time to play with Daddy."

Claude was still in the after-hours joint, staring at Kalish's death notice. He was startled when a sixteen-year-old girl popped into existence in the chair opposite him.

"Are you awake?" was the first thing she asked him.

Taken aback, Claude had to think about it before answering. "No, I don't think so."

"Damn! Then I'm still dream-walking. I need to get back before she gains control." The girl got to her feet and began to pace the confines of Hagerty's dreamscape. She turned and stared hard at him. "You're not one of the patients, are you?" It wasn't a question.

"No, I work here . . . I mean, at Elysian Fields. Hell! Why should I bother explaining myself to a dream?"

"Am I?"

"What else could you be? You're not that god-awful nightmare. At least I don't think you are."

The girl stopped smiling. "She's been here? In your dreams?"

Claude felt his conscious mind starting to rebel. He didn't want to dream anymore, but his subconscious was forcing the issue. The walls of the club began to melt. The girl drew her legs under herself and floated in midair, hands locked across her knees. There was something familiar about her, but Hagerty couldn't place it.

"Pretend you never saw us. Pretend we never existed. Leave this place and go somewhere nice and peaceful, Claude Hagerty . . ."

"How do you know my name?"

"You created me, didn't you? I'm your dream, aren't I?"

She fell silent, as if listening to something far away. Hagerty thought she was beautiful. "I'm afraid I can't stay. She's in control now. And she's decided it's time to go." The girl unwrapped herself and kicked upward, soaring through layers of dream with the ease of a championship swimmer.

Hagerty moved to follow, but his feet were mired in syrup. "Wait! Tell me who you are! Are you the woman in Room 7?"

She did not pause in her ascent, but her voice sounded as if she was standing beside him. Or in him.

"My name is Denise Thorne. Her name is Sonja Blue."

Time to go.

She'd had enough of this place, with its endless drugs and intravenous feedings. Her defenses against the narcotics were complete. The madhouse was not without diversions, but they did not justify delaying her departure.

Time to go.

She stood up, tossing matted hair out of her eyes. She felt the drugs as her system purged the intruders from her bloodstream, reducing them to phantoms. Her mind was clear and her body her own. She could hear Malcolm as he wept in his sleep. She smiled and shrugged her shoulders once. Twice. The canvas fabric fell away, revealing naked white flesh. She lifted her arms, studying the scars studding the inner forearms. They had not bothered to trim her fingernails during her imprisonment. Good. She'd need them.

Moonlight limned her in silver and shadow, beckoning her to leave. She sank her nails into the padding of the wall and chuckled as it tore in her grasp.

Lizardlike, she scaled the wall of her prison until she was level with the window. It was three inches thick, interwoven with wire mesh, designed to withstand repeated blows from a sledgehammer. It took four blows from her right fist for it to break, although every finger in her hand shattered on the third try. She pulled herself through the narrow window into the darkness, midwife to her own rebirth. Her ribs groaned then snapped as she forced herself through the opening, spearing her left lung. She spat a streamer of blood into the night air.

She clung to the brick face of the building, luxuriating in the feel of cold air rushing past her naked flesh. For the first time in months, she was alive. The wind caught her laughter, sending it across Elysian Fields' grounds. Behind her she could hear the Danger Ward's inmates shrieking and wailing as their nightmares dumped them back into the reality of their madness. Her right hand was beginning to burn, but she was used to pain. It would pass.

Sonja Blue began to crawl, headfirst, down the wall of the madhouse.

Claude Hagerty woke to find himself standing outside Room 7, the keys in his hands. He came to his senses with a startled intake of breath. A wave of disorientation struck him and he reached for the doorframe to steady himself. Looking down the corridor, he could see the security gate standing open.

Then he heard the patients. How could he have slept through that, much less sleepwalk?

The dream was still with him. He could see the young girl with the honey-blonde hair, dressed in clothes that were just coming back into style. He saw the sadness in her eyes and heard the weariness in her voice. What was it she had said?

"She's decided it's time to go now."

Hagerty unlocked Room 7 and pushed the door open. He wasn't concerned about the patient escaping or worried about getting hurt. He already knew what he'd find.

The straitjacket lay on the floor like an empty snakeskin. He tracked the vertical rips in the canvas wall padding. Cotton ticking oozed from the rents. Cool air gusted into the room, dispelling the closeness. Even in the half-dark he could make out the jagged teeth of the broken safety glass lining the window. The blood drying on the wall was the color of shadow.

Affidavit of William "Billy" Burdette, Night Manager of Hit-n-Git #311

Burdette: Look, I told you guys this shit five times already. If you don't believe me, why don't you give me one of them lie-detector tests?

Officer Golson: It's for our files, Mr. Burdette. We have no reason to doubt your account of what happened. We just simply need to have it transcribed by a departmental steno, that's all. It'll save you from coming back downtown should we have any further questions . . .

Burdette: Oh . . . all right! So where do you want me to begin?

Officer Golson: Start from the beginning, Mr. Burdette.

Burdette: Huh? Oh, okay. Uh, my name is William Burdette, I work at the Hit-n-Git over on Claypool. I'm the night manager there and I work the graveyard shift—that's from eleven at night to seven in the morning—by myself. It's a rough part of town. Lots of street people and junkies. I've been held up a couple of times before this. This morning, I guess it was around 4 a.m., I was in the back of the store, near the canned-food section, when she comes in. We've got one of them chimes that goes off when someone comes through the doors. So I look up and see this bag lady come in. I think, oh, great! That's all I need is some old scuzz coming in and tracking up my store! So's I put up my mop and go behind the counter so I can keep an eye on things, right? But when I get up front, I sees she's no bag lady. At least I don't think so. She's real young—early twenties, maybe—and she's wearing these grungy clothes that look like she took them off a wino or something.

Officer Golson: Could you describe what she was wearing in more detail, Mr. Burdette?

Burdette: Oh, sure. Let's see . . . Well, the shirt was a long-sleeved flannel jobbie, like they give out at the mission. It was three sizes too big for her and she had the sleeves rolled up over her elbows. That's how I seen them marks up and down her arms.

Officer Golson: Marks? You mean the type left by hypodermic needles?

Burdette: Yeah, I guess, so. I didn't get too good a look. And she was wearing a pair of tan workpants a size too big for her. They were seriously gross . . . smeared with mud and God knows what else. I noticed she weren't wearing no shoes. Her hair was hanging down in her face and it was real long and dirty, like it hadn't been washed in a month of Sundays. She was one fucked-up chick, I can tell you. I'm used to the junkies wandering in at all hours. But what was weird about this chick was what she didn't do. Most junkies usually head straight for the snacks and load up on Cheetos, Chocodiles, Suzy Qs, Popsicle Bombs . . . that kind of crap.

But this one went to the far aisle, where we got this carousel rack full of sunglasses, and started trying on shades. She had her back to me and hair in her face, so I never got a real good look at her head-on, but I watched her try on a few of them. She moved kind of jerky. Real weird. I knew she was going to try to steal some shades. Didn't have to be Sherlock to figure that one out. I was so busy watching her, I didn't notice the guy who walked in at, oh, I guess it must have been half-past.

I heard the door chime and glanced up, long enough to see it was some white guy. I was keeping an eye on the junkie when the next thing I know there's this sawed-off staring me right in the face. The white guy says, "Hand over what's in the register." I forgot all about the girl. All I could see is that damned shotgun. So's I open the till. I got forty bucks and some food stamps, and that's about it. I give it to the holdup man and he says, 'That's all?' I know right then he's going to wipe me. I can hear it in his voice and see it in his eyes. He was going to blow me away because I didn't have enough money. I had this picture of my brains getting splattered all over the cigarette display and dripping off the funny-book rack.

Then I hear this . . . noise. Sounds like cats being boiled alive. For a minute I think the cops are coming. Then I realize it's coming from inside the store! I remembered the junkie was still there. I don't think the holdup guy even knew she was in the store. He turns around and shoots blind, blowing hell out of my Dr. Pepper display. That's how I got this cut on my cheek, from flying Dr. Pepper glass.

Anyways, the junkie chick runs at the dude like she's going to tackle him, and all I can think is that she's going to get us both killed. She's screaming her head off when she plows into him. Now you got to understand, this guy was big. An ex-jock or a biker or something. And she takes him out! Drives her left shoulder blade into his gut and grabs his gun hand at the same time and forces it back. That's when the second barrel went off, knocking that damn big hole in the ceiling. Damn thing went off inches from my head. Felt like someone up and hit me with a two-by-four! Guess that's when I blacked out, because the next thing I know there's a cop bending over me asking me if I'd been hurt. My ears were still ringing pretty bad and it took me a while before I could hear good enough to understand what people were asking me. I guess I was in shock or something, because I kept asking the paramedics about the girl. They didn't know what the fuck I was talking about.

When I got up off the floor, all I saw was a bunch of shattered Dr. Pepper bottles. No dead girl. No blood. The stickup man's gun was on top of the counter, wrapped in a plastic bag. The cop that found me said it had been on the floor. I couldn't figure it out. Then I saw the doors.

You see, the store's got these swinging glass doors. During the day both of them are unlocked, but after midnight I lock one side so's I can keep better track of who's coming in and going out, see? Both them doors were hanging off their hinges and there was busted glass all over the parking lot! Looked like someone rode a motorcycle through them . . . from inside the store!

I don't know what the hell she was on, but judging from them doors, I'm glad I didn't get in her way. That's all I can tell you about what went on, save that I never saw her before and I hope I'll never see her again. I'm quitting this chicken-shit job.

Officer Golson: Mr. Burdette, what exactly was stolen from your store?

Burdette: Well, the money the holdup guy took from the till was scattered on the floor, near the gun. So the only thing I know for sure was taken from the store was a pair of sunglasses. The mirrored kind. And that's only because I saw her wearing them just before she plowed into the asshole.

Officer Golson: You're sure that's all that was stolen? A pair of mirrored sunglasses?

Burdette: You got it.

Irma Clesi opened the door to her apartment. She was dressed in a shapeless housecoat and fluffy houseshoes, her head lumpy with rollers.

Five-thirty in the god-damned morning! Every day for twelve years she woke up at five-thirty so she could fix that lazy slob's breakfast. And what thanks did she get for sending him off to the factory with something beside cold cereal in his gut? A kiss? A hug? A simple 'Thanks, honey?' No fucking way. The bastard didn't even have the common decency to offer to take out the garbage.

Irma Clesi struggled down the front stairs, cursing her husband, Stan, under her breath, the shiny black bag bouncing against her thighs with each step. Metal cans and glass bottles clanked in the predawn quiet.

The trash cans for their apartment complex were set flush with the pavement, the lids opened by foot pedals. It was an old, uniquely urban form of trash collection. Irma wasn't sure how the garbage men got the cans out; Stan claimed they used special hooks to lift the aluminum containers out of their dens. Irma didn't really care, just as long as it kept the neighborhood dogs from scattering trash all over the sidewalk.

Irma's left houseshoe, a wad of pink synthetic cotton candy, slammed down on the pedal and the trash can's lid popped up. Irma caught the lip of the cover with her hand and opened it further, leaning over to drop the plastic bag full of coffee grounds, beer bottles, and chili cans into the hole in the sidewalk.

There was someone looking up at her from inside the trash can.

A man in his early thirties, his long hair bunched around his face, lay crumpled in the Clesis' rubbish bin. Whatever it was that killed him had stuffed his corpse into the garbage bin a couple of hours earlier, for now his limbs were stiffened into obtuse angles, like those of an abstract sculpture.

Irma dropped the lid and her bag of garbage. Her screams were short but explosive as she ran back to the safety of her apartment.

The neighborhood dogs, drawn by the aroma of chili, tore at the plastic bag, spilling garbage all over the sidewalk.

Claude Hagerty sat in his booth at the Cup 'n' Saucer, a greasy spoon specializing in the early breakfast trade. He'd been taking his breakfast there for twelve years and the waitresses knew him on sight. A plate with two eggs sunny-side-up, biscuits, and hash browns with country gravy appeared without his having to order.

The morning newspaper was unfolded before him, the updated edition having hit the stands just after he got off work. He stared at the front page while his eggs congealed, searching for traces of her passing. He found it on page three: Man Sought In Connection With Armed Robbery Found Dead In Trash Can.

Claude shut the newspaper, resting his brow on the heel of his palm. His stomach roiled and the sight of breakfast made him even queasier. He was back at Elysian Fields, listening to Dr. Wexler have hysterics.

Wexler was a tall, tanned, conventionally handsome man in his late fifties who looked like his dust jackets. Except when he was angry. And he'd been real angry at four o'clock in the morning. Angry enough to fire Claude for "not doing his job."

Tired as he was, Hagerty couldn't bring himself to go home and sleep. Something was eating at him. He couldn't help but feel that he'd been given a clue, but he was too stupid to recognize it. His dream had faded during the excitement and recriminations following Blue, S.'s escape, and his attempts to recall the details met with frustration. As he sat and stared at the columns of newsprint, Claude's vision blurred and his mind began to drift.

"Denise Thorne."

The voice sounded as if someone had spoken in his ear. Claude started awake with a muffled shout. Several of the Cup 'n' Saucer's patrons stared at him. He pulled himself out of the booth and left a ten-dollar bill next to his untouched meal.

His mother, bless her, had tried her best to get him to use his brains and not just rely on his brawn. And, to a certain extent, she had succeeded. Claude was a voracious reader, and he was familiar with the public library.

He was the first one through the library doors. He'd had to wait an hour before they opened, but he used the time to read the newspaper from front to back, attempting to find further evidence of her activities. He'd even scrutinized the want ads and lost-dog notices. Except for the dead man stuffed in the trash, he could not find anything he could link to her. That made him feel a little better.

He checked in the subject catalog and found a single entry for Thorne, Denise. It was a nonfiction book called *The Vanishing Heiress*. When he had no luck locating it in the stacks, he asked one of the librarians where it might be. The woman checked her computer terminal and scowled.

"I'm sorry, sir. That book was checked out over six months ago and it's never been returned. People can be so thoughtless. The computer says it's an out-of-print book, so there's no chance of us being able to reorder it . . ."

"There aren't any other books on Denise Thorne?"

"No. That's the only one I've ever heard of."

Hagerty's hands curled into fists. It was all he could do to keep from smashing them against the countertop.

"However, you could check our newspaper morgue. Everything's on microfiche. I'm afraid I couldn't give you the exact date. Late 60's, early 70's. That's all I can recall."

"You know something about her?"

The librarian, an older woman, nodded. "I remember when it happened. I had a daughter the same age, so I guess that's why. Those things have a way of making you stop and thank God it wasn't you."

"What happened to her?"

The librarian shrugged. "No one knows."

Wexler was shaking. He moved to the wet bar and fixed himself a Scotch on the rocks, eyeing his surroundings with distaste.

He'd never liked the house. She'd bought it after her husband's death. It was a twenty-room mansion, decorated like a bordello and filled with icons of Zebulon Wheele.

Images of the deceased televangelist covered every wall; a tasteful, if unexceptional, portrait in oils hung alongside a picture composed of 125 varieties of pasta. A charcoal study commissioned from Andrew Wyeth was displayed next to a life-sized Zeb executed in Day-Glo colors on a black velvet background.

Catherine Wheele's personal study—the one she used to receive visitors—had to be the worst example of kitsch iconography in the entire house, and that was saying something. The walls were covered by murals depicting the life and career of Zebulon Wheele.

The "story" began with a cherubic, barefoot urchin in ragged overalls holding a bible to his narrow chest, his Keane-ish eyes cast heavenward. It ended with the silver-haired Zebulon, attired in his trademark powder-blue three-piece suit, mounting a celestial stairway. The Pearly Gates sat atop the stairs. Two robed, Aryan-looking men bedecked with halos stood on the steps, welcoming Zebulon with open arms. Zebulon was looking over his shoulder at the woman standing at the foot of the stairs. Although weeping, Catherine Wheele's likeness somehow kept its makeup dry.

Wexler remembered how feverishly she had spoken of Zebulon's "crusade" that night. He recalled how bright her eyes had been, the pupils large and unfocused. She'd spoken unceasingly of her late husband, the words blurring into one another to form a tapestry of sound, until she pushed him onto the love seat and fellated him. Wexler found himself staring at the same love seat and shuddered.

That was the first night he'd been in the house and the night he'd been made aware that one of her dummy companies controlled the board of directors at Elysian Fields. That was the night she'd told him she knew about the money he was embezzling from the hospital and how she was going to "overlook the whole thing" if he simply agreed to take on a special patient. No questions asked.

Raymond Wexler stared at the love seat and contemplated the unraveling of his life. He finished his drink and was starting on his second when she entered the room. He started guiltily, slopping liquor onto the polished surface of the bar.

"Raymond," she said frostily.

Abandoning his drink, Wexler tried to smile and look concerned at the same time. It didn't work. Catherine Wheele was not a woman who took bad news graciously.

She was dressed in a peach chiffon negligée, its décolletage and hem lined with ostrich feathers. Her wig showed signs of having been put on in a hurry. She wasn't wearing any makeup, and the feral intelligence he saw in her eyes disturbed him. Wexler realized that he'd never seen her real face before, even during their brief sexual tussles.

"You must have your reasons for waking me at this hour, Raymond." She walked toward her desk, her body moving like a ghost underneath the opaque chiffon. Wexler tried to recall what she looked like naked and failed. "You could have at least phoned . . ."

"She's escaped." He grimaced after he'd said it. He hadn't meant to blurt it out like that, but he was afraid she would look into his mind. Anything was better than that.

Her back stiffened but she did not turn to look at him. Wexler felt a sharp twinge in his forebrain, but could not tell if it was her doing or simply a nervous headache. She was studying the large framed photograph of Zebulon that rested on the corner of her desk. Zebulon was standing next to the governor, smiling into the camera as they pumped each other's arms. Catherine stood behind and to one side of her husband, watching him with coon-dog devotion.

"I see. Does anyone know?"

"She's killed someone already, Catherine. It's in the papers!"

"That's not what I asked."

Wexler was sweating. His skin felt cold. "The orderly on duty at the time, name of Hagerty. But I've already had him dismissed."

She swung around to face him. He knew it was going to be bad, but he hadn't expected it to be *this* bad. The rage gave her eyes a weird shine, like those of an animal. "I'm afraid that won't do, Raymond. I'll have my boys . . . take care of it."

Wexler opened his mouth to protest, but she closed the distance between them, pressing her body against his. Her perfume was overpowering. He could feel a cold pressure in his head as she reached inside. He wondered if she would tell him to stop breathing.

"I'm afraid you've failed me, Raymond. Failed me in a big way."

She lifted a hand to his face. Her fingertips stroked his cheek, then dipped beneath the surface of his skin. She traced the tilt of bone and sweep of muscle as if trailing her fingers through the waters of a still pond. The ripple that went through him in ever-increasing circles was pain. Wexler tried to scream, but nothing would come out of his distorted, gaping mouth.

When it was over, his face was unmarred, although fierce muscle contractions threatened to grind his teeth to chalk. Catherine Wheele's fingers were stained bright red.

Hagerty passed a hand over his eyes, gently massaging them in their sockets. After hours of searching the microfiche archives, scanning the front pages of the nation's major newspapers for a face he'd glimpsed in a dream, he'd finally found what he was looking for.

The face smiled at him from a news item dated 1969. Now he realized why she'd looked familiar.

Denise Thorne.

That Denise Thorne.

She was the daughter and only child of Jacob Thorne, founder of Thorne Industries. Her net worth was estimated between ten and fifteen million, making her one of the world's richest teenagers at the time of her disappearance. She'd been educated in exclusive schools and vacationed in exotic locales. Her entry into Vassar was assured. Then she vanished from the face of the earth.

Every year or so one of the news services would do an article on missing celebrities, and certain names were sure to pop up. Names like Judge Crater, Jimmy Hoffa, Ambrose Bierce, D. B. Cooper . . . and Denise Thorne.

Along with some school friends and a hired traveling companion, she had jetted to London in the summer of '69. They were rich young Americans out to sample the forbidden pleasures of "Swinging London." Three days after arriving at Heathrow, the group decided to investigate the discotheques in the Chelsea district. They may have been underage, but they were wealthy and that made all the difference.

Denise Thorne was last seen talking to an older, aristocratic-looking gentleman. When questioned later, her companions could not recall his name but were under the impression he was of the ruling class. No one saw either of them leave. That was August 3, 1969.

Kidnapping was a natural assumption, and suspicion automatically fell on the hired companion. As he read the news accounts—weeks condensed onto a single fiche—Hagerty could feel the mounting frustration as the authorities ran out of leads. After a week they dropped all lines of inquiry involving the companion and focused their suspicion on radical political groups—the IRA in particular. But the persistent absence of a ransom note or a statement claiming responsibility for the crime forced Scotland Yard to abandon that line of questioning as well.

By the end of 1969 the case was still open. Some optimistic souls speculated she had run off to India with a band of hippies. The general consensus, however, was that Denise Thorne was lying dead in a ditch or, more likely, moldering in a shallow grave out on some lonely moor. By New Year's day of 1970 she was old news and the papers had more than their fair share of new atrocities to report.

Hagerty sat in the dark and stared at the face of a girl missing and believed dead for over eighteen years. The face of his dream intruder. She had been a pretty girl, with a strong jawline and high cheekbones. She wore her hair in the fashion of the day: long, parted down the middle, and straight as a board. He tried to superimpose the features of Sonja Blue. His mind rebelled. She couldn't be the same woman. Denise Thorne—if she were alive today—would be close to thirty-five, and Sonja Blue couldn't be more than twenty-four.

Claude vaguely recalled the newspapers reporting the case when it first happened. He'd been nineteen at the time, and the bum knee that'd kept him from being a college draft pick had also kept him out of Vietnam. He'd been working nights at the state hospital when the Thorne disappearance made the papers, over eighteen years ago. So what was the connection?

Maybe if he rested his eyes he could think better.

The librarian shook his shoulder, waking Claude from the first decent sleep he'd enjoyed in over forty-eight hours.

"Sir . . . sir? I'm afraid you'll have to leave. The library closes in ten minutes."

Hagerty stumbled from the library and entered the parking lot, fumbling for his keys. He was suffering from the disorientation that accompanies sleeping while sitting upright; his mouth felt like a ball of damp cotton and his back ached from his hours in the chair. He had the car door open before he realized he was no longer alone.

There were two of them, dressed in conservative dark suits with narrow lapels and even narrower ties. Their hair was short and brushed away from their foreheads. They were wearing sunglasses after dark. They had come up from behind and were now flanking him. Hagerty felt his scalp tighten as he realized his was the only car left in the parking lot.

One of them spoke. It didn't matter which. "Claude Hagerty?"

Cops. That was it. They were police. They'd found out about the escape and were asking questions. Nothing to be worried about.

Smiling his relief, Hagerty turned to face them. "Yes? Can I be of some help?"

The air in his lungs escaped in one agonized gasp as a fist sank up to its wrist in his stomach. The blow knocked Claude against the car door, slamming it shut. His hands opened in reflex, dropping his car keys to the pavement.

The man who sucker-punched him withdrew his fist from Claude's gut. Light glinted dully off the brass knuckles. He drew back to deliver another blow, but Claude's instincts were in gear. He lashed out with his right arm, catching his attacker across the chin with a closed fist.

The stranger staggered backward, his sunglasses askew. Blood dribbled down his chin. The second man drew a blackjack from his coat pocket.

"Wexler didn't say nothing about no linebacker," growled the man with the blackjack.

The recognition was sharp, like a needle jabbed in a boil. The last time he had seen these men they were grasping the ankles of Archie Kalish. There was only a moment for Claude to realize that they meant to kill him, then the back of his head exploded.

Claude fell to the pavement. He did not see which one kicked him in the ribs or who dealt the blow to his kidneys.

The last thing he saw before he passed out was one of the identical strangers standing over him. The stranger was saying something, but Hagerty's ears were roaring too loud to make it out. The stranger gestured to his companion and Claude saw the streetlight reflecting off his cuff links. Cuff links shaped like little spoked wheels. Hagerty wanted to know where the man had gotten his cuff links, but they kicked him in the head before he could ask.

He came to in the train yards.

He was sprawled over the hood of a car. The engine's warmth was pleasant against his back. He wanted to go to sleep, but there was a horrible roaring in his head that actually shook the ground. Then he heard the train whistle.

Someone grabbed him by his shirtfront and hauled him upright. Hagerty screamed aloud. It felt as if his head had been sewn together with carpet thread and the sutures were ready to pop. The identical strangers, the ones who accosted him in the library's parking lot, were still there. They had removed their sunglasses, revealing eyes as cold and flat as those of sharks. Claude preferred the sunglasses. One of them had a split lip, which he kept fingering as he looked at Claude.

The other one was talking, asking him questions, but Claude's hearing kept fading in and out. He realized he was suffering from a mild concussion. When he didn't answer their questions, one of them held his arms while the other went to work on his stomach. When the man holding his arms let go, Hagerty collapsed on the ground.

"Who you workin' for, huh? You workin' for Thorne?"

The stranger with the split lip gathered twin handfuls of Hagerty's hair, lifting his head off the ground. The pain was immense and tears streamed from his eyes, but all he could do was stare in stupid fascination at the killer's spoked cuff links.

"Leave it, Frank. Look at him. We're not gonna get anywheres with him. Better just get it over with."

"She's not gonna like it. She'll want to know." Frank's voice took on the whine of a petulant child, but the other waved him quiet.

"What difference does it make as long as he's dead? Here, help me with this bastard. The next train will be along in a few minutes. Christ, this fucker's heavy."

Panic gnawed through the gray cotton of the concussion. Claude wanted to scream, but his tongue had been transformed into a swollen wad of flesh blocking his throat. They were trying to pull him to his feet, one tugging on each arm. Frank was swearing.

Good. If you're going to kill me, the least you can do is get a hernia, he thought.

Both men bent over Claude, sweat dripping from their brows and ruining their impassive masks. Hagerty was amazed by the purity of the hatred he felt for these killers. It swelled against his breastbone like a helium balloon. Fine. He would die hating.

The hands emerged from the darkness, moving like moths dancing in the night. They landed on the shoulders of the hit man who'd kicked Hagerty in the head. Hagerty found satisfaction in the look of fear that crossed his attacker's face. The man let go of Hagerty's arm and reached for the gun inside his jacket. He never made it.

The hands snapped upward, the left clamping over his ear and bottom jaw while the right grabbed his forehead and jerked. The sound of breaking vertebrae was like a gunshot.

Frank freed his gun and kept his grip on Claude. Adrenaline gave him the strength to pull Hagerty off the ground and splay him against the car. He kept his hand on Claude's throat while he held his gun inches from the orderly's face.

"Cute trick, whore! Real cute trick. Try anything else and I'll blow your boyfriend's brains all over the fuckin' countryside, understand?" Frank shouted into the dark. His eyes jerked back and forth, but they kept straying to his companion sprawled in the dirt.

There was only laughter in response.

Frank turned and fired in the direction of the sound. The muzzle flashes revealed only gravel train beds and empty boxcars.

The hit man's face was the color of clay. Dark crescents had appeared under his arms. He let go of Hagerty, who managed to stay upright by hugging the hood of the car. Frank wrapped both hands around the grip of his gun and fell into a wary shooter's stance.

She landed on the roof of the car, hissing like a cat. Frank jerked around, his mouth a lipless line, and fired. The bullet struck her in the left shoulder, the impact spinning her backward. Hagerty heard her cry out, then the sound of her body striking the ground on the other side of the car.

Frank stood and blinked at where she had stood, then began to inch his way around the front of the car, his gun at ready. It was obvious he wasn't worried about Hagerty sneaking up on him from behind or doing anything but falling down.

Frank cleared the hood of the car and stared at where her body should have been.

"Oh, shit."

Her fingers dug into the back of Frank's neck before he had time to realize she was behind him. Her grip was so tight it pinched the nerves, temporarily paralyzing him. She reached around with her free hand and squeezed the wrist on his gunhand. Delicate bones ground together and collapsed, splinters spearing the pulse point. Frank screamed like a girl.

Hagerty wasn't surprised when Frank came flying over the hood of the car. Sonja Blue followed at her leisure, boot heels ringing against Detroit steel.

Frank wallowed in the dirt, clutching his ruined hand to his chest. It was black with congested blood and resembled an inflated surgeon's glove. The hit man's face was white with shock and his lip was bleeding again. He babbled to himself in a sibilant whisper, "Antichrist, Antichrist, Antichrist."

Sonja Blue bent over and grabbed a handful of suit, pulling him upright without any noticeable effort. "Now, is that any way to talk?"

Frank's only answer was a high-pitched, nasal whine.

She dragged him back to where Hagerty stood propped against the car. She glanced at him and Claude saw his own battered, bleeding face reflected in twin mirrors where her eyes should be. Still more sunglasses after dark.

"Tell your playmate good night, Mr. Hagerty." Placing her hand at the base of Frank's skull, she slammed his head against the hood of the car. It sounded like a watermelon dropped on a gong. Frank's body jerked spasmodically under her hands. Claude was reminded of the full-body immersions he had witnessed as a child at the Baptist church his grandparents attended, only there wasn't any water this time. Just a spray of brains and blood and bone.

But that's not what made him faint.

It was when she pulled her lips away from her teeth, revealing canines that belonged in the mouth of a wild animal, and tore open the throat of the ruined thing that had been Frank. That's when he fainted.

Hagerty's dreams were not empty.

He was wandering through a library with bookshelves as tall as skyscrapers. He could hear a train roaring down one of the aisles, its passage shaking the stacks.

He glimpsed movement ahead, where the bookshelves intersected. He didn't want to go any farther, but felt trapped in the book-lined maze.

Two men loitered on either side of the shelves, watching Claude as he approached. They wore dark suits with narrow lapels and narrower ties. They both wore sunglasses. Claude recognized them as the identical killers. Only they were no longer identical. One of them stood with his head propped against his left shoulder; when he shifted his weight to the other foot, the head lolled onto his chest so that he was staring at his feet. The other's hands resembled a cartoon animal's. His forehead was cracked open and the brains spilling out of the wound ruined the cut of his suit.

They moved in concert to block Claude's path.

"Get out of my way, assholes."

The mismatched killers turned sideways and disappeared. Claude kept moving.

Archie Kalish leaned against one of the bookshelves, smoking a cigarette. Or trying to. Most of the smoke escaped through the ragged hole in his throat. He grinned at Claude, as sleazy in death as he was in life.

"Hey, Hagerty! So what d'ya think? Some kinda piece, huh?"

Claude watched Kalish's larynx vibrate as he spoke. Claude kept walking. Kalish's laughter sounded like whistling.

Dr. Wexler was thumbing through a leather-bound volume of Freud. There was something wrong with his face. He did not offer to speak to Hagerty.

There was a door up ahead. An exit sign glowed over the threshold. Claude picked up his pace. He could see someone waiting for him by the door. A woman.

Denise Thorne looked very sad. Her long, straight hair was the color of raw honey. She was wearing a paisley miniskirt with a buckskin vest, the fringe longer than her dress. She was wearing white go-go boots and held a bouquet of flowers in her hands.

"I told you to get away while you still could," she said.

Claude felt it was important to speak to her. He stopped and tried to touch her shoulder.

Denise Thorne shook her head. "Too late."

Lozenges of mirrored glass dropped from her brow ridge, merging into the cheekbones and sealing away her eyes. Her hair writhed, drawing in on itself. Darkness welled from her scalp, radiating outward like ink in a water glass.

She opened her mouth, letting the lower jaw drop impossibly low, like a snake swallowing an egg. Her teeth were way too long and sharp to fit into a human mouth. Claude could hear the train coming. The whistle blasts sounded like a woman screaming.

And he woke up.

mavrides 1999

He was surrounded by white. At first he thought he was in a hospital, then his eyes focused and Claude found himself staring at egrets. The birds were frozen in a ritual dance on the translucent surface of a rice-paper screen.

There was a sound from the other side of the divider. The egrets folded in on themselves, allowing Sonja Blue to come forward and place a damp washcloth on Claude's brow.

Hagerty dug his elbows into the mattress, desperate to avoid the touch of the woman who'd saved his life. He wanted to scream, but all that came out was a stream of profanity.

"Stay the fuck away from me. Get your goddamn motherfucking hands off me!" His throat tightened as if the words meant to choke him.

To his surprise, she flinched.

"I should have expected this." She sounded tired.

A sledgehammer caught him between the eyes as he tried to sit up. He struggled to keep from fainting. He did not want to lose consciousness in the presence of this woman.

"Don't move so fast, you'll black out again." Her voice carried a note of concern. She stood at the foot of the cot and watched him with twin panes of polarized glass in place of eyes.

Hagerty cursed and dragged the washcloth off his forehead. He didn't want to look at her. Her very existence made his forebrain swell until it threatened to leak out his sinuses. It dawned on him that he was very thirsty.

She suddenly moved from out of his line of sight. Claude fought a surge of hysteria; as much as he hated having her around, at least he knew where she was. Careful of the malignant throbbing in his skull, he studied his surroundings.

He was in a warehouse loft; the ceiling loomed far above him and the room was poorly lit. He could barely make out the geometric shapes of the rafters overhead. He wondered how he might escape, but his mind refused to stay on the subject.

Sonja Blue returned with a Mason jar filled with water. Hagerty stared at the proffered glass but made no move to take it from her hand.

"Okay. If that's how you want it." She set the water on an upended orange crate next to the cot and stepped away.

Hagerty lifted the container with shaking hands, slopping water onto his bare chest.

"It's after ten p.m., you've been out for nearly two hours. Thought you might like to know." She crouched at the foot of the bed, hands dangling between her knees. Without wanting to, Claude found himself looking at her.

Her hair was shoulder-length and black as goddamn, as his grandpa used to say; styled in the bristling fashion made popular by music videos, it rose like the crest of an exotic jungle bird. She wore a battered black leather jacket a size too big for her over a sleeveless French-cut T-shirt of the same color. The jacket was going out at the elbows, and an attempt had been made to repair it with electrician's tape. The legs of her tight-fitting black leather pants were tucked into a pair of scuffed, low-heeled engineer boots. Her hands were encased in fingerless black leather gloves. And, of course, there were the mirror shades. Claude's dream tried to resurface, but it was quickly banished.

"You, uhhh, look different," was all he could come up with.

"I no longer look like a drugged-out madwoman, is that what you mean?" She laughed without smiling. "Yeah. I guess I do look different."

Claude heard himself speaking before he knew what he was saying. "What are you?"

She did not seem to take offense. She cocked her head to one side and regarded him with polarized eyes. "Do you really want to know?"

"Do I have a choice?"

She shrugged. "Not anymore."

She stood up. It was a simple, fluid motion, like the uncoiling of a snake. She moved across the floor of the loft to the opposite wall and drew back the heavy blackout curtains that covered the windows. The staccato glow of neon illuminated the room, revealing a maze of rice-paper screens. Sonja Blue leaned against the windowsill, arms folded. Claude sat upright, clutching the mattress with both hands until his knuckles ached.

"You must have an idea as to what I am. And it's not an escaped lunatic, is it, Mr. Hagerty?" She pushed the mirror shades onto her brow, exposing the eyes they hid. Hagerty began to shiver like a man with fever. She let the glasses drop back into place.

"Welcome to the Real World, Mr. Hagerty."

Can't push it too fast. I'll lose him if I force too much on him. I wanted it to go down quick and clean, damn it. Just go in there and take out those bozos and get him to safety. An impersonal kill, that's all I wanted. But I lost control! It couldn't resist playing with them. I've got to be careful. Ever since the escape, the Other's been strong. Too strong. It's just waiting for me to screw up. Looking for a chance to get out. I can't let my guard down. Not with him around. It's not his fault he was drawn into this. He's innocent.

Since when did that make any difference?

Shut up, damn you. Just shut up!

Hagerty wished he knew what was going on. As dangerous as Sonja Blue might be, that wasn't as disconcerting as his not knowing what part he was playing in this horror show. Was he the hero or the victim? And if Sonja Blue was the monster, why did she go out of her way to rescue him?

She was no longer in the loft, although he could not recall hearing her leave. He shuffled around his "prison" in his underpants, trying to decide what kind of movie he was in. If he could figure out the movie, then he stood a chance of surviving to see the credits. But only if he could figure out the rules. If it turned out to be one of those slasher films . . . The thought depressed him so badly he gave up on the analogy and focused on exploring the loft.

The room was subdivided into cubicles by a network of painted rice-paper screens. He walked among sock-eyed carp, grinning lion-dogs, grimacing dragons, prancing monkey lords, glowering no-tail cats and stalking tigers, their presence oddly comforting. He moved from compartment to compartment, searching for clues to what was going on. What he found made his head hurt.

One cubicle contained a videoplayer and monitor. The extension cord hung from the rafters like an orange python. An unmarked cassette jutted from the mouth of the player. Claude nudged the cassette, and the machine obligingly swallowed it. For a moment Claude felt safe, involved in the mundane ritual of technology. Then the tape began to play on the monitor: a woman in a gold lamé pantsuit exhorted her audience to stand up and sway from side to side, hands held over their heads. The sound was off, but Claude knew what she was saying. He watched the mascara mingle with her tears and trickle down her cheeks. It looked like her face was melting. He hit the stop button and the monitor screen returned to the gray nothing of an empty channel.

Another cubicle contained a low, Japanese-style table. Three books rested on the table. One was a large, very old-looking tome with metal edges and leather binding. Claude did not recognize the language, but there were several pages of complex, overlapping illustrations that made his eyes throb when he tried to decipher them. The second was a slender, hardbound volume in German. The third looked to be far more accessible. Claude turned the book over in his hands, noting the brittle plastic binding protecting the dust jacket and the shelving code affixed to its spine. The title was *The Vanishing Heiress: The Strange Disappearance of Denise Thorne*. The book fell open to a page with two photographs on it.

The larger picture was a photoportrait of the Thornes in happier days: Jacob Thorne stood in the background, looking every inch the self-made captain of industry. His women were seated on a small divan in front of him, his hands resting on their shoulders. Shirley Thorne, a delicate woman with a gracious smile, held her daughter's hand in her lap. Claude was surprised rich people could look so normal.

The smaller picture was blurred, obviously blown up from a snapshot. It showed a slightly older Denise Thorne in a crowded nightclub. She was not looking at the photographer. She seemed distracted but otherwise enjoying herself. She held a champagne glass in one hand. The caption read: *Last known photo of Denise Thorne, taken by club photographer the night of her disappearance at the Apple Cart Discotheque, London, August 3, 1969.* A ballpoint circle hovered just over her shoulder. Inside it was the blurred outline of a man. The man remained a grainy, ill-defined blot even on close inspection. Scrawled in the margin, in the same blue ink as the circle, was the word "MORGAN."

Claude shut the book and replaced it on the table. For the first time since waking up, he noticed the dust coating everything. His hands were grimy with it and the soles of his bare feet itched. His hostess obviously had not yet found the time to catch up on her housekeeping.

The kitchen was located in a corner where the raw brick met the jutting angle of the roof. The only piece of furniture was a Salvation Army–issue dinette set. A pair of midget iceboxes, stacked one atop the other, sat on the rickety table. Claude tried the taps on the double-basin sink, only to be rewarded with the plumbing equivalent of an epileptic seizure and water the color of rust.

His stomach growled. He opened the top cooler and heard glass containers clink together. He reached inside, fingers closing around chill glass. Soft drinks, milk, anything would be welcome.

He stared at the pint container of blood for five seconds before dropping it. The bottle shattered, splattering his naked legs. Claude clamped his hands over his mouth and staggered into the tiny bathroom located off the kitchen.

He sounded like a cat sicking up a hair ball.

When he was through, he remained hunched over the sink, his palms against the cold enamel, and stared at his reflection in the medicine chest. Although the swelling was going down, it was surprising he'd woken up at all.

His right eye was covered by a bruise the color of a hybrid rose. His bottom lip looked like a piece of raw liver. A knot the size of a pigeon's egg hung over his left eyebrow, and it felt like his nose was broken. Again.

He let his hands stray to the Ace bandages wrapped around his chest. It hurt a bit when he moved too fast; otherwise his ribs seemed okay. He spat into the sink and studied his saliva for traces of blood, then tried the same experiment with his urine. He was damned lucky to have escaped without serious internal injuries. If you consider being held captive in your underwear by a vampire as being lucky . . .

Claude laughed in spite of himself. Funny how good that felt. He was surprised to discover he was no longer in mortal terror. He experienced a sense of relief, not unlike emptying his bladder after a long road trip. He decided that while he did not fear Sonja Blue, neither did he trust her. He'd learned the hard way never to rely on the semblance of sanity.

Back when he was younger and his hair longer, he'd come to trust a patient who, on the surface, seemed perfectly harmless. Then one day the patient turned into a screaming, hissing wild thing and pulled out a handful of Claude's hair by the roots. Now he wore his hair cropped close to his skull in order to camouflage the missing piece of scalp.

He remembered the hit man called Frank and the way she'd toyed with him before the kill. Hagerty had no love for the man, but he could not repress revulsion at the memory of his murder.

When he was fifteen, he'd found the family cat—a fat, good-natured old tom—"playing" with a mouse. The cat snapped the rodent's spine, leaving the creature alive but paralyzed. Then, gripping the mouse by the head, it repeatedly hurled the tiny rodent against the garage door. The crippled mouse squeaked each time it rebounded onto the pavement. This prompted the cat to swat the mouse again; *squeak*-thud. The rodent's eyes had gone white with pain and fear, its rib cage shuddering with every breath while blood leaked from its twitching nostrils. The cat continued its grisly game of handball for a minute or two more, then it grew bored and bit the mouse's head off. After that, Claude was never able to look at the old tomcat in quite the same way, just as he could not look at Sonja Blue without sensing the feline sadism lurking below her surface, waiting for a mouse.

"There you are. Made a mess, didn't you?"

He reacted as if she'd poked him with a cattle prod. She stood in the bathroom doorway, a grocery sack in one arm and a suit of clothes draped over the other. Claude was acutely aware of being dressed in nothing but a baggy pair of BVDs.

"Thought you might like some clothes. The ones you had on were covered in blood. Hope these fit." She shoved the clothes at him. "You can change in here while I clean up." The door closed in his face.

Getting dressed in the bathroom was like changing clothes in a broom closet. Claude stopped swearing after the third time he slammed his knee into the toilet tank. The dungarees fit him well enough, although his neck overflowed the collar of the flannel shirt and the cuffs ended an inch above his wrists.

He opened the door in time to see Sonja Blue wringing a mop in the kitchen sink. The water was the color of cranberry juice.

"What the hell are you looking at? Expect me to lick it up off the floor with my tongue?" she snapped.

Her feelings were hurt. Claude was taken aback by the realization. It occurred to him that he was a lousy, ungrateful house guest. He didn't know what to say, so he watched her mop the floor in guilty silence.

"I picked up something down at the corner superette. *Haute cuisine* it ain't, but it'll do for now." She didn't look up from her work, but motioned with a curt nod to the sack resting on the table.

Stepping over the pool of blood and tap water, Claude rummaged through the bag and produced a jar of peanut butter, a loaf of white bread, a quart of milk, and three cans of potted meat. He stared at the cartooned demon on the can of deviled ham and smiled.

The smile grew wider. He felt as if his lips were going to split.

"What's so funny?" Sonja Blue glanced at him as she wrung the mop for the last time. The water was now the color of pink lemonade.

Claude began to laugh. Tears squeezed from the corners of his eyes. His laughter carried the shrill edge of hysteria. He realized that if he lost control he would laugh until he blacked out. Which is what he did.

Alive. I'm only really alive when I'm on the prowl. Alone. Unobserved. I'm glad Hagerty is too unsteady to leave the loft. I could not track my prey with him queering the game.

The night is an origami rose, unfolding itself for those unafraid to look. As much as I hate them, my eyes allow me to know the half-glimpsed marvels and nightmares that fill this world. Sapphires among the rot.

My eyes are windows to hell, enabling me to spot those who Pretend. Their spoor hangs in the air, as obvious as street signs.

Over there, lounging in a doorway, sharing a cigarette with its unwitting prey, is a *vargr*. It rests its shoulder against the doorframe, holding a Marlboro between thumb and overlong index finger. I can see the animal in its eyes as it studies me with the detached speculation of a predator. But I am not interested in such beasts tonight.

I round the corner and enter the city's tenderloin district. The porn shops, titty bars and adult cinemas are all very busy, like maggots in a corpse. I like downtown. It's my element.

Sensing my intrusion, a succubus glances up from her transaction. As she leans into the open passenger window of a nondescript rental car, she looks like all the other whores working the neighborhood. She lifts her head, tossing back a mane of copper curls, and scans the streets. Is she on the lookout for vice cops or other wayward children of Gehenna? The faltering neon of the Triple X Sinerama's marquee illuminates her true face as it shifts and roils beneath the carefully constructed facade. I do not meet her gaze and hurry away. Out of my league.

The Pretender population in America is nowhere near that of Europe, but immigration is picking up. Standing in line at the Pussy Kat Theater, its deformities masked by a shapeless raincoat, an ogre watches me with the eyes of a rabid rat. I make a note of him. Child-eaters are a rarity nowadays, but missing children aren't. The ogre's gaze follows me as I walk past. He knows I'm not human, but cannot identify my clan. That makes him nervous.

I smell roasting flesh and burning hair, and I nearly collide with the pyrotic before I see it. It sidesteps me, leaving a vapor trail in its wake. It wears the flesh of a middle-aged man in a business suit, his skin the color of a boiled lobster. His hair is ablaze and smoke billows from his ears and nostrils. The pyrotic is either very strong or has been in possession too long. Now it is looking for another body, male or female. It doesn't matter. Once elementals get a taste of being incarnate, they often end up addicted to the earthly plane. Kind of pathetic, really. No one pays any attention to the burning man as he hurries down the street.

Something catches the corner of my eye and I discover the reason for the Pretenders' uneasiness. It seems I am only partly to blame.

It sits on the bottom stoop of an old brownstone, rummaging through its shopping bags, muttering the litany of the out-patient.

To the humans it is just a bag lady, another bastard child of Reaganomics. But I see the seams in the costume and the stage makeup on its face. It is a *seraph*, come for a brief visit. The aura that surrounds the wrinkled, grime-caked face is blue fire. It looks up from the Macy's bag and stares at me. Its eyes are golden and have no whites or pupils. It smiles and speaks, but its language is beyond me. I am too base a creature to understand. All I hear are wind chimes. If I try to answer, all the *seraph* will hear is a cat being skinned alive.

The Other is frightened of it, just as the succubus and the ogre were afraid. *Seraphim* never interfere with Pretenders. But they could if they wanted to, and that is why the Pretenders are fearful of them. The Other digs its claws into my brain. If I do not leave it will try to gain control. It knows I cannot afford to let it do that. Not tonight. Not while I still have to find Chaz.

I turn and run from one of the nine billion faces of God.

She stood in the doorway of the bar, sucking in ragged gulps of air. Her heart rabbited in her chest and her hands trembled. That was close. Too damn close.

She could feel the Other raging just below the surface, and bile burning the back of her throat. For the first time since she'd ducked in to escape the *seraph*, Sonja noticed her surroundings.

The bar was located in the basement of one of the old brownstones fronting the street. A frosted pane of glass faced the stairwell. It didn't have a name, but she recognized it as one of Chaz's haunts. The drinks were cheap, the lights dim, and the clientele sleazy—Chaz's kind of place.

The front room was large and had a low ceiling. It stank of stale beer and decades of trapped cigarette smoke. The actual bar was against the far wall, situated under the only decent lighting in the joint. Clustered against the opposite wall were a handful of arcade video games, their cases covered with graffiti and cigarette burns. A Rockola jukebox strained the Ramones' "Pinhead" through failing speakers.

The tables and booths scattered throughout the room boasted three hookers, a ferret-eyed dealer, two glowering skinheads and a couple of hard-core alcoholics. None of them was Chaz. She noticed a doorless passageway flanked by twin cigarette machines. Taped over the lintel was a yellowing sign that read: POOL.

Why not check it out? Maybe the little shit was back there, hustling the marks. She walked past the sentries posted by the tobacco company, aware of being watched by the people at the bar.

For a moment she thought she'd stumbled into a nest of minor demons. She'd expected to find a roomful of teenaged boys, but not ones with blue hair. She paused as her vision shifted spectrums, scanning the faces for traces of Pretender energies. Low-level demons were identifiable by the sworls of power marking their features, like the tattoos of Maori tribesmen. But every face she scanned was clean, at least of Pretender taint.

One of the blue-haired youths leaned across the scuffed green of the pool table, his back to her as he lined up his shot. He wore a black leather jacket garnished with loops of chrome chain at the shoulders. Emblazoned across the back of the jacket was the grimacing face of a bright-blue ape. Jesus, she had been away too long! These were members of the Blue Monkeys, one of the city's more volatile youth gangs. And she'd just walked, unawares, onto their turf.

The Blue Monkey made his shot and moved back to watch the break go down. His competition grunted and the others made rude noises. No one bothered to look up. She moved about the room, scanning the audience for a sign of Chaz. Unless he'd taken to dyeing his hair, her prey wasn't there. She turned to go.

A hand grasped her upper arm, just above the elbow. "Hey, baby. Looking for someone?"

The Blue Monkey was seventeen—maybe eighteen, if he pushed it—his indigo hair short and spiky. Despite the acne that pitted his cheeks like a spray of buckshot, he was moderately good-looking. He wore an Iron Maiden T-shirt under his club jacket.

She shook her head. "Just looking for . . . a friend who isn't here."

The Blue Monkey smiled in what he imagined was his best James Dean imitation. The gang members gathered around the pool table were watching them now. "You can forget that asshole, baby. Rafe's here."

She shook her head a second time, smiling wanly. "No, I don't think so." She slipped out of his grip and started for the door.

Sniggering laughter ran through the gang. Rafe flushed red all the way to his indigo roots.

The hand was on her arm again, only tighter this time. "Maybe you didn't hear me so good," Rafe ground the words out between clenched teeth. "I said I'm your friend now."

She felt her patience begin to melt. The Other strained on its leash. It sounded almost friendly this time.

C'mon! Let's settle this little fucker's hash. Just this once . . .

No! It was so tempting to give in, to indulge her dislike for these swaggering, no-necked little Hitlers. But once the jinn was out of the bottle, it took blood to get it back in. Better to leave now and avoid the risk, before things got any worse.

"I don't think yer her type, Rafe," jeered one of the gang. More snickers. Rafe's face was the color of a fire hydrant.

"I have to go now." She disengaged herself a second time.

"Whassamatter, whore? Ain't I good enough for ya?"

Rafe's eyes were no longer sane. She recognized the madness in them. Rafe was the Blue Monkeys' pet psychotic, their own personal whirling dervish. He might look like a teenage boy, but he was something far more dangerous, and the gang knew exactly what it took to set him off. They knew which responses were guaranteed to trigger his transformation into the living incarnation of the Tasmanian Devil from the old Bugs Bunny cartoons.

Rafe grabbed a fistful of her hair, moving so fast she could not dodge his attack. He jerked her off-balance so her palms were planted against his chest for support. His breath reeked of dope and Jack Daniels.

That's it. I'm not gonna play pattycake with this jerk.

She levered herself backward, ignoring the tearing at her scalp. She'd endured far more pain in her past than the loss of some hair. Rafe was staring, mouth open, at the hank of hair he was left holding in his hand when she hit him. She still had the self-control to deliver the blow with the back of her hand, but it was enough to send Rafe sprawling into the arms of his tribe. Blood leaked from one nostril and his lower lip was split. His eyes rolled like an enraged mule's.

The Blue Monkeys clotted around her, blocking the exit. There were nine of them. His friends struggled to put Rafe back on his feet.

"You bitch," Rafe mumbled through rapidly swelling lips.

One of the older gang members chuckled. "Looks like we got us a gash that knows *jew*-jitsu!" He reached out to snag her mirrored sunglasses. "Bet you got trouble seein' with them fancy-ass shades on, bitch."

Her hand flashed up fast as a cobra, and her fingers closed around his wrist before he could touch her. There was a sound of balsa wood crunching and the Blue Monkey screamed like his namesake.

One of the gang tried to back away, but the others held him in place. "Fuck. Oh, fuck. It's her. The chick Chaz was talkin' about."

Rafe spat a wad of blood and phlegm on the floor. "Shaddup, you goddamn lit'l queer. Chaz was jackin' us, and you know it! This here's just some poon with fancy moves." His eyes were unfocused. "Clear off the table. We gonna have ourselves one wingding of a gangbang." Rafe glanced contemptuously at the Blue Monkey with the shattered wrist. The youth was whimpering, his lips white with shock as he cradled his arm against his chest. "Somebody shut that fuckin' whiner up."

The gang took up its war cry. The backroom sounded like the monkey house at feeding time. Rafe lurched forward, wrapping his arms around her waist. He intended to slam her onto the pool table and fuck the bitch until she bled.

Her knee pistoned up, smashing into his denimed crotch and rupturing his testicles; it was as if a napalm bomb had gone off in Rafe's jeans. He managed one high, thin scream before collapsing. The agony of his ruined *cojones* was so great he didn't even know she'd fractured his pelvis.

The Blue Monkeys watched as Rafe spasmed on the floor, clutching his groin, their ape yell fallen silent.

That was when the Other made its move.

"You fuckers think you're tough, huh? You think you're bad? You shitheads can't even handle a girl!"

Shut up. Shut up. It's bad enough without you provoking them. Let's go! Let's just walk out of here, damn you!

Two of them lunged at her, one from behind and one in front. The one behind grabbed her arms, pinning her elbows to her side. The Other laughed and stamped on his instep, breaking it in two places. The Blue Monkey yowled and let go of her arms. The Other grabbed her frontal assailant by the throat and crotch, lifting him off the floor.

No, stop. Please . . .

The Other tightened her grip on the boy's crotch. He made a bleating sound as she castrated him.

No. God, no. Stop . . .

She lifted the struggling youth over her head.

Don't!

The Other laughed as she hurled the boy against the wall. The sound his spine made as it snapped was delightful.

Someone swung a pool cue. She absorbed the blow across her back, although it cost her a couple of ribs. No big deal. Her laughter grew louder. The Other hadn't enjoyed herself so much in months.

A burly youth with a royal-blue mohawk grappled with her. She caught a glimpse of the knife seconds before he slid it between her ribs, puncturing her left lung. She wrapped her arms around the mohawked punk, pressing him to her breasts. They looked like a high-school couple slow-dancing at the prom. The Blue Monkey stared into her upturned face, expecting her to die. The Other grinned and belched a gout of blood into his face. The Blue Monkey began to panic. He backpedaled, desperate to break free of her embrace, but she refused to let go. His face was a blood-slick mask, his eyes bulging like a vaudeville minstrel's. The Other unsheathed her fangs.

Every synapse in the tough's brain overloaded and blew. "Get her offa me! Get her offa meeeee!"

Two of his friends grabbed the Other's shoulders and wrested her from her unwilling dance partner. They stared dumbly at the knife buried to the hilt in her chest. The Other plucked it out as if it were a bothersome thorn.

"Hey, lover! You forgot something." She flicked her wrist and the blade buried itself in the punk's Adam's apple.

The Other leapt atop the pool table, surveying the carnage: two dead, two crippled, one maimed. Not bad for starters.

One of the boys made for the door. No, no, no. Mustn't have that. Not while the party was still in full swing and she was having such a good time. She snatched up one of the cue balls on the pool table and lobbed it at the fleeing Blue Monkey. The crunch it made upon connecting with his skull was satisfying. The Blue Monkey staggered drunkenly for a step or two, the seepage from his head turning his hair purple.

Fun was fun, but the thrill was losing its edge. She better split before the cops finally decided to show up. Only three loose ends left. She hopped off the pool table and ducked a roundhouse from a Blue Monkey with a sterling-silver skull pinned to one earlobe. She punched his face and felt his jaw restructure itself. She let him fall without a second look.

The next-to-last Blue Monkey almost had the fire exit open. She let fly with an empty beer bottle. It struck the fleeing gang member in the right knee. The boy fell to the floor, clutching his shattered kneecap.

The last of the Blue Monkeys was smaller than the rest. Fifteen years old, at best. He was the one who'd mentioned Chaz. Figured. Chaz liked 'em young, rough and stupid. She held the boy by his club jacket's lapels. The toes of his boots brushed the floorboards.

"Where is Chaz?"

"I . . . I . . . ." The kid was terrified beyond speech. His eyes were as blank as her mirrored glasses.

She pushed against the wall of hysteria surrounding his mind. (*Tell me where he is.*) The boy's will folded like a Chinese fan.

"Don't know! Truth! Truth!"

"Now, that can't be true. Surely you know where he likes to hang out? You can tell me."

"Hell Hole! Look in Hell Hole. Don't hurt me."

"Hurt you? Now, why would I want to do that?"

The Other lowered the boy until his feet once more touched the floor but did not relinquish her hold. There was a gnawing pain in her chest from the knife wound, her scalp itched and she was breathing like a bellows. It would take an hour for the damage to heal on its own, but she could boost the process with some blood. Not much. Just enough.

The littlest gang member stood trembling in her hands like a trapped rabbit. She had glimpsed his sins during their brief touching of minds. Gang rape. Hit-and-run. Mugging. Liquor-store robbery. Street-fighting. Quite impressive, for a squirt with parrish-blue hair.

It'd have to be fast. She could hear the sirens in the distance. Her fangs unsheathed, wet and hard. She pulled him to her in a lover's embrace. He had an erection.

They always did.

The Other watched the cop cars fishtail to a halt outside the bar with no name. She stood in the shadows of the alley across the street, arms folded. The bartender broke down and called the police when he heard the gang screaming. She'd slipped out through the fire exit before any of the patrons worked up the nerve to check out the pool room. *A wonderful establishment. I'll have to go there more often.*

The Other smiled as she walked away from the flashing lights and ambulance sirens. Marvelous workout. Simply marvelous. Just what she'd been needing. She hawked a piece of lung onto the pavement without breaking stride. Just the thing to take the edge off before she got her hands on Chaz's sweet little butt.

The Hell Hole was proud of being a dive.

A lot of time and money had gone into selecting the proper decadence for the club. That way its patrons wouldn't notice it was just another bar. It was a natural for Chaz.

The walls were festooned with rubbish salvaged from the city dump and places even less savory. Baby doll heads were affixed to the walls by nails driven through their eyes. The front end of a '58 Chevy jutted onto the dance floor, a moth-eaten moose head mounted in place of the hood ornament. Instead of glass eyes, golf balls graced the creature's sockets; sawdust dribbled from its nostrils, while a used jockstrap dangled from its antlers. Loops of Christmas-tree lights hung from the ceiling, none of them flashing in sequence.

Chaz sat at his table in the corner, staring at the centerpiece: a Barbie doll shoved headfirst into a Suzy Homemaker oven. Christ, the place was dead tonight. London had the States beat when it came to the clubs. Sometimes he wished he'd never left England. But things had been different then. His meal ticket was in danger of being nicked, and America seemed as good a place as any to escape to.

Chaz frowned and took another swallow of gin. Wouldn't do to think about Sonja. He'd learned long ago to put people out of his mind. He erased them from his memory so well it was like they'd never existed. That was the best way. The only way. Attach yourself to 'em, become "indispensable," use 'em up then throw 'em away. He'd done it hundreds of times in the twenty years since he first hit the streets. You have to learn fast if you're on your own by age twelve and want to stay alive.

Then there was Sonja. Their relationship had lasted the longest. What had Sonja called it? Symbiotic, that was the word. Yeah. She needed him to lure her prey into the open. It'd been dangerous, but she paid him well. And the sweet rush of adrenaline and fright involved in the hunt got him higher than any street drug. He could have lived without her, sure. But it was so easy to keep hanging around. Hell of a lot easier than peeping into the heads of dope peddlers so he could be at the right place at the right time when a deal went down. Yeah, it was much easier being Sonja's judas goat. Safer, too, providing he stayed out of her way during her "spells."

But, in the end, he'd committed a major sin, as listed in the Gospels According to Chaz. He'd become dependent on her. Now *that* was scary.

Bloody hell, where was everybody? He glanced at his Rolex. He'd agreed to meet that little shit and his blue-haired friends here, so where were they? If they didn't show up soon, he'd be forced to go looking for a party. Chaz hated that Muhammad-and-the-mountain jazz. He enjoyed being the focal point. Make 'em dependent on me, that's the way it should be.

Still, the little Yank had his points. Maybe he'd take him along to Rio. On second thought, Rio was full of beautiful boys with skin the color of café au lait. He could buy any number of dark-eyed Cariocas, so why bother importing a petulant, blue-haired punk? No, Rio would definitely be wasted on his pet Blue Monkey.

God, he hated this depressingly young country and its populace of bourgeois mall-crawlers. He just had to be patient. Come Carnival he'd be spending his days drinking espresso and eyeing the samba dancers as they paraded down the streets.

He'd dreamed of Brazil for years, ever since he saw the poster in the window of a West End travel agency. He was seventeen at the time and already well-versed in the language of exploitation. He was posing as houseboy for a withered old pouf while wringing him for whatever he could get. It wasn't a demanding job, really—the odd suck and fuck—mostly the old queen simply wanted a handsome boy following him around. They went to the theater a lot. That's how he happened to be walking past the travel agency.

The poster's layout consisted of two figures, male and female, photographed against an aerial view of Rio de Janeiro at night. Fireworks filled the sky like chrysanthemums made of colored fire. Both the man and the woman were the color of milk chocolate, with the dark eyes and exotic features of true Cariocas. The man wore skin-tight white satin pants that flared at the knee, the vents lined with red silk. His white satin shirt boasted the billowing, layered sleeves of the samba dancer and stopped just below his breastbone. Chaz admired the muscles that rippled across the dancer's exposed stomach. He wore a simple domino mask and the sunniest smile Chaz had ever seen. The samba dancer held a pair of brightly painted maracas in his slender hands.

The woman was also outfitted in white satin, her dusky skin in sharp contrast with her clothes. One beautifully naked leg was extended from the voluminous ruffles of her skirt. Her midriff was also bare, but far more subtle in its muscularity than the male's. A white halter concealed breasts the shape and color of chocolate kisses. Her head was covered by a carefully wound turban the color of snow, and she wore a mask identical to her partner's. But where the male samba dancer held maracas, she balanced a magnificently plumed parrot on her wrist.

Chaz stood and stared at the samba couple until his patron, having lost his temper, stormed off. There was a row later that night and within two weeks Chaz was back on the streets. The fact that the relationship was over didn't bother him, except that it meant he couldn't "visit" his beautiful dancers as often as he would have liked. After a time, the samba couple was replaced by a poster advertising package tours to Sorrento, but the smiling Cariocas were never far from his mind.

Sometimes he woke with the rhythm of steel drums echoing in his head and the smell of the Amazon rain forest clinging to his pillow. Now he was going to Rio. All he was doing was waiting for the right time to leave. For some reason, it hadn't felt right yet, and for Chaz that was important. He still had enough money to live—and do it well—in his precious Rio. A man with his savvy and unique abilities could do well for himself down there. Maybe he'd buy into a cocaine plantation. Or perhaps he'd found his own escort service, specializing in handsome, smooth-skinned Cariocas of both sexes. And, if his luck failed him, there were always the *turistas* . . .

He cast his thoughts outward and touched the minds of those in the bar. His talent was slight but he'd become its master years ago. He was proud of his skill. Better to be a dead-on shot with a .22 than a blind man armed with an assault rifle. Like that painted, holier-than-thou bitch. He groaned. Thinking about Sonja was bad enough, but he refused to let that whore preoccupy his thoughts. He returned his attention to his probes. At least it'd keep him from being bored.

Hmmmm . . . the manager, Rocky, was lounging near the door. Rocky didn't like him. Didn't like the crowd that Chaz attracted. Thought he was a dealer. Didn't want him hanging around, but business was real shitty.

Chaz was not upset by the manager's low opinion of him. You didn't remain sensitive if you were a telepath, otherwise you went psychotic or ended up with your head in the gas cooker. Like poor ole Mum; she couldn't handle knowing what the neighbors *really* thought. Silly cunt never learned how to screen herself.

Lise the barmaid's mind, however, was more to his liking. Where Rocky's thoughts were chunky, Lise's internal monologue was mental champagne. She was bored. Bit lonely. She knew he had money. Knew he had access to drugs.

She was debating whether she should let him pick her up. She thought he was a bit creepy, but the prospect of free drugs sparked a vague heat between her legs.

Chaz smiled into his drink.

"Hello, Chaz. Long time no see."

The hand on his shoulder pinned him to his seat.

Chaz's skin grayed and sweat jumped from his brow. "Sonja."

She smiled without revealing her teeth. "Sure is. Mind if I join you?"

"No. Of course not. Have a seat."

As she slid into the chair opposite him, the barmaid left her station to take the new customer's order.

"Get your friend anything, Chaz? Cocktail? Beer?" There was a trace of jealousy in her voice.

Sonja did not bother to look up at the barmaid. "We are not here, is that understood?"

The girl wobbled and blinked a few times, then left the table, rubbing her forehead with the heel of her palm and looking slightly confused.

"What did you do?" he hissed.

"Nothing serious. I just don't want our little discussion interrupted. After all, we haven't seen each other in such a *long* time. I take it your employers didn't see fit to tell you I'd escaped?"

"I don't have the slightest idea what you're talking about."

"Cut the bullshit, Chaz. You can't lie to me. Not that I don't know it, anyway. They must have paid you well; I can't see you slitting your throat for tuppence." She studied him for a second. "Jesus, you look like shit."

It was true. Nearly every dollar he'd earned had gone up his nose or in his arm. Back in London, during his peak, he'd been handsome. Some even called him beautiful. But his dissolution had brought out the rodent in his features. She marveled at the transformation; not even her own fall from grace had been so thorough.

Chaz lit one of his foul French cigarettes, his eyes searching the bar for some hope of escape.

"Where is it, Chaz?"

"What?"

Her voice was as sharp and cold as a surgeon's scalpel. "I don't have time for games, Chaz. I know you have it. You filched it from me when you kissed me. I thought, at first, that was why you shot me."

"Sonja—"

"I want what belongs to me, Chaz." She extended one hand and waited. It was an elegantly menacing gesture.

Chaz reached inside his breast pocket and withdrew a folded switchblade. The handle was six inches long and made of lacquered teak. A golden dragon winked its ruby eye in the dim light of the club. Chaz held it in his palm, admiring the gold leaf one last time, then handed it to its rightful owner.

She turned the weapon over with trembling hands, caressing it like a lover. She pressed the dragon's eye, and the blade leapt from its hiding place within the hilt. She turned it so the braided silver surface caught the light. In the erratic flashing from the Christmas lights the knife resembled a frozen flame.

"I'm surprised, Chaz. I thought you would have pawned it by now."

"I kept meaning to . . ." He stared at the silver blade, his eyes focused on something far away. "I dunno. Maybe I wanted a keepsake . . ."

"Something to remember me by. How sweet." She grinned and Chaz shuddered. "How much did you get for setting me up?"

"I don't know what the fuck you're going on about!"

"You were checking out Catherine Wheele for me, man. You told me to meet you at the playground at midnight. I went there, Chaz, but you weren't alone. You had Wheele and her goons with you. Your new friends. You didn't tell me she was Real! You somehow forgot to mention that, mate. I woke up in an insane asylum. I hope you got your thirty pieces, Chaz."

"Look, Sonja, it's not what you think . . . I'm your mate, ain't I? I wouldn't do anything to hurt you. I'm glad you escaped. But I didn't have a choice. Honest! That Wheele slut, she sussed me out. She would have turned my brains inside out! She's powerful, Sonja! Too powerful for the likes of me. She was gonna burn my brain. What could I do, eh? What could I do? You believe me, don'tcha?" He reached across the table and took her hands in his. "C'mon now, luv. We're friends. We've been more'n friends. It could still be like that. Like the old days. You got away from that loony, right? We could go somewheres safe. Mexico. Brazil, maybe. What d'ya say, pet? Rio sounds nice, don't it?"

He looked into her face, searching for signs of her weakening. He'd played the game before. He'd gotten rather good at it, over the years, despite the lack of eye contact. He'd have to fuck her, but that was the easy part. He'd long since learned how to get it up and keep it up, regardless of his partner. It was sidestepping her wild, sadistic rages that was tricky.

"I'm sorry, Chaz." The Other smiled. "But Sonja isn't in right now. It's a good thing, too. She'd probably do something really stupid. Like forgive you."

Chaz tried to pull away, but it was too late, she'd already reversed the grip on his hands. "Let me go! Sonja, let go!"

Her voice was politely detached, like that of an airline stewardess. "How about if I broke one of your bones for every day I spent locked up in that stinking loony bin? That sound fair to you, Chaz? I was in there for six months. That averages out to one hundred and eighty days. Did you know there are two hundred and six bones in the human body, Chaz? That'll leave you with twenty-six unbroken bones. That's not too bad, is it, now?"

She tightened her grip. Chaz screamed as the bones in his left hand snapped like a bundle of dry twigs. "That's twenty-seven . . ." His right hand crunched and became a mess of right angles. He yelled for someone—anyone—to help him. No one seemed to hear. ". . . and that's fifty-four. Only one hundred and twenty-six more to go. Oh, and don't bother yelling for help, Chaz. I told the manager we weren't to be disturbed. He was very obliging." She smiled, her fangs unsheathing like the claws of a cat.

Chaz's brain wrapped itself in shock, refusing to allow the pain in his ruined hands to escape past his wrists. He noted with detached fascination how the jagged ends of the finger bones pierced his flesh. His thinking was astonishingly clear now that his pain receptors were on hold. He was going to die, but it was up to him as to how horrible it would be.

"I'll tell you . . . who paid me."

"You don't need to. Wheele paid you. Really, Chaz, I thought you could do better—"

"Not Wheele, that bitch! She thought leaving me alive and whole was payment . . . enough. No, he paid me the hundred thousand to shut up. Told me to leave the country. They think I'm in Brazil."

He had her hooked. She leaned across the table, her face inches from his own. He could see himself reflected in her shades. He didn't look good.

"Why didn't you leave, Chaz? Surely you must have known I'd come looking for you."

Chaz blinked. That was a genuine puzzler. One he'd asked himself every night for six months. He should have jumped the first flight to Rio de Janeiro the minute he'd received that nice flight bag full of twenty-dollar bills. But he'd gone against his nature. He knew, better than anyone, that nothing short of death—and maybe not even that—would keep her from tracking him down.

"Dunno. Maybe I had some unfinished business." The numb throbbing was starting to creep up his forearms. He had to hurry. His hands would be waking up soon. "He paid me the hundred thousand . . . almost gone now. Should have gone to Rio. The coke's cheaper there. Could have sailed up the Amazon . . . learned how to chew the coca leaves, just like the Indians do." He smiled at the idea. Flocks of brilliantly colored macaws fluttered at the corners of his eyes.

"Who paid you, Chaz?"

"Sonja, my hands hurt . . ."

The Other was losing its patience. Chaz felt a shadow flicker through his forebrain, like a pig rooting for truffles. He wasn't so far gone she could invade him as easily as that. Besides, he had every intention of telling. But he had to do it right. He raised a barricade and the dark thing in his head hissed its displeasure. The shield would not hold for long, but it didn't have to.

"Who paid you, Chaz?"

"Jacob Thorne."

There was a heartbeat's worth of silence. Then the face below the sunglasses writhed. Chaz was pleased to see how deeply he had hurt her.

"Liar!"

She grabbed Chaz by the throat and dragged him from his seat. She shook him, determined to flail the truth out of his pale, wasted body. Chaz's head lolled backward, the weight of the skull no longer supported by the neck. The bastard was smiling.

Hustled again.

Lise finished cleaning the countertop and tossed the damp bar rag into the sink. God, what a slow night. The only customer in the joint was that Brit, Chaz. Lise still wasn't sure what to make of him. He was kind of creepy and he hung out with sleaze like the Blue Monkeys. She always felt like she was naked when he was around. But he was sort of good-looking, in a Keith Richards kind of way. And no American girl's completely immune to a British accent, even one by way of the council blocks. Besides, he tipped well and occasionally offered a little crystal meth if the service was good. She'd screwed guys for less than that.

Time to check up on him. He was bound to have finished his gin and tonic. She winced. Her head felt like it was about to split open. Probably her sinuses again. Oh, well, Chaz no doubt had something for a nasty headache.

As she approached the table, she noticed Chaz was slumped in his chair, hands folded in his lap. His chin was propped on his chest, a shock of dirty blond hair obscuring his face. Lise groaned aloud. The asshole was strung out. Rocky didn't like the customers nodding out before they settled their bar tabs, and he didn't like Chaz, straight or not.

"Hey, Chaz! Hey, man. You want Rocky to see you?" She grasped his shoulder, her hopes for a big tip and a free line of meth rapidly disintegrating. "C'mon, man, wake up!"

His head rolled forward, the eyes turned up so only the whites were visible. His mouth flopped open. Blood and saliva dribbled onto the floor.

Her screams were audible from the street.

He was walking through a featureless maze. There was no sky. Every turn led him down a corridor that looked the same as the last. Claude did not know where he was or how he got there.

He realized he was being led through the identical passageways. At his side walked a huge lion with a long black mane. The lion guided him as a seeing-eye dog would a blind man, except that it held Claude's right hand in its mouth. Claude could feel the gentle pressure of its jaws against the flesh of his palm. Although Claude was not afraid, he was somewhat perturbed to find his hand in the mouth of a lion. The beast showed no signs of harming him and it seemed to know the way. Still, it *was* a lion . . .

He awoke in darkness. What time was it? Three o'clock? Or had an entire day slipped past without his being aware of it? No. Only a couple of hours, he was certain. Something had woken him up. But what?

Somewhere in the dark, a door closed.

That was it. His enigmatic hostess had returned. He sat up in the narrow cot, fumbling with the orange crate that served as a nightstand. His hands closed on a plastic cylinder.

How considerate. After tucking him back into bed, the vampire left him a flashlight in case he had to find the john in the middle of the night. He bit back another fit of hysterical giggles and thumbed the flashlight on.

The beam wasn't very strong and did little to illuminate the blackness of the loft. The painted animals on the screens seemed to move in the weak light as if stalking him.

He found her leaning against a brick wall, her back to him. Claude noticed for the first time the rungs sunk into the brick face and the trapdoor set in the ceiling. He watched for a couple of minutes as the shoulders of her leather jacket hitched in short, sharp spasms before realizing what she was doing.

She's crying.

Claude stepped forward, lifting the flashlight so he could see her better. He felt awkward and intrusive, but he could not stop from trying to comfort her.

"Denise?"

She whirled about, startled by his presence. Claude heard himself cry out as if from somewhere far away. Her mouth was smeared with blood, but that wasn't the bad part. The bad part was she didn't have her sunglasses on.

The whites of her eyes swam with blood and were red as fresh wounds. There were no irises, just overexpanded pupils the size of shoe buttons. There was no humanity in them. They were the eyes of a wild thing.

She recoiled from the light, lifting a forearm to shield her horrible, flat eyes. The hiss that escaped her made Claude's testicles crawl.

"Don't look at me! Don't touch me! Don't talk to me! Just leave me *alone!*"
She struck out blindly, knocking the flashlight from his hand.

Claude watched the beam of pale-yellow light as the flashlight cartwheeled through the darkness before shattering on the floor. He felt her jacket brush his elbow and then she was gone, swallowed by the labyrinth of rice paper.

Claude stood in the dark and massaged the fingers of his right hand. They were numb from where she'd knocked the flashlight out of his grip, but otherwise he was unharmed.

Somewhere in the loft, Sonja Blue wept dry tears of frustration.

RESURRECTION BLUES

This year I slept and woke with pain
I almost wished no more to wake.
—Lord Tennyson, *In Memoriam*

She lay silent and still, hands folded on her chest in mimicry of the dead. Her pulse slowed itself, her breathing becoming so shallow her chest did not rise and fall as she entered the sleep of the undead. But vampires are denied the luxury of dreams. They can only remember.

I do not remember *being* Denise Thorne.

I can recall events, dates, and names from the time before, but they are not my memories. They are dry facts, summoned from an impersonal computer file, snapshots from someone else's life.

Her dog's name was Woofer.

Her best friend in the third grade was Sarah Teagarden.

The chauffeur's name was Darren.

The names have faces and information attached to them, but the emotion is gone. I feel nothing for them.

Except for her parents.

I am amazed there is still a spark of emotion left for them. I'm not certain if this is anything to celebrate. That is where the pain comes from.

I remember her last hours vividly; I guess that's because they are the hours of my conception and lead directly to my birth in the backseat of a Rolls Royce. No human can claim such memories. Guess I'm one lucky bitch.

I remember the discotheque with the loud psychedelic music—the Apple Cart—and the pulsating amoebas on the wall and the bored-looking girls in miniskirts dancing in cages suspended from the ceiling. Really Swinging London, man.

Denise splurged on champagne cocktails. No society child is a stranger to alcohol, but she had yet to master it. Being treated like an adult and ogled by men was intoxicant enough. She was giddy. And careless. And stupid.

I do not recall the exact moment Morgan made himself known. He was just there, as if he'd been present all along. He was tall, distinguished, and looked early middle-aged. He was elegant and debonair and Cary Grant-ish, with streaks of silver at his temples and an impeccable Saville Row suit. He called himself Morgan. *Sir* Morgan. He was an aristocrat. The way he carried himself, the way he moved, his tone of voice, made it evident he was a man used to issuing commands and having them obeyed. He looked out of place in the club, but no one would have dared challenge his right to be there.

Sir Morgan plied her with champagne and produced an endless stream of urbane banter. Despite her millions, Denise was a teenage girl and, therefore, susceptible to romance and fantasy. She imagined herself the Poor Little Rich Girl with Morgan as her Prince Charming. Unaware of her fortune, he had picked her, out of all the older, more experienced women in the nightclub, to be his companion. Stupid little get.

A girl with savvy would have pegged Morgan for an upper-class rake with a taste for squab. She would have been wrong, but that was closer to the truth than the romantic sap sluicing through Denise's overheated imagination.

She could not take her eyes off him. Every time he looked at her, she was certain he saw all the things she kept secret inside herself. She wanted to fuck him real bad.

I'm certain he did not know who Denise Thorne really was. Careless of him. If he'd known, he would never have approached her. Had things gone as planned, the resulting headlines would have spoiled everything and eventually spelled not only his death, but the ruination of centuries of careful planning.

After succeeding in separating her from the herd, Morgan suggested a midnight ride through the streets of London. How romantic. Stupid! Stupid! Stupid!

The Rolls was the color of smoke. The chauffeur opening the door wore livery so black it didn't reflect light. The windows in the rear of the car were also heavily tinted. For privacy, he assured her. A bottle of champagne awaited them, nestled in a bucket full of ice. Denise felt like she was in a movie. All it needed was a soundtrack.

After her second glass of champagne things began to go wrong. The interior of the car rippled and warped. It was very warm and close. It hurt to breathe. She had trouble keeping her eyes from rolling like greased ball bearings.

But worst of all, Sir Morgan . . . changed.

He opened his mouth and his canines grew, extending a full inch. His tongue flicked over his teeth, wetting the razor-sharp points. His eyes seemed to shimmer. The pupils wavered, like candle flames caught in a draft, then narrowed into reptilelike slits. The whites surrounding his eyes looked like they were bleeding.

Denise screamed and threw herself against the car door. She clawed at the space where the handle should have been, then pummeled the wall of glass that separated her from the driver. The chauffeur glanced back at her and smiled, displaying sharp teeth. She dropped back against the upholstery, clutching her elbows. She was too frightened to scream. All she could do was shiver.

Morgan smirked and shook his head. "Silly girl."

She felt his will enter her, hot as pig iron. She started to cry as Morgan pulled her to him without using his hands. He reached into her head and ordered her to crawl across the backseat, and her body obeyed. She struggled against him the best she could, but Morgan was far too old and far too powerful to be denied by a sixteen-year-old girl. Her body was a marionette fashioned of meat, and Morgan the red-eyed puppet master.

Her prayers were incoherent by the time she reached his lap, her fingers numb as she opened his fly.

His penis was huge and marble-white. It was erect, yet empty of blood. It was cold in her mouth and felt dead, despite its pretense of life. Her facial muscles cramped and it felt as if her jaw would dislocate. Her fear turned into shame, then blazed into hate. She tried to force her teeth down onto the meat violating her throat, but her body refused to cooperate. She nearly choked on her own vomit when the glans of his penis struck her tonsils.

Morgan eventually grew bored with oral rape and retracted his control over her flesh. Denise collapsed in midstroke. Her throat was scalded by bile and her face ached. Her cheek lay pressed against the wool blend of Morgan's pant leg. His crotch was stained with her tears and saliva. She could hear the Rolls purr as it wound its way through the streets of London with no particular place to go.

Morgan flipped Denise onto her back. She was in shock, beyond reacting to what was done to her. She watched him shred her clothes with detached interest. His hands were cold. Dead man's hands.

He lifted one of her arms, turning it so the inner forearm was exposed. He ran cool, dry lips over the pulse point in her elbow. He drove his fangs into her arm the instant he shoved himself between her legs.

Denise cried out once. Her scream was so shrill the dogs in the neighborhood the limo rolled through howled in sympathy.

The horror of what was being done to her broke through the shock barrier her mind had erected to protect itself. Everything that was Denise Thorne disappeared, raped into oblivion by her demon prince.

And I was born.

My first sensation was pain—pain as Morgan punctured my forearms with his blood kisses, pain as his ice-cold dick rammed into my blood-slick vagina. His jism burned like battery acid. He slammed against my bruised and bloodied crotch for a few more minutes after his orgasm before finally growing bored with the game.

I ceased to exist the moment he disengaged his dick. He was too busy buttoning up to notice I was alive.

I couldn't move. I was still weak from being born. I noted his clothes were covered with blood, mucus, and sperm. Morgan enjoyed a sloppy fuck.

The car rolled to a stop and the doors unlocked themselves. Morgan threw me into the gutter like a passing motorist tossing out a fast-food wrapper. I heard a bottle shatter under me, but I couldn't feel anything. I was dying.

Death's funny. It fans whatever spark of self-preservation is left in your carcass into an inferno. Somehow, I found the strength to pull myself onto the sidewalk. I dug my fingers into the cracks in the pavement and hauled myself along the concrete an inch at a time. The blood kept making me lose my grip.

Even though I was horribly bashed up, I kept thinking about how badly my teeth hurt. The pain in my upper jaw overwhelmed my other injuries.

I remember hearing a man yell, "Oi!" And I can remember the pavement vibrating under my belly as he ran toward me. But the very last thing I recall before sliding into my coma was a weird tingling in my fingertips, like bugs were crawling all over them. It wasn't bugs.

It was my fingerprints changing.

I woke up nine months later. But that's not the point. The thing is, I woke up empty.

I wasn't a complete tabula rasa; I knew that two plus two equaled four, I could still speak and understand English, and I knew all the words to "Strawberry Fields Forever." But as to *who* I was and where I came from, I drew a blank.

That didn't bother me, at first. When I came to, I was lying on my side in a hospital bed with tubes up my nose and an IV stuck in my arm. I woke up thinking, *I gotta get outta here.* I didn't know my name, or even how old I was, but I did know I couldn't stay in that place anymore. Time to leave.

I sat up for the first time in nine months, my joints cracking like dry timber. Pain bit into my calves and spine as I forced my muscles to flex and bend, but the pain seemed very far away. Numb fingers pulled at the tubes sunk into my nostrils. There was a brief sunspot of pain, then blood streamed from my nose. I ignored the warmth dripping off my upper lip and clawed at the needle sunk beneath the surface of my wrist. Another flash of cold light and the smell of saltwater flooded the room.

I fumbled with the protective railing for a couple of minutes. There was a click and the side collapsed. I felt a quick jolt of hurt in my crotch. I had just performed a rather crude decatheterization on myself.

I felt giddy and numb. Maybe I was dreaming of escape. I lowered myself to the floor and stared at my surroundings, wobbling on thin, uncertain legs like a newborn colt.

I was in a hospital ward. Beds were lined up to the left and right of me, each housing a silent, motionless mound of blankets and meat. I tottered toward the door, peering through the gloom at my wardmates. They lay curled in their beds like giant fetuses, umbilical cords emerging from their arms. It was night and the lights were off; but that made little difference to the sleepers. It was always night in that ward.

I passed through the door into a corridor. I hesitated on the threshold, blinking back tears. The light in the hall hurt my eyes, but I hunched my shoulders and continued to stagger along. I did not see a single doctor, nurse, or patient, but I could feel their presence nearby. I did not want to be discovered. I did not want to stay in that antiseptic, brightly lit place any longer. I rebounded off the door to the fire escape before I saw it. The fading letters on its surface read FIRE EXIT. I pulled on the handle with both hands, painfully aware of how weak I was.

A gust of cold air mixed with light rain struck my face. I stumbled onto the landing and sucked in a lungful of fresh air. Old cigarette butts littered the metal floor. The interns no doubt used it for quick smokes while on duty. I might be found out if I stayed too long.

I began the long climb down to street level, my body finally starting to wake up. The pain and discomfort were no longer ghost sensations. Blood and phlegm leaked from my nostrils, and my hands were stained orange by a mixture of blood and rusty metal. It was bitter cold and all I had on was a faded hospital johnny. My legs cramped violently and I was afraid I would overbalance and fall over the railing into the alley below.

After what felt like an hour, I reached the bottom of the fire escape. My legs trembled and I felt feverish. I was ten feet above street level and couldn't figure out how to work the mechanism that released the ladder. I rattled the escape ladder, tears of frustration running down my face. I was terrified of being caught.

I tried lowering myself to the sidewalk. My arms felt like they were being pulled from their sockets. Probably were. Everything went gray and my fingers slipped. Then I was lying on my back in the middle of some garbage cans. All I saw was a tiny strip of night sky sandwiched between two old buildings. It was drizzling and raindrops dripped on my face.

I got to my feet and stumbled away. I had no idea of where to go, but I knew I had to get away. London is an ancient city, full of crooked streets and dead-end mews. It's easy to get lost there. I don't know how long I wandered the back alleys, avoiding the lights and traffic, but it was dawn when I collapsed in the doorway.

It was late April, and it's bloody cold in London that time of year. I was wet to the skin and shivering. I ached horribly and was badly bruised from my fall. My bare feet bled, but I didn't care. I sat in a shallow doorway that faced the alley, shoulders hunched and knees drawn to my chest. I felt unconsciousness boiling up inside me, but I was afraid to close my eyes. I remembered the beds full of unborn sleepers, their eye sockets filled with shadow. I started trembling and could not stop.

Suddenly, there were hands on me, lifting me from my deathwatch.

"See Joe? There she is, just as I said . . ." The voice of a woman, shrill and sharp.

"Yeah, yer a reg'lar blood hound, Daphne. Here now, help me with her . . ." A man's voice, barely more than a bass rumble.

Faces swam into view: a thick-featured man with a broken nose and a pinch-faced woman wearing too much makeup bent over me. The pinch-faced woman clucked her tongue solicitously, sounding like a cockney hen. The big man wrapped his jacket around me and lifted me in his arms.

"Cor, look at th' state she's in! Looks more like a drowned rat," grumbled the man.

"But she's young, Joe," whined the woman. "You'll be makin' more than a bleedin' fiver off 'er, ducks."

"Awright! Awright! Here's yer bloody finder's fee! Now, sod off. I got business t' attend to."

I relaxed in the stranger's arms. I was warm and, for the moment, safe. I listened to his heart thump in his chest and the rasp of his breathing. I felt secure. My world had a focal point.

My savior's name was Joseph Lent. Joe was a pimp.

He was a big man in his early thirties. He resembled a Mick Jagger who'd gained fifty pounds and decided to play goalie for the Hammers. He wore his dirty blond hair long enough to touch his collar. He dressed flash—nicely tailored suits that could pass for Saville Row jobs. He used to laugh at how the "poncey bastards" who ran the shops sniffed while they waited on him.

"Like they was afraid of smellin' somethin' bad. Har! Har! Har!" He'd laugh and show his tooth—the gold bicuspid. That was always a bad sign. He'd laugh with his mouth but his eyes would never join in. Later on, he'd get drunk and use his fists.

Joe didn't know what to make of me, but he had his guesses. Shortly after

I was strong enough to sit up and keep down a little soup, he laid down the law. He sat on the bed and stared at me with his dark eyes.

"I dunno what yer game is, but it don't take much to figure yer runnin' from somethin'. Or someone. Izzat it? You some kind of runaway?"

I blinked. I really didn't know what to say. His guesses concerning my origins were as valid as anything I could volunteer.

"You escape from a government scheme? Mebbe th' methadone clinic, eh? I seen th' scars on yer arms. Y'into smack? Coke? Morphine? Don't make me no never-mind, love. Whatever turns y'on, like they say. I've put a lot o' time in on you, girl. If y'works f'me, you can have anything yer heart desires. I'll protect ya. I'll see that th' bobbies never get a hold of y'again. Is it a deal, now? Yer Joe Lent's girl now, ain'tcha?"

Joe became my man. Not just any man. He was *the* Man. He was my father, brother, lover, boss and personal terror. He schooled me for my role in life. He taught me how to walk, talk, dress, and tell vice plants from the regular tricks. I was a good student. I was desperate for an identity. Any identity. And Joe Lent was more than happy to define my world. He's the one who named me Sonja Blue: "Sounds exotic. Like one o' them long-legged Danish birds."

It was perfectly natural that I should walk the streets and proposition strange men and give my money to Joe. Didn't every woman? I was barely a year old. How was I to know any different?

My life revolved around Joe. I fixed his meals. I cleaned his flat. I turned tricks for him. I gave him my money. I had a name, a function in life, and I belonged to someone. I was happy. The only time I wasn't happy was when Joe beat me.

Pimps are an insecure lot. They live in fear of their meal tickets walking out on them for someone bigger and better. Joe was *real* insecure. He'd lost his last girl to the competition, and that hurt. That's why he carried the cane. The one with the bronze knob on the end shaped like an eagle's claw. The bobbies might not approve of him walking down the street with a cricket bat, but a cane . . . Well, that was gentlemanly. Style made all the difference.

Whenever Joe got bad drunk, he'd use his fists. He was good at slapping girls around. He knew how to beat the bloody daylights out of a woman without messing up her face or putting her out of business. And he knew how to do it so I'd lie on the floor, my nose gushing like a fire hydrant, and beg him to forgive me. And mean it, too.

Joe was my life, my love, my universe. If I lost him, where would I be? Who would I be?

Things went on like that for a year. We'd go through periods where Joe would alternately shower me with gifts, then beat me until it hurt to breathe. I always recovered quickly and rarely needed to see a doctor. The only time I had any problems with my health was when I developed anemia. I grew very pale and my eyes couldn't handle direct sunlight, so I took to wearing sunglasses.

When my appetite began to seriously dwindle, Joe dragged me to the aged quack who "fixed up" all the working girls in the district. Joe was terrified of losing me to disease or pregnancy. I was quite successful on the street; I attracted the odd fish out looking for a bit of kink. You could charge extra for that.

The old charlatan prescribed ox blood and milk to "strengthen my constitution." It actually worked. For a while.

Occasionally, Joe tried to get me to talk about my past. He entertained the notion that I was the daughter of a rich man and doubted the extent of my amnesia. His attempts at making me remember never worked. As far as I was concerned, Joe was my real family. For some reason, I never told him about the hospital and the roomful of empty sleepers. Perhaps I was afraid he'd try to take me back there.

I was two years old when it happened. Joe was drunk again. He'd gotten it into his head that I was trying to cheat him on his take and planning to walk out on him. He was out of his mind. I'd never seen him so angry. He didn't use his fists that night. He went after me with the cane, instead.

The first time the cane struck me, all the air went out of my lungs in one big *whoosh!* The second blow caught me in the pit of my stomach. I fell onto the floor. I couldn't draw in a second breath. It felt like I was drowning. The third stroke caught me on the right shoulder. I heard, rather than felt, the bronze eagle's claw break my collarbone. Then he started kicking, all the while calling me foul names and raving at the top of his lungs.

I tried crawling away, but he followed me. He wouldn't let me be. And, for the first time since he found me, I began to hate Joe. The hate surprised me with its strength. There was so much of it! It seemed to grow in direct proportion with the pain. I was so full of hate it threatened to pour out my mouth and nose. I was so astonished by my capacity for it I nearly forgot my beating.

Joe brought his cane across my back and I felt ribs snap. Suddenly, my hate changed. I felt it curdling and churning inside of me, transforming itself into a force I couldn't contain. I opened my mouth to scream, but all I could do was laugh. And laugh. And laugh.

I do not remember what happened after that.

I woke up on what was left of the bed.

Every muscle in my body ached. I had at least two broken ribs, a broken collarbone, and my left eye refused to open. There was blood in my mouth. I squinted through my rapidly swelling right eye, expecting to see Joe sitting in his favorite chair, the cane propped across the armrests. Joe was always serene and composed after a beating.

Joe wasn't in his chair.

In fact, the chair was a jumble of kindling.

Then I noticed the blood on the walls, and how high some of it was splattered. I felt dizzy and looked down at my hands. My fingers were digging into the mattress and I could see the mattress ticking through the huge rents in the bedclothes. My ears were ringing. I looked up again, afraid of what I might see.

I saw Joe.

He was sprawled in the corner like a big rag doll. He didn't move when I called his name.

I got to my feet, although I almost swooned when I stood up. My stomach was the color of a ripe eggplant and hurt with every step I took. I staggered over to where Joe lay.

There wasn't much left of him.

His arms and legs were bent funny, like a scarecrow's; then I noticed all the long bones had been snapped in two. The jagged edges stuck out through his clothes.

His head was a mass of hairy pudding attached to his neck. His eyes were pulp and his teeth lay scattered like mah-jongg tiles. Maybe it wasn't really Joe. The corpse could be anybody . . . Then I saw the gold bicuspid. I shivered and looked away.

There was a ragged hole just above his breastbone, as if someone had attempted a tracheotomy with a can opener. Then I noticed the rest of him.

His killer had torn off his trousers and shoved the cane up his ass. An inch or two of wood and the bronze eagle's claw protruded from between his buttocks. The eagle's claw was clotted with blood, hair, and brains. That meant Joe was probably already dead when his killer rammed three and a half feet of mahogany up his rectum. At least, I hoped so.

I stumbled backward, clamping a hand over my mouth. My guts heaved, angering the bruises purpling my abdomen as I hobbled to the loo. My brain was starting to wake up; what if whoever killed Joe was still in the flat? Maybe it was the gang from the next district. Joe had a lot of enemies. That was his way. But no one hated him enough to do that kind of job on him. No one.

The bathroom was empty. I tried to make it to the toilet but got as far as the sink before throwing up. God, how it hurt. I forgot about Joe and clung to the washbasin. My knees tried to buckle but I forced myself to stand. I didn't like the idea of fainting with a dead man in the other room. I opened my eyes and found myself staring into the sink, at what I'd sicked up.

The sink was full of blood. But it wasn't my blood.

I began to shake. Sweat trickled down my back. It felt like a spider crawling down my spine. I was startled at how easy it was for me to identify the blood I'd puked as belonging to Joe. Blood has its own identity, just like fingerprints, voiceprints, or semen. It tasted of Joe.

I was right. Nobody hated Joe Lent enough to do such horrible things to him.

Except me.

I looked in the mirror and saw the blood smeared across my lips. I opened my mouth in dumb protest and saw, for the first time, my own fangs. They emerged from my gums hard and wet, stained with stolen blood. I cried out and pressed my hands over my mouth in an attempt to hide my shame.

I remembered.

I remembered who I was and where I'd come from and how I got there. I remembered what I was. I heard Morgan's dry farewell laugh as he tossed me from the car. I recalled the weird writhing in my fingertips just before I went into hibernation. I stared at my hands, fearful that they might turn into the claws of a monster. Suddenly, the room flexed and I watched as the whorls and lines on my fingers and palms melted. New ridges and patterns emerged, only to be swallowed by yet another set. I forced myself to look away and caught sight of my face in the mirror. No wonder they never found me. Even my face . . . I tried to scream but all that came out was a dry choking sound. My flesh halted its dance.

I think I went insane then, at least temporarily. The part of me that fancied itself human went on vacation. My memories are fuzzy, as if I were drunk the whole time. I came back to find myself on a small boat owned by an Irish fisherman sympathetic to the IRA. I told him I was in trouble because I'd killed an English soldier. That was good enough for him. Money was no problem. Joe Lent taught me well, and now I no longer had to share the wealth.

I entered France through Marseilles, one of Europe's most glamorous hellholes. I spent a few weeks trawling the narrow streets and open-air cafés of the Pigalle, earning my keep and learning the language. I also discovered what Joe had referred to as "the Etonian vice" was not limited to England. I was pursued more than once by prospective "protectors," but always managed to escape. I lived in mortal terror of losing control again and killing someone. The beatings my clients paid for . . . Well, that was different. I also feared remembering. I did my best to live in the present and limit the future to my next meal. However, my condition, once awakened, could not be ignored.

My eyes, already sensitive to strong light, now required protection in the dimmest surroundings. I could deal with that. The hunger was my biggest problem.

The hunger was a balloon in my belly; when the balloon was full, I functioned normally; I even felt good enough to fool myself into thinking I was human. But when the balloon was empty, the hunger was released, threatening to destroy me from the inside out. It felt like a massive meth overdose: my heart and pulse nearly shook me apart; my lungs were filled with cold lead and my guts full of bamboo splinters. Compared to the pain I've endured since then, the early stage of my addiction was a cakewalk.

I bought live rabbits and geese from the markets—a benefit of being stricken with vampirism on the Continent—and drained them as humanely as I knew how. The salty hotness of blood as it filled my mouth was appallingly delicious. A warm, pleasant feeling replaced the pain as I drank. But it was never really enough. Deep down, I knew I wanted something more than the blood of animals.

I left France within two months of my arrival. I was afraid of being picked up by Interpol. I did not fear being punished for Joe's death. I was terrified that Denise's parents would discover the truth. Better they should believe their daughter dead.

I drifted from city to city, using stolen passports to cross the borders. Finally, I got tired of fighting off pimps and signed up with a Norwegian brothel catering to the North Sea oil trade.

Bordellos servicing wildcatter rigs aren't posh joints; they resemble frontier cathouses from the turn of the century. They're loud, cheap, vulgar, and rowdy. Gangs of drunken, horny men constantly squabble over a handful of available women.

The launches came in with the men from the rigs on a regular basis. The usual crowd consisted of Swedes, Norwegians, Brits, and the occasional American, but they were all the same by the time they made it to our place— roaring drunk and ready to fuck. There were always twice as many tricks as girls and at least one john who didn't want to wait his turn. Brawls over girls were pretty common.

The madam was an old whore named Foucault. She liked to brag about how she'd "seen service on all fronts" during the Second World War. Maybe the First one, too. She knew the business and kept a bouncer on hand for when the brawls got out of control. Which proved to be almost every night.

The *Amphitryon* was a rig so isolated its crew managed shore leave only once a year. The men came in loud and rowdy, bragging about their dicks and their staying power. It looked like a typical workshift.

Madame Foucault greeted the "gentlemen" at the door and ordered a round of drinks on the house. She explained that since there were over twenty men and only twelve girls, there would be a slight delay in attending to their needs, but she promised that everyone would be "taken care of."

She ordered us to come out and model for the customers. The girls were decked out in their work lingerie, which was starting to show signs of wear and tear; the feather boas needed dry cleaning, the fishnet stockings sported badly patched ladders, and some of the Frederick's of Hollywood-style costumes fit a bit too snugly.

The men of the *Amphitryon* didn't give a damn. They argued among themselves as to who'd go first and who'd get which girl. One of them swaggered over to me and began to feel my tits. He reeked of peppermint schnapps.

"That one's mine," one of them slurred in Swedish.

"Hell she is," retorted the bigger man, fumbling with my bra straps.

I looked past the man attempting to undress me and stared at the Swede. He was smaller than his fellow and stood clenching his fists. There was anger in his face. The other man was built like a linebacker and it was clear he was used to being deferred to. The Swede wanted to kill the big man, but was afraid of being humiliated in front of the others.

Waves of hate emanated from the Swede. It felt as if I were standing in front of a heat lamp. I started to get excited, and the big drunk thought I was responding to his pawing.

"See? She likes a *real* man," he jeered.

The Swede's rage was exquisite. He stared directly at me and I felt a brief connection between us, like the spark that detonates a keg of dynamite. He wanted to see the big man's blood. So did I.

The smaller man's face reddened and seemed to swell, as if trying to contain an internal explosion. His eyes glazed and he began to tremble. One of his companions touched his arm and the Swede bellowed like a bull and lunged at the big man.

The drunken giant was taken by surprise, stunned by the ferocity of the attack. The Swede slammed a fist into his tormentor's kidney. The big man's jaw dropped in mute pain. I stood, motionless, and watched the two of them writhe on the floor at my feet. The hatred radiating from the Swede was of tsunami proportions.

The Swede was astride the other man's back, delivering vicious punches to his head. Some of the victim's friends grabbed the Swede and pulled him off the prone figure. The Swede swore and struggled violently. They tried to calm him down, but the little Swede kept kicking and clawing, his curses degenerating into a wordless shrieking.

The bouncer, a muscular German, emerged from the backroom and immediately jumped to the wrong conclusion; he thought the men restraining the smaller man were responsible for the fight, so he grabbed one of the men holding the Swede. The big man was on his hands and knees, staring uncomprehendingly at the blood from his nose puddling on the sawdust-strewn floor. The Swede landed on his spine feet first, forcing the big man back into the floorboards. Then he began to throttle him from behind. The big man's back was broken and he was helpless to shake off his attacker.

The big man's face purpled. His tongue stuck out and his eyes looked like deviled eggs. Four men grappled with the crazed Swede in an attempt to dislodge him, but he refused to be budged.

By this time the men from the *Amphitryon* were either trying to pry the Swede off his victim or they were fighting the bouncer. The girls fled to the safety of their rooms. I didn't move a muscle; I was basking in the Swede's homicidal frenzy.

The riot was in full swing. The men arguing with the bouncer were now brawling among themselves. Furniture was trashed. Bottles were smashed. All I could hear was men swearing and women screaming. The smell of blood was sharp and brassy. I felt wonderful.

The Swede finally succeeded in killing his foe. The big man lay prostrate on the floor like a Muslim at prayers. However, this obvious conquest didn't appease the Swede's bloodlust. He grabbed a chair and renewed his attack on the corpse. He screamed and laughed at the same time. His mouth was fixed in a rictus grin and tears streamed down his face.

There was a loud noise and something warm splashed my face.

The Swede let go of the chair. He stood for a second, staring at the hole in his middle and the loops of shiny pink intestine dangling around his knees, before falling to the ground. The hate was gone; it was as if someone had thrown a switch, allowing me to move and think again. I looked at myself. I was covered in the Swede's blood. I had to fight to keep from licking my hands.

Madame Foucault held a smoking shotgun, her face unreadable. The fight was over as suddenly as it'd begun. Everyone gathered around and stared at the dead men.

Madame Foucault finally spoke. "He went crazy. That's all there is to it."

I felt her looking at me. I stared at the blood congealing on the floor. I left the next day.

I realized there was more to being a vampire than simply drinking blood. I had been one of the undead for nearly four years and I had yet to understand my powers and their corresponding weaknesses. My knowledge of vampirism was incomplete; it was shaped by popular fiction, old superstitions, and other faulty attempts to mythologize a reality imperfectly perceived. I was trying to divine my true nature in a funhouse mirror.

According to folklore, vampires have their own set of rules, just like cricket or Monopoly. Vampires drank blood and only came out at night. They couldn't stand daylight or the sight of crosses. They were repelled by garlic. Silver was anathema. Holy water had the same effect as battery acid. They could be killed by a stake through the heart. They could not enter a church. They never aged. They turned into bats and wolves. They had powerful hypnotic powers. They slept in coffins during the day.

I was confused by these rules and fearful of testing their validity. It had been over three years since my birth in the backseat of Sir Morgan's Rolls, but I had yet to make an attempt to explore my dark heritage.

Some things didn't need much in the way of proving. I didn't like going out in direct daylight; it made my skin itch and caused headaches that threatened to separate the lobes of my brain. However, I did not burst into flame or crumble to dust the moment I set foot outside. As long as I wore heavy clothing and sunglasses, I could function with only a minimum of discomfort.

The only noticeable effect garlic had on me was bad breath.

I did not experience revulsion or pain in the presence of crucifixes. However, visions of Christopher Lee, the flesh of his stigmatized forehead bubbling like molten cheese, kept me from touching one.

Silver did not bother me, whether in the form of crosses, flatware, or coin of the realm. As for the stake through the heart bit, well . . . I didn't consider it a feasible test.

I was still ageing, although my years of hard living did not show; there were girls in the business younger than myself who could have passed for my older sisters. My stamina was incredible; I was rarely sick and I healed quickly. Too quickly. I was strong, although nowhere near as powerful as I would become. I had nothing to fear from even the roughest trade.

I ventured into a church and was not seized by epileptic fits the moment I crossed the threshold. Half-expecting to be struck by lightning, I approached the altar. Old women, their heads covered with babushkas and dressed in widows' weeds, knelt at the prayer rail. A priest dressed in a long, flowing cassock moved about in the shadows, tending the votive candles flickering at the feet of wooden saints.

The baptismal font was built into the altar rail. The lid pivoted to expose a shallow silver basin. I stared at the holy water. I'd intended to immerse my hand, but my resolve faltered at the possibility of my flesh being stripped to the bone. I noticed the priest, standing by the image of St. Sebastian, was watching me.

I hurried from the church, the holy water untested.

I wasn't too hot on turning into a bat. Did I need a magic potion or a special incantation to trigger the metamorphosis? And if I did succeed in becoming a bat, how would I reverse the transformation? Cinema vampires changed by lifting their capes and flapping their arms, but that was too damn silly. Perhaps if I concentrated real hard . . .

My body felt as if it was covered with ants. I cried out and leapt to my feet, swatting my arms and legs. I was afraid to look in the mirror, but I knew my flesh was dancing again. I rode out the skin tremors, and when they'd finished, I was still human. At least physically.

The hypnotic powers I'd experienced firsthand, although none of the legends I'd ever heard mentioned vampires drawing sustenance from the emotions of others. Nor did they mention telepathy, as I was becoming increasingly aware of the thoughts of those around me.

At first it was a mental variant of white noise; thousands of different voices merged into a backwash of unintelligible gibberish. Occasionally a snatch of coherent thought would bob to the surface, but nothing more.

I thought I was going mad. Then I realized the voices in my head weren't telling me to kill small children or derail streetcars; they seemed preoccupied about what to have for dinner and who stood a chance of winning the football pools. The only time I had problems was when I got too close to drunkards, madmen, or the truly evil. Their thoughts came through all too clear.

By spring of 1974 I found myself in Switzerland. I was employed in a house operated by Frau Zobel. Brothel-keeping was something of a family tradition for her, stretching back to the Napoleonic era. While Frau Zobel did not pretend to like me, she realized the financial benefits of having an employee specializing in "fancy passions."

I enjoyed working for Frau Zobel. She ran a first-class house, discreetly located in a respectable Zurich neighborhood. The girls were clean and the clientele genteel. It was light-years removed from my apprenticeship under Joe Lent and my time with Madame Foucault. But despite her grand airs and left-handed pedigree—she claimed to be the illegitimate granddaughter of Napoleon III—Frau Zobel was made from the same stuff as old Foucault; tenpenny nails and boot leather.

I had no friends among the girls in Frau Zobel's stable. I'd made it a practice not to get friendly with anyone, for fear of being discovered. Not that I had to actively discourage anyone from making overtures. Most women dislike me on sight. Men, on the other hand, react in one of two ways: either they are uneasy while in my presence, or they want to involve me in a minor sex atrocity.

I didn't mind being tied up with clothesline or beaten with a bundle of birch twigs, but I rarely played the submissive role. I attracted those who wanted to be dominated and degraded, and I assumed the mantle of dominatrix without complaint. It wasn't a one-way relationship; I experienced a diluted version of the pleasure I'd received from the Swede's berserker rage. I thought I was keeping that part of me in check. Instead, I was nursing it.

One of my regular clients was Herr Wallach, a pudgy man in his late fifties whose particular fancy passion involved a block-and-tackle and ice water enemas. Herr Wallach was a tenured mathematical theoretician. He also belonged to an esoteric fellowship composed of thinkers, artists, and poets. At least that's how he described it. Every year the group held a party at the home of one of its members. The host for the 1975 party was Herr Esel, a professor of metaphysics. Wallach wanted me to be his guest. The prospect of attending what sounded like a dreadfully dull evening in the company of Herr Wallach was far from appealing. Then he showed me the evening gown he'd bought for the occasion. It was a strapless dress made of black velvet, stunning in its simplicity, complete with matching silk opera gloves. Wallach told me I could keep it after the party.

Funny how something as trivial as an evening gown changed my life.

Professor Esel's estate was located on the outskirts of Zurich. It was an old mansion, inherited from an ancestor who made his fortune with pikemen and timepieces.

Herr Wallach made a great show of introducing me to his associates. The only time he seemed self-conscious was when he realized I meant to wear my sunglasses during the party. We argued about it on the way over and he sulked for a little while. However, parading around with a beautiful girl on his arm restored his good spirits. There were a few raised eyebrows, but the Swiss are nothing if not polite.

Wallach introduced me to Professor Esel, a florid little man who resembled a burgermeister more than a metaphysicist.

"Ah, Herr Professor, I would like you to meet . . . a friend of mine, Fräulein Blau."

"*Guten tag, Fräulein Blau.*" Esel bowed smartly. I received a mental image of myself tied naked to a canopied bed, surrounded by frisky dachshunds. Esel spoke to Wallach, although his eyes never left me. "You'll never guess who has shown up tonight, Stefan. Pangloss is here!"

Wallach was genuinely surprised. "*Nein!* You must be joking. After all this time? It must be ten years since he last attended one of our gatherings."

Esel shrugged. "See for yourself. He was in the music room, the last time I looked. The bastard hasn't changed at all."

"Come along, Sonja. You simply must meet Pangloss." Wallach led me away, unmindful of Professor Esel winking me *auf Wiedersehen.*

Pangloss was in the music room, seated on an antique sofa, flanked by two lovely women who listened to him avidly and laughed at his witticisms. There was a feverish gleam in their eyes as they followed his every movement. Their laughter was synchronized; it reminded me of the clockwork toys the Swiss are so adept at creating. They did not look away from Pangloss when Herr Wallach introduced me.

"Herr Doktor Pangloss, I would like you to meet Fräulein Blau."

Pangloss halted in mid-anecdote and gazed at Wallach. My first impression was of a man in his early fifties, his longish black hair randomly streaked with gray. He wore an evening suit and wire-rim glasses tinted dark green. He smiled frostily at Wallach, then focused his attention on me.

"I am delighted to make your acquaintance, Fräulein."

Wallach cried out as my fingers bit into the soft flesh of his upper arm. I was close to fainting, but I could not look away. Wearing Pangloss's clothes and seated between the twin automatons was a dead thing, resembling an unwrapped mummy, its flesh the color and texture of parchment. There was enough nose left to keep the wire-rims in place, and I caught a glimpse of banked embers deep within the sockets. A few strands of silvery hair clung to the yellowed, flaking scalp. The creature lifted a skeletal hand—its fingers capped by filthy, splintered talons—and fitted an ebony cigarette holder in its lipless mouth.

"What is the matter with your lovely companion, Wallach? It is Wallach, is it not?" rasped the dead thing. "She seems to have taken ill."

Flustered, Wallach hurried me onto the balcony. Pangloss followed. His lady friends, forgotten for the moment, blinked like mediums emerging from deep trance.

After seating me on a bench, Wallach babbled something about fresh air and scampered off in search of a glass of water. I caught the odor of dust and cobwebs and found Pangloss standing beside me. He no longer looked like an unraveled pharaoh. I wondered if I was going mad.

"Perhaps I can be of some assistance, Fräulein Blau. After all, I *am* a doctor . . ." He reached to feel my pulse, but his hand was bone and desiccated flesh. I recoiled.

His features flowed and hardened into a mask of normalcy. "I was right. You can see." He stepped closer. The smell of rot threatened to choke me. "Who's get are you? Who sent you here? Was it Linder? Answer me!"

I staggered to my feet; I did not want that dead thing near me.

"You dare?" Red fire flickered behind green glass and something cold stabbed my brain. I remembered Sir Morgan and how he raped Denise's mind before he raped her body.

Not again. Never again. I pushed back, desperate to force the intruder out of my mind, even if it meant my eyes popped out on their stalks. I felt Pangloss's frustration boil into rage, then I was alone in my head.

We stood facing each other, both of us shivering. Pangloss was furious, but I sensed uncertainty in him.

"How old are you?" he hissed. His image flickered like a failing fluorescent light. One moment he was a well-dressed bon vivant, the next an animated corpse. It was rather distracting.

I told him the truth. There was no point in lying. "I was born in 1969."

"Impossible! You could not possibly have such power!" He grabbed my wrist, forcing me to look him in the face. The flesh sloughed away, revealing a death's-head. "Don't lie to me. I don't know whose get you are, but you aren't going to count coup with me. You may have caught me off-guard that time, but I won't make the same mistake twice. Oh, you're strong, that's true, but you don't know what to with it, do you?"

"Ah, Herr Doktor! There you are. Herr Wallach mentioned you were looking after Fräulein Blau for him . . ."

Pangloss and I stared at the man framed in the french windows. He was a small, slender man in his sixties with a dapper little mustache. Hardly a knight in shining armor, but he'd do.

Pangloss dropped my wrist as if it were leprous. He bowed stiffly in my direction. "I am relieved to hear that you are no longer ill, Fräulein. Now, you must please excuse me. He pushed past my savior, who regarded him with a wry smile, and disappeared into the house.

"A most unusual man, the Herr Doktor, is he not?" the little man mused aloud. "Ah! But I have not introduced myself. How rude! I am Erich Ghilardi."

"Do you . . . know Doktor Pangloss?"

Ghilardi shrugged. "Let us say I know *of* him. I fear Herr Wallach will be returning with your drink soon, so I shall dispense with small talk. May I visit you at your place of employment, Fräulein? Ah, do not look so surprised! Your behavior this evening was most proper. It was no failure on your part, I assure you. Everyone in our little clique knows how Wallach locates his companions."

I smiled and handed him my card. He bowed neatly and slipped it into his breast pocket. "*Auf Wiedersehen*, Fräulein Blau."

I watched him leave. Such a polite old gentleman. It was hard to imagine him dangling from the chandelier or groveling on all fours with a rubber ball in his mouth.

Wallach frowned when he returned with my glass of water. "What was Ghilardi doing out here?"

"Simply making sure I was all right. Nothing you need to worry about."

Wallach continued to fret. "I don't like him paying attention to you. He's disturbed, you know."

"No, I didn't know. Who is he?"

Wallach didn't approve of me asking about Ghilardi, but his love of gossip overcame his misgivings. "He's one of Europe's leading scholars on fantasy and the occult. Rather, he used to be. He wrote several volumes on the masters of the genre: Poe, Lovecraft, and the like. Then he went over the edge. In fact, ten years ago he suffered some form of fit while hosting our little event. Most unfortunate. After that, he started claiming werewolves and vampires were real, or some such trash. He even wrote a book about shadow races living in secret coexistence with humanity for thousands of years. Of course, the book was widely ridiculed when it was published. Made himself a complete laughing stock."

It was late when I returned to my room. I stripped down to my skin and sat in the dark, thinking about what had happened at the party.

I'd finally come face-to-face with one of my own. What had Morgan really looked like? The thought was enough to make me shudder.

I contemplated the cheval glass in the corner of my room. What about me? What did *I* really look like?

I'd dismissed the belief that vampires hated mirrors as an old wives' tale, like the inviolability of sacred ground. Maybe *I* was the ignorant one.

Perhaps vampires loathe mirrors not because of what they *don't* see, but because of what they *do*.

It was dawn before I mustered the courage to stand before the mirror. I was terrified of what might stare back at me, but too curious to remain ignorant. Although my reflection wasn't that of a withered hag, I was outlined in a faint nimbus of reddish light. It was strongest about my head and shoulders; I was reminded of the corona glimpsed during an eclipse. My reflection smiled at me. I put my hand to my mouth, but my mirror twin didn't. A long, pointed tongue, like that of a cat, emerged from my duplicate's lips.

"No!" I struck the cheval glass hard enough to make it spin. I backed away, watching the mirror as it flashed reversed images of the room. It came to a halt with its back to me, the mirror facing the wall. I left it that way.

Ghilardi came to visit me within a week of our encounter at Herr Esel's party.

I received him in the parlor and, after sampling the house wine, escorted him to my room. He had a black valise, like the ones doctors carry. I didn't think anything about it, since my clients tended to rely on props.

Once we were alone, I excused myself and ducked behind a screen to change. I told him to make himself comfortable; he nodded politely, glancing about the room nonchalantly. He looked at the inverted mirror for a long moment before moving to the bed. I tried to engage him in conversation, hoping to divine his kink.

"So, Herr Ghilardi, what is it you like?"

"Like?" He sounded distracted.

"*Ja*. What is it you would like me to do to you? Or you to me? Don't be shy, *mein herr*, there's nothing you could say that could possibly shock me."

"I see." He didn't sound convinced. "Fräulein Blau . . ."

"Sonja."

"Umm, very well, then. Sonja, I would like you to do nothing to me."

I stepped out from behind the screen. "Are you quite sure about that, Herr Ghilardi?"

Ghilardi was standing beside the bed; he was still fully clothed and had the black bag open. He opened his mouth to answer but nothing came out. My work clothes often affected the customers that way.

I was dressed in a black chamois Merry Widow corset that lifted and separated my breasts like jelly molds. My legs were sheathed in black nylons with seams up the back, held in place by a black lace garter belt. I walked toward him slowly so I wouldn't overbalance on my spike-heeled patent-leather pumps. I still had my shades on. Most of my clients didn't mind that I kept my eyes hidden while I serviced them. Those who demanded to see my eyes never returned.

"Lilith!" It was a gasp of recognition and repudiation.

Before I could tell him he could call me whatever he liked, Ghilardi thrust a hand into his valise and withdrew a silver flask.

"*Verdamt Nosferatu!*" he cried, and dashed its contents in my face.

I staggered backward, spitting out a mouthful of lukewarm water. My makeup was ruined.

Pressing his advantage, Ghilardi produced a large silver crucifix and slammed it against my forehead, knocking off my shades and throwing me off-balance. I landed solidly on my rump.

I clapped my hands over my face and screwed my eyes shut. I was vaguely aware of Ghilardi intoning the words to the Lord's Prayer in Latin. I was too dumbstruck to notice if the skin had been flayed from my skull.

I'd been found out! I'd been identified as a monster and was going to die like one, that was the important thing. I thought of Denise's parents; how it would hurt them to find out what had really happened to their child.

There were hands on my shoulders. "Forgive me. Forgive me, *bitte!* You must think me a crazy old man, *nicht wahr?* How can I explain why I did such a cruel, insane thing . . ." He pulled a neatly pressed linen handkerchief from his breast pocket and began to daub at my face. "Please, Fräulein. I'm sorry if I frightened you. Are you hurt? Let me see . . ."

I took my hands from my face, and to my surprise as much as Ghilardi's, I began to cry. It was the first time I'd done so since Joe Lent's death.

"I am *Nosferatu*. You're not mistaken."

"*Nein.*" His voice was soft, comforting. His hand strayed to my damp, unmarred forehead and patted it reassuringly. "You are not one of the Damned, child. Forgive me for thinking such foolishness."

A flare of anger sparked deep inside me. "What do *you* know about it, old man?" I tried to pull away from him, and when he would not let me go, I bared my fangs. He sucked in a sharp breath, but did not draw away.

"Let me see your eyes."

I complied. Even the dim light of my room was painful.

"How long have you been like this?"

"Since 1970. Maybe 1969."

"*Unmöglich!*" He seemed as astonished as Pangloss. He wiped away my tears and told me to blow my nose. "You are something very rare, Fräulein Blau. Maybe something that has never happened before." He handed me my shades, which I gratefully slipped back on. "But you are confused, aren't you? And you do not want to be *Nosferatu*, eh? Maybe we can work out an agreement between us, *ja?*" The old man smiled and rocked back on his heels. "How would you like to come live with me?"

Herr Ghilardi bought my contract from Frau Zobel and promptly installed me in his home, changing my life forever, if not for better.

He was independently wealthy. The Ghilardi fortune originated from a series of arranged marriages between minor Italian princes and the firstborn daughters of Swiss moneylenders. The family estate was located on the shores of Lake Geneva, far removed from city life and nosy neighbors.

The manor boasted a private library devoted to the fantastic, although Ghilardi's filing system was an anal-retentive's nightmare; leatherbound first editions sandwiched between garish paperbacks, while secondhand book-club volumes were thrust among rare folios.

I was surrounded by fictionalized reflections of my affliction. Ghilardi allowed me the freedom to examine whatever I wanted, but did not steer me in the direction of any one book.

I searched countless volumes for information, no matter how distorted, that might shed some light on my condition. I had access to Ariosto's *Orlando Furioso*, Rabelais' *Gargantua*, Walpole's *Castle of Otranto*, Beckford's *Vathek*, Radcliffe's *Mysteries of Udolpho*, Huysmans' *Là Bas*, and even the infamous

Malleus Maleficarum. I met with nothing but frustration. There were no fictional counterparts for the likes of Morgan and Pangloss—or myself; Rymer's Varney was a penny-dreadful scarecrow and Stoker's Dracula a pathetic Victorian sex fantasy.

I sifted through the works of Polidori, Poe, Le Fanu, Wilde, Machen, Hodgson, Lovecraft, and a score of others and came away with nothing. Whatever clues I succeeded in plucking from the morass were inevitably contradictory. It was six weeks after my arrival when he finally gave me the book.

Ghilardi was on the terrace, studying a storm building in the mountain tops. The lake had grown dark and choppy. When storms break on Lake Geneva, they are awesome testimony to nature's potency. Ghilardi liked to watch.

"Did you know, my dear, that it was on the shores of this very lake, while watching a storm, that Mary Shelley first conceived the idea for *Frankenstein?*" He did not take his eyes off the darkening clouds as he spoke, a brandy snifter cradled in one hand.

I did not answer. I had already learned to recognize his rhetorical questions.

"So, you did not find what it was you were searching for?" His eyes flickered sideways, regarding me carefully. "Then, perhaps, this might be of some assistance." He removed a slender hardbound volume from a nearby table and handed it to me.

The book was entitled *Die Rasse Vorgabe*. The Pretending Race. This was the book Wallach had mentioned at Esel's party. The one that had ruined Ghilardi's reputation, reducing him to the level of von Däniken, Churchward and Berlitz. It became my bible, the revelation on which I built my world.

Humans insist on defining reality by their standards. They are poorly equipped to do so, since they are selectively deaf and blind in one eye. They are beings with an insatiable need to categorize the universe that surrounds them, but demand that the facts reveal a universe suited for human cultivation and exploitation. Things must remain status quo.

The Pretenders dwell in the cracks in mankind's perception of reality. To the untutored eye they are nothing to look at: beggars, cripples, prostitutes, anonymous strangers. Their faces are unremarkable, their demeanor bland. They aren't the type that like to draw attention to themselves. That is why Ghilardi referred to them as Pretenders; they pretend to be human, hiding their demonic *otherness* behind a mask of carefully constructed banality. Only to the trained eye do the beasts stand revealed, their auras suffused with fearsome energy.

Ghilardi held the belief that mankind possesses a genetic trait for telekinesis, telepathy, clairvoyance, and all the other sixth-sense stuff. Aeons of civilization and trickery by Pretenders led to the gradual withering of these psionic powers, the extrasensory equivalent of an appendix. Ghilardi was convinced he held the key that would awaken these dormant powers in any human, be they sigma cum laude or a hod carrier.

According to Ghilardi, Pretenders are the creatures found in human myth and legend, twisted beyond recognition: vampires, werewolves, incubi and succubi, ogres, undines and demons too numerous to mention. They escape detection by hiding in plain sight. The various species have only two things in common: they can pass for humans, and they prey on them.

Five years after the fact, I finally discovered how vampires—or what humans refer to as vampires—reproduce.

The bite of the vampire is not the factor that taints the victim; it's the saliva—in some cases, the sperm—that triggers the transformation. Once the victim dies, the corpse undergoes radical physical and genetic restructuring, readying itself for the new occupant. Once the transmutation is complete, a minor demon enters the host, but that is far from the end of the process.

The transition from the spiritual plane to the material world is traumatic. The newborn vampire enters the host body without a personality or past. It has no frame of reference, only raw instinct. The neonate monster uses as its template the only thing on hand: the brain of the victim. This is either a good or bad move, depending on how long the victim has been dead.

If the host is freshly dead—say, two or three days—the fledgling vampire resembles, for the most part, a normal human, complete with memories and intellect. However, if the resurrection takes too long, what arises is a shambling mockery, all but brain-dead. These hapless monstrosities are revenants, the idiot children of the vampire race. Humans call them zombies or ghouls. They are far more plentiful than the traditional vampire, but their stupidity ensures their inevitable destruction. Many are so slow-witted they forget to hide during the day and die their final death, burned to the bone by the sun's rays.

True vampires of power—like the fictional Count Dracula and his Real-World counterpart, Sir Morgan—are rare. Even under ideal resurrection conditions vampires are born with imperfect brains. It takes decades for them to learn how to master their powers. Most end up killed, either by humans, rival predators, or their own ignorance, long before they gain enough experience to lay claim to being a Noble, one of the vampiric ruling class.

Nobles are proud and arrogant. They are not afraid of being discovered; they flaunt their powers, often going out of their way to attract attention to themselves. They can control the minds of others, their strength and vitality are immense, they practice a form of astral projection, and, by human standards, they are practically immortal.

The most interesting difference between Nobles and their wet-mouthed country cousins is that they do not feed on blood alone. In fact, they prefer feasting on human emotion—the blacker the better. Nobles are skilled in summoning and manipulating the darker aspects of man's nature, cultivating it so it provides them with an excellent vintage. Ghilardi claimed that Nobles had been covertly involved with the Nazi death camps and the Stalinist pogroms.

It was easy to see why Ghilardi had been treated like a pariah dog by his peers. If I didn't know better myself, I would have dismissed the book as the ravings of a crank. Ghilardi claimed that the key to his discovery of the Real World was an ancient grimoire called the *Aegrisomnia* or, loosely translated, *Dreams of a Fevered Mind*.

I asked to see this so-called tome of forbidden lore, still uncertain whether or not Ghilardi might be a good-natured crackpot.

"It is a most wondrous book, the *Aegrisomnia*," he explained as he unlocked the display case. "I came across it while researching the folklore of the vampire. Most interesting. Shortly after I read it for the first time, I discovered I could . . . see things. That was ten years ago. I was hosting our little *klatsch* that year. When Herr Doktor Pangloss arrived I . . ." He fell silent, then glanced up at me. "I am told I had a collapse of some kind. I do not remember very much. But after that, Pangloss did not attend our parties for nearly a decade. That is when I began working on my book."

The *Aegrisomnia* was a large, rather awkwardly bound volume with metal hasps and an Arabesque lock. It looked like a medieval teenager's diary. The text was in Latin, although some passages looked to be Greek. There were alchemical tables, conjuring diagrams, and what Ghilardi claimed were non-Euclidean geometric formulas. Every other page was covered in complex, multilayered patterns that, at first glance, resembled a child's collection of Spirograph drawings. However, when I looked at it a second time, I detected words hidden amid the esoteric scribbles.

Although my Latin was rusty enough to inflict lockjaw, I managed to decipher the opening line: "Greetings. You have regained that which was lost." I had to rely on Ghilardi's translation of the "secret text," which detailed the habits of the various Pretender races.

There were discourses on the matriarchal structure of the *vargr*, treatises on the reproductive cycle of incubi and succubi, and essays on the diet of ogres. Ghilardi was convinced that the *Aegrisomnia* was a Rosetta Stone for viewing the Real World. In theory, once exposed to its wisdom, the readers' "inner sight" would awaken, allowing them to pierce the veil and see the Real World. Unfortunately, Ghilardi's attempts to prove the existence of the Real World were disastrous. Most of the hand-picked initiates saw nothing but meaningless scribbles. The last one started screaming and didn't stop until he was sedated. After that, Ghilardi kept his precious volume of forgotten lore under lock and key.

Once I accepted him as my mentor, Ghilardi outlined the details of our arrangement. He would provide me with shelter and an identity while I would permit him to observe my evolution into a Noble.

Ghilardi stated that I was a fluke, a freak even by Pretender standards. I was proof of man's tampering with the reproductive cycle of the vampire. Human technology had interfered in the unnatural order of things. Morgan had left me for dead in the gutter—and by all rights, I should have died—but new blood was forced into my veins, diluting, if not completely neutralizing, the virus polluting my flesh. The demon was trapped inside a living host, not a piece of dead meat. Most irregular. Since I never died and my brain was in perfect working order—well, almost—I was evolving into a Noble, a "king vampire," at an unheard-of pace. Ghilardi was thrilled by the prospect of documenting my progress. I was to be his proof that he wasn't a crazy old fool.

He also had other, far less academic plans for me. He'd spent his entire life steeped in the romance of the occult investigator. He fancied himself in the role of Professor Van Helsing, tracking down the scourge of humanity and driving a stake through its heart at cockcrow. But he was too old and infirm for such heroics. It wasn't until much later that I realized how insanely brave his attack on me at Frau Zobel's had been. Ghilardi had stepped into that room expecting to be killed, yet determined to play the role of fearless vampire hunter. Now he had the chance to vicariously experience the danger and adventure through his pupil.

I should never have allowed him to do it; it was stupid and foolhardy—neither of us had any idea of what the consequences might be. But I had come to trust Ghilardi as a wise man who knew what he was doing, and if he wanted to hypnotize me so he could talk to the demon trapped inside my psyche . . . well, who was I to tell him no?

It didn't take very long for him to put me in a trance. I felt as if I was sliding down the throat of a huge animal. I was surrounded by red darkness; part of me started to panic as I felt control of my body slip away. I realized I'd made a big mistake, but it was too late to do anything but fall. I thought I heard something begin to laugh. I regained consciousness thirty seconds later.

He kept insisting it wasn't my fault. That I wasn't responsible for what happened. Maybe he was right, maybe it *wasn't* me. But they were *my* hands. The bones are so brittle at that age—so fragile, like a bird—and broken arms don't heal as fast as they used to. I'm sorry; I'm so very, very sorry. Wherever you are, please forgive me. Forgive *us*.

From then on, the Other was my constant companion. It had always been there. At first it was too weak to assert itself, except during times of extreme stress, such as Joe Lent's beating. For years it had been my silent, parasitic partner, feeding on the emotions generated by my clients. Now it was my intangible Siamese twin, joined at the medulla oblongata, and I could no longer ignore its existence. I was unable to predict its behavior or, worse yet, safely control it.

My first outing as a vampire hunter was in Frankfurt, since Ghilardi deemed it wise to avoid a ruckus in our own backyard.

The neighborhood had been a ghetto before the Nazis emptied it. Then the Allies had bombed it until nothing remained but the cellars. Although rebuilt after the war, the neighborhood's soul never recovered. The nice new apartment buildings quickly withered, transforming the district into a slum. There was so much despair permeating the area the half-life would last for another thirty years. Perhaps that's what attracted him.

He was new; he still had grave dirt behind his ears. He wasn't experienced at Pretending; he'd forgotten the basics, such as breathing all the time. That's a problem among the recently resurrected: most of them suffer from massive brain damage. This one didn't look too zombed-out, although he was far from MENSA material.

I watched the derelict, fascinated and appalled. I'd never seen a revenant before. Morgan was as far removed from the thing huddled in the doorway as *homo sapiens* is from *homo erectus*. The human eye could see nothing but a starveling junkie, shirtless and barefoot, shivering on the doorstep of an abandoned building. He was just another street person, made invisible by poverty. How long? How long had I been walking among the dead?

The revenant wore the body of a white male in his mid-thirties; he stood in the shadows of the doorway, thin arms wrapped around a narrow, sunken chest that did not rise or fall. His clothing consisted of a pair of ill-fitting pants held up by a length of rope and an old greatcoat the color of smoke. The uninformed would have attributed the derelict's shivering to the cold, but I knew better. He was a junkie, but it wasn't smack he was hurting for.

Ghilardi wrinkled his nose in disgust. "*Mein Gott!* I can smell him from here."

I nodded, never taking my eyes off him. "Probably a bum to begin with. The district's full of them; they sleep in condemned buildings and in the piles of uncollected garbage in the alleys." I put one hand in my coat pocket, caressing the silver blade Ghilardi had presented to me in Geneva in anticipation of our first kill.

"Stay put, *verstadt?* I don't want you getting hurt."

Ghilardi said nothing, but we both glanced at his arm resting in its sling.

I walked across the street, aware of being watched from both sides. I prayed the old man would not try to interfere. If anything else happened to him . . . I suppressed the thought. I was going into battle and I needed to concentrate my attention on my prey . . . the enemy.

The revenant straightened as I drew near, his eyes gleaming hungrily. I spoke to him in German.

"You look like you're in a bad way, friend."

The undead thing nodded. He still wasn't breathing. Bad camouflage: the creature was seriously ignorant of the laws of supernatural selection.

"I can fix you up, if you can meet the price. You *do* have it, don't you?"

The revenant stuffed a pale hand into his pants pocket; the fist emerged bristling with deutsche marks. Following a dim memory from his previous existence, he rolled his victims after he finished draining them. He had no intrinsic understanding of money, except that it made good bait.

I smiled and nodded in the direction of the alleyway. The revenant complied, his movements insectile.

Once we were in the solitude of the alley, the revenant hissed; his pupils dilating rapidly until they swallowed the entire eye. He expected me to scream and try to escape. Instead, I grinned, baring fangs as sharp as his own. The growl percolating in his chest became a confused whine. This had never happened before, and the revenant was unsure as to how to proceed.

"C'mere, dead boy."

The derelict tried to flee; I grabbed a fistful of greasy hair and jerked him back into the alley. There was a wet tearing sound and I found myself holding a snarl of matted hair and dripping scalp. The revenant fell among the overflowing garbage cans, disturbing a small army of rats. He hurled one of the writhing bags of fur and teeth at me. I batted it aside with a swat of my hand. The undead thing leapt at me, shrieking like a tea kettle. His ragged nails raked my face, leaving wet trenches. I stumbled backward and instinctively tried to shield my face with my forearm.

The derelict grabbed my wrist in an attempt to throw me off-balance. I lunged forward, slamming him against the cold brick wall. Pressed belly-to-belly amid heaps of rubbish, we resembled low-rent lovers enjoying a sleazy tryst. I kept my left forearm wedged under the revenant's chin, forcing his fangs away from my face. The beast reeked of clotted blood and dried feces.

The thing whined piteously when he saw the knife, the blade forged to resemble a frozen silver flame. I realized I was grinning.

The blade went in easy, piercing skin and muscle like rotten sailcloth. The knife slid home between the fifth and sixth ribs, puncturing the heart as if I'd jabbed a pin into a toy balloon.

The revenant yowled and thrashed like a landed fish, but showed no signs of dying. Frightened for the first time since the fight began, I stabbed his chest three more times. Nothing. Obviously the old legend concerning impaling a vampire's heart was unreliable. I began plunging my knife into every organ I could think of, clinically, at first, but with increasing frenzy as I realized I was beginning to tire. The Other laughed at me as I stabbed the struggling revenant. She was amused by my ignorance.

Don't take it too badly. It's your first time, after all. The first time is always messy and clumsy. You've got to expect it to be bloody. But it leaves you with a taste for more.

"Get out of my *head*, damn you!" The knife buried itself in the revenant's neck, severing the spinal cord.

The screams stopped as if I'd pulled the plug on a stereo system. The derelict's eyes disappeared into their sockets, retracted by withering eye stalks. Repulsed, I stepped back and let the thing fall; his limbs curled inward, like the legs of a dead spider. I moved away quickly, clapping a hand over my nose and breathing through my mouth. It didn't help.

"*Mein Gött . . .*"

It was Ghilardi. He stood at the mouth of the alley, staring at the corpse as it continued its accelerated deterioration. The body bloated and grew black, its head resembling the release valve on an overinflated tire.

"How long have you—"

"Since he screamed. I was afraid for . . . Jesus!" Ghilardi's face was the color of oatmeal. The corpse exploded with a ripe gush of gas. Ghilardi vomited before he could finish his sentence. I grabbed his good elbow and hurried him onto the street.

Ghilardi was visibly shaken. The vampire-hunting fantasies of his youth were full of adventure and suspense. They never mentioned the stink of putrefaction and the taste of vomit.

I looked at my hands; they were trembling, but not out of fear.

It leaves you with a taste for more . . .

". . . you're hurt." I realized Ghilardi was speaking to me. "We'll have to see about those gashes on your face."

We halted beneath one of the remaining functional street lamps so he could examine my wounds.

"Gashes?" I replied dreamily. "What gashes?"

All that remained were four pencil-thin, rapidly paling lines of pink.

Ghilardi lost interest in vampire hunting after Frankfurt. I didn't. The mass of hate and frustration knotted in my guts was sated by my hunts. I wanted to feel Morgan's unlife squirting between my fingers, but was willing to settle for killing lesser beasts.

I talked myself into believing it was a safety valve that allowed me to keep the Other in check, that I was performing a public service. Idiot. I was doing it because I got off on it.

I traveled all over Europe—even going so far as to make raids into Czechoslovakia, Yugoslavia, and Poland—while Ghilardi stayed home and filled his notebooks with information relating to the care and feeding of a vampire.

Time begins to blur at this point. Ghilardi warned about that. Vampires can go to ground for years, not because they're superhumanly patient but simply because they have such a lousy sense of time. The years begin to run together. I can recall fragments . . .

1975: She looked so out of place, wandering among the burn-outs and old hippies. Her blond curls, starched pinafore and patent-leather Mary Janes made her strangely archaic, like a child lost in time as well as space. She drifted in and out of the crowd, plucking at the sleeves of passersby.

It was very late for a child to be alone on the streets of Amsterdam, and the neighborhood was not one where mothers normally let their children roam unattended. I was lounging in front of a live-music club, waiting for the band to start playing. Several other patrons milled outside the front door, smoking their foul tobacco-and-hash cigarettes. Inside the club, locked inside a special kiosk, an elderly woman sold state-approved hashish, morphine, heroin and clean syringes.

Most of the people clustered outside the bar were young. Many were dressed in faded denims sporting "Give Peace a Chance" and "Eco" patches. Amsterdam was a favorite spot for aging hippies fleeing the growing complacency of the '70s and the inevitability of their adulthood. The hippies looked stoned and bitter, as if perplexed by society passing them by. Judging by their accents, a good number of them were American. Amsterdam was also popular among draft-dodgers.

The little girl—surely no more than five or six—flitted from person to person, her small voice lost in the noise from the street. I couldn't hear what she was saying, but I had a good guess; "Please, won't someone take me home to my mother? I'm lost. I want to go home, but it's too dark and I'm scared. Please, won't someone take me home? I don't live too far away . . ."

A tall, thin hippie with long hair and a longer face stooped so he could listen to her. He straightened, toying with the hash cigarette he held in one hand. He glanced back at the doorway to the club, then down at the pale little face. He shrugged his bony shoulders and she slipped her tiny hand into his large one and started down the street.

I followed at a discreet distance, listening to the little girl as she chattered away about her mother, her brothers and her kitten. The hippie nodded every so often, the scent of Turkish tobacco and hash marking his passage.

The neighborhood began to decline and soon the little girl was leading the hippie through one of the uglier districts in the city. The row houses were red brick and had once been pleasant, well-scrubbed homes, with pleasant, well-scrubbed families living in them. But that was before the Second World War. Something happened in that neighborhood during the Occupation—something nasty—and the neighborhood never recovered from the wound dealt it by the Nazis. I paused, fascinated by its similarity to the place in Frankfurt. It felt the same.

I shifted my vision, curious to see what marked this spot as a Bad Place. The buildings shimmered, as if I was looking through a curtain made of rising heat, and I was standing on the same narrow cobblestone street. A large flag marked with a swastika fluttered over the doorway of the center house. The banner fluttered in a long-ago breeze as unsmiling men dressed in black leather topcoats escorted frightened men, women, and children into the house. The vision burst like a soap bubble, dispersing in time for me to see the little girl leading the slack-faced hippie across the same threshold.

I dashed across the street and up the flight of stone steps that led to the front door of what had been, thirty years ago, Gestapo headquarters.

The hippie must have been exceptionally stoned or too thoroughly tranced not to notice that the little girl's "home" was an abandoned building marked for demolition. I came to a halt in what was once the foyer.

Strips of yellowed wallpaper hung from the wall like soiled bandages. Broken glass and a decade's accumulation of filth gritted underneath my heels. There were discarded wine bottles and syringes scattered about, but the pungent aroma of human piss and vomit was missing; this wasn't squatter territory.

The first floor was a long central hallway flanked by two rooms on either side. At the end of the hallway was a rickety staircase that led to the second story.

I moved cautiously down the hall toward the stairs, glancing into each of the abandoned rooms. None of the rooms had doors. I felt a buzzing in my skull and the curtain of shimmering heat reappeared. The foyer changed; the wallpaper was no longer peeling and a thick carpet ran the length of the hall.

Everything looked very cheery, except for the Gestapo agents putting out cigarettes on a young man tied to a chair. In the next room a pudgy man in a spotless white smock—like a kindly doctor sent from Central Casting—carefully adjusted the connections on the car battery attached to an older man's genitals. And in the third room a screaming woman was raped by a German shepherd while three Gestapo agents smoked cigarettes and laughed.

I staggered backward, my guts convulsing. One of the Gestapo men—a short, rat-faced man with wire-rim glasses—swiveled his head in my direction, scowling as if he'd seen something.

The buzzing stopped and I was back in the deserted hallway, shivering like a junkie. No wonder there weren't any signs of recent squatting; even the most insensitive *Lumpen* could feel the evil in this place! I fought to control my trembling. How many other slices of hell did the Nazis leave scattered across Europe?

I turned to look into the fourth and final room before ascending the stairs to the second story. The hippie lurched forward, one hand clamped against the wound in his neck, trying to staunch the flow of blood spurting from his jugular. His Hawkwind T-shirt was already muddied beyond reading, and his long, sad face was horribly white.

The hippie wobbled drunkenly for a second, his eyes empty of sanity. His mouth opened and shut like a landed fish. I could hear the high-pitched tittering of a child echoing through the empty house. The hippie pitched forward, collapsing in my arms. I let the body drop onto the bare boards. My hands were slick with his blood. My revulsion was heightened by the thrill sparked by the sight and smell of the red stuff.

The thing was upstairs. I mounted the staircase carefully, grimacing as the stairs groaned and creaked under my weight . . .

Something small with crimson eyes landed on my back, tearing at my throat with sharp nails and needle-like teeth. I tumbled down the stairs, the hell-child riding me like a demented jockey. Pain raked my shoulders and the back of my neck as the thing tore at me. I had a vision of the unholy creature chewing away at my neck like a harbor rat on a rope.

I slammed against the walls, attempting to shake loose the thing clinging to me. Plaster fell from the ceiling in gritty clouds, mingling with my blood, but the child-beast held tight. Desperate to free myself, I did a running cartwheel down the hall and was successful in dislodging my attacker.

The child-vampire lay among a pile of discarded wine bottles and strips of wallpaper. She no longer resembled the golden-haired little girl who'd coerced the hapless young man into walking her home.

When I looked at the child-thing I saw a hideously withered crone's face set atop tiny shoulders. Her mouth was toothless except for two sharp little fangs and her eyes glowed like molten steel. The child-thing straightened her blood-soaked pinafore and stared at me for a moment. Then the little girl was back, weeping and shivering and calling for her mother.

It was a good illusion. The urge to protect children is strongly ingrained in humans—especially the females. I wavered, suddenly overcome with the desire to lift this darling child in my arms and hug her . . .

Trick! It's a trick! The Other's voice was like ice water in my brain.

"I. . . " I was going to pick that thing up," I muttered aloud in astonishment.

Hissing her anger, the child-vampire sprang at me, fangs unsheathed. The beast was as fast as an ape, but I managed to catch the girl-harridan in midleap. My hands tightened around her wizened neck. There was no way I could get to my knife without exposing myself to another assault, and I was already weakened by blood loss.

The hateful thing twisted and writhed in my grasp, slashing my hands with her fangs and claws. Her eyes shone like a trapped rat's. A surge of hate and disgust swept over me, and I began to throttle the child. Her yowls and curses grew in volume and she kicked at me with her tiny Mary Janes. A reddish froth rimed her lips, a combination of her saliva and my blood.

It felt as if all of my willpower was being channeled down my arms and into my hands. The vampire-girl's struggles became more and more frenzied as her eyes started from their sockets. I glimpsed exposed muscle and finger bones gleaming wetly in the dim light, but I did not loosen my hold.

I didn't notice the buzzing, at first, as my attacker's screeching served to camouflage it. But I had the feeling I was being watched . . .

There was someone standing in the doorway of the room the hippie had staggered from. It was a man in early middle age, his hair touched by silver at the temples. He was dressed in a German SS colonel's uniform, the stainless-steel skull on his hat glinting in the light. He stood holding a pair of black leather gloves in one hand, and it was evident from the look of mild surprise on his face that he could see me.

That face. I *knew* it. I knew it all too well.

It was Morgan.

The Nazi Morgan flickered, like the picture on an old television set, then disappeared.

I looked down at the vampire-child. She'd stopped struggling because her head had come off in my hands. The tiny body lay on the cold floor; a liquid with the same color and consistency as congealed spaghetti sauce oozed from her neck.

I stared at the little head I held in my hands. The child's face had returned.

God, ohGodno. I've gone mad and killed a child. I hallucinated the whole thing. I kidnapped some poor little girl and took her to this terrible place and I murdered her.

The little girl's smooth, baby-soft face turned the color of antique ivory and the skin cracked and peeled like parchment.

I dropped the vampire's head and kicked it like a soccer ball. It bounced once and came to rest against the corpse of the hippie in the Hawkwind T-shirt.

The old Gestapo headquarters did not offer any further glimpses of Morgan, although I stumbled across evidence of far more human monsters.

Although I searched the house from front door to attic, I could not bring myself to investigate the cellar. I took five steps into the darkness, then began to shiver uncontrollably. Whatever went on down there thirty years ago was unspeakable; it was the source of the evil that tainted the neighborhood like a ghostly cancer. I had no doubt that was where the vampire-child had nested during the day.

I fled the house, choking on bile and fear.

1976: It was the cemetery Morrison was buried in. It was also the same place Oscar Wilde, Balzac, Voltaire, Molière, Sarah Bernhardt, Victor Hugo, Edith Piaf, Max Ernst and Gustav Doré, among others, happened to be interred. But as far as the teenagers were concerned, Jim Morrison was the only noteworthy occupant.

Père Lachaise is a fantastic necropolis located on the northeast side of Paris, off the Boulevard de Belleville. It was once the gardens attached to the villa of François d'Aix de Lachaise, confessor to Louis XIV; now it is home to over 20,000 monuments and 800,000 graves.

There were more famous dead people in Père Lachaise than live ones in New York City. Sublime masters of the written word lay next to petit-bourgeois shopkeepers. Infamous hedonists and adulterers rest alongside proper Christian ladies who would have been scandalized by their proximity to such sin while alive.

Like any great city, Père Lachaise attracted a steady stream of tourists and vandals. The tour guides were fond of recounting how a Victorian lady was so shocked by the rampant griffon guarding Oscar Wilde's tomb she removed the offending organ with a hammer she just happened to have in her purse.

The French are pragmatic in regard to such acts; it's the price you pay for fame.

However, the vandalism perpetrated by the thousands of young pilgrims who flocked each year to the tomb of the Lizard King transcended mere desecration and approached true folk art.

Outside of a modest marble bust depicting the singer at his peak—the nose smashed by a recent incarnation of the Victorian castratrix—Morrison's grave was simple and not very big. The graffiti radiating from the doomed poet, however, was far from simple.

It had been added to over the years, layer by layer, in a thousand different hands and a dozen different languages, until it formed a dense, interlocking mural. Whether the medium was aerosol spray paint, felt-tipped marker, or pocket knife, the messages all boiled down to WE MISS YOU.

Once Morrison's plot could no longer contain the scrawled endearments, they began to spread onto the surrounding monuments, until the testimony of the fans' love for their fallen hero obliterated the inscription on the plaque marking the resting place of Abelard and Héloise.

There were always young pilgrims wandering through Père Lachaise, the majority of them tripping their brains out. Normally, vampires avoid such well-trafficked areas, preferring to haunt lonelier locations.

I was lured to Paris by the rumors circulating among the counterculture diehards that Morrison's ghost wandered Père Lachaise at night in search of groupies. While in a nearby bar I overheard a gang of teenage fans discussing "visiting Jim" that night. I followed them from a safe distance.

There were four pilgrims, three boys and a girl, full of wine and acid and exhilarated by the prospect of glimpsing their idol's ghost. Since they'd never seen Morrison in concert, this was as close as they'd ever get to actually meeting him in the flesh.

I followed them over the fence into the graveyard, watching as they wove through the field of tilting stones. It was obvious they had made the trip dozens of times; they threaded their way through the maze of marble and granite with the surefootedness of sherpas. This was their shrine and as much a part of their lives as the prayer wheels of Katmandu.

Of the four, the oldest couldn't have been more than fourteen at the time of their messiah's death. It was a chilly October night and they were outfitted in American jeans and sneakers; two of the boys wore leather jackets while the third shivered in a flannel shirt that was no protection against the autumnal wind. The girl wore a heavy denim jacket with an intricately embroidered slogan on the back that read NO ONE HERE GETS OUT ALIVE.

The boy in the flannel shirt carried a large wine bottle, which he stopped to drink from every few steps. His companions hissed at him to keep up. Looking cold and disgruntled, he hurried after them.

One of the boys in the leather jackets had a knapsack with him, which he proceeded to empty once they reached the grave site. He produced several candle stubs, two more bottles of wine and several joints.

"Think we'll see him?" whispered the girl as she hugged her elbows for warmth.

The older boy nodded. "Sure. Philippe—you know, Jean-Michel's cousin?—he saw Jim just last week."

The boy in the flannel shirt snorted derisively, shifting from foot to foot in order to keep from freezing. "Philippe sees lots of things. He virtually lives off acid and Vichy water."

The girl's tone was colder than the wind knifing through the graveyard. "I don't think you *want* to see him, Pierre. You're going to ruin *everything.*"

Pierre looked wounded. It was painfully obvious that the only reason he was standing in the middle of a cemetery in the middle of the night, waiting for a ghost to put in an appearance, was because she was there.

The boy who unloaded the knapsack arranged the candles into a lopsided circle atop the marble slab covering Morrison's grave. "Céleste is right," he said, touching each wick with his lighter. "If you don't want to see him, you *won't*. You can't think negative, Pierre, or you'll scare him away."

The candles flickered wildly in the wind gusting through the cemetery, throwing strange shadows on the disfigured bust situated at the head of the grave. The group uncorked the remaining wine bottles and huddled around the meager light. Soon the odor of marijuana mingled with the smell of lichen and dead leaves.

After a half-hour's vigil, Pierre stood up and kicked at the extinguished candles. "This is bullshit! I'm going to end up with pneumonia because Philippe Daigrepoit thought he saw something while he was tripping!"

The other members of the group shifted uneasily, but it was evident they had each come to similar conclusions.

"I don't know about you"—this was addressed to Céleste alone, although she was unaware of it—"but I'm going home to . . . Oh, my God!" The half-empty wine bottle slid from his numbed fingers, smashing onto the grave slab. Pierre stared down the narrow alley that wound between the tombs opposite the Morrison site.

His companions turned to see what he was staring at. Céleste gasped aloud and put her hands over her mouth.

"It's . . . it's him. It's Jim!"

From my hiding place among the monuments I could see a slender masculine figure standing a hundred yards away, its skin as pale as moonlight. I felt a momentary shock of recognition as I stared at the face of the dead rock star. Was it possible? Was Morrison a Pretender?

The Lizard King, resplendent in jeans and a leather jacket, beckoned with one languid hand but did not come any closer. Despite the cold, he was bare-chested underneath the jacket.

"Céleste, he wants *you*," whispered the older boy. "He wants *you* to go with him." His voice contained awe and envy.

Céleste's eyes had the glaze of someone discovering her fondest fantasy brought to life. "Me . . . he wants *me* . . ." Her voice was dreamy and detached, as if she was talking in her sleep. She stepped forward, eager to embrace her one true love.

"Wait a minute, Céleste! Hey, are you going to stand there and let her go with that thing?" Pierre stared at his friends, then at Céleste. He sounded genuinely frightened and more than a little jealous. He grabbed her forearm, trying to force her to look at him. "Céleste! Céleste, listen to me. Don't go with him. You can't!'

"Let go of me, Pierre." Her gaze remained fixed on the Lizard King.

"No!"

"What are you worried about? It's only Jim. He won't hurt me."

"Céleste . . ."

She wrenched herself free of his grasp, hurrying toward the dead singer.

I moved from my place in the shadows, bowling over the leather-jacketed youths. I saw the Lizard King touch her cheek and take Céleste by the hand. He was going to lead her deep into the necropolis, where he could feast undisturbed. If he disappeared into the labyrinth of crypts and tombstones, I'd never find them in time.

I tackled the retreating vampire, knocking it free of Céleste. The thing thrashed violently underneath me, but couldn't break free of my hold. On closer inspection I could see the leather jacket and jeans he wore were filthy, the jacket moldering. Morrison's face snarled at me, but the vampire wasn't the dead singer resurrected.

Vampires are the chameleons of the Real World; they can remodel their faces into any semblance they choose. It's the supernatural equivalent of protective coloration. And this vampire had chosen the semblance that would ensure him good hunting. The vampire's features were exactly the same as those on the funerary bust— right down to the smashed nose. At a distance of a hundred yards, the illusion was good enough to attract prey; and by the time they were close enough to notice something was wrong, the vampire had them securely tranced.

The Lizard King hissed, exposing his fangs. I kept one hand clamped on his throat, pinning him to the ground, as I reached for my knife.

"Leave him *alone*. You're spoiling *everything!*" Céleste brought a memorial vase filled with rank water and withered daffodils crashing down on my head. I fell back, momentarily stunned.

"Jim! Oh, Jim, sweetheart! Are you all right?" She helped the vampire to his feet.

The Lizard King grinned at her, his eyes glowing and fangs unsheathed.

"*Nooooo!*" Her denial was thin and high-pitched, like a child refusing to go to bed.

The Lizard King grabbed her by the hair, pulling her closer to his mouth. Céleste struggled, her screams bursting from her like the cries of frightened birds.

Although blood from my head wound was trickling down behind my shades and dripping into my eyes, I got to my feet.

"Let her go, dead boy."

The Lizard King snarled again, tightening his grip on the girl. Céleste sobbed hysterically, too frightened to scream.

"Céleste! Merciful God . . ."

It was Pierre. The boy was still there, even though his companions had fled the minute the girl began to scream. The youth stood just beyond reach of the vampire. I could tell the young idiot was getting ready to jump the monster.

I stepped forward, hoping to draw the Lizard King's attention from the boy. It worked. The vampire snapped his head in my direction, baring his teeth like a cornered rat. I could hear the keeper's hounds baying close by. So did the vampire, his stolen face registering fear. There were too many witnesses. He'd have to abandon his catch. He propelled the hysterical girl into Pierre's arms. The boy did not bother to question his luck and ran in the direction he and his companions had come from, Céleste in tow.

The Lizard King turned and ran, but I was right after him. He sprinted through the graveyard like a broken field runner, but I managed to keep up with him. I caught him by the fence. He was clambering over the ancient spikes when I buried the knife to the hilt in the meat of his left calf.

I'd discovered that while *I* was impervious to silver, most Pretenders were hyper-allergic to it. The vampire screamed as silver penetrated flesh and muscle, but succeeded in boosting himself over the wrought-iron fence. I could tell the vampire's nervous system was already affected by the silver toxins in his bloodstream; he dragged a rapidly degenerating left leg as he plunged into a knot of late-night party-goers, bleating and waving his arms. Luckily, they thought he was just another geek visiting Jim Morrison's grave. I took my time killing the bastard when I caught up to him.

That was also the year I noticed I'd stopped aging . . . at least to human eyes. For some reason, my metabolism decided twenty-three was the ideal time of life, and stayed there. That was also the year I began buying black-market blood. After years of living off the blood of animals, the thirst upped the stakes.

1977: In Rome people walk the most chaotic streets in Europe, unaware that twenty-two feet below the soles of their shoes lies a kingdom that extends nearly six hundred miles, with an estimated population of six million.

I was seated at a sidewalk café, nursing a glass of red wine while I watched the evening crowds, when the messenger arrived.

He was a thin, pasty-faced young man with unhealthy purple blotches under his eyes. I divined by the flicker of his aura that he was a human sensitive. He was also quite mad.

"You are Blue?" His English was execrable, but I knew no Italian.

"What do you want?" I stared at the black halo crowning his head; the rays emanating from his skull snapped and fluttered like banners caught in a high wind. The sensitive's eyes were wet and bright, the pupils oscillating to a secret beat. He was dressed far too warmly for a Roman spring. Not only was he a crazed esper, he was a junkie as well. What a combination.

"He says tell you come." The sensitive's eyelids twitched as he dry-washed his hands.

"Who told you?" I didn't relish the idea of tapping into the junkie's mind to get my information. God only knows what lay coiled behind those eyes.

"He say you know. Tell me say Pangloss."

The smell of old death came back to me. "Very well. I'll go."

The sensitive grinned, revealing crooked teeth. Was this pathetic creature Pangloss's renfield?

I followed the sensitive through a series of twisting back streets that took us deep into the city's oldest neighborhoods. I could feel myself being watched by scores of dark, suspicious eyes as we hurried through the narrow alleys. I glanced skyward. Although my view was hampered by a Jacob's Ladder of laundry lines, I could see the moon of Islam hovering over Christendom's city.

The sensitive led me to an ancient, crumbling villa with an overgrown garden. The ground floor was deserted of life and furniture, but the door to its cellar stood open. The young man hurried down the stairs without bothering to see if I was following.

The basement had a dirt floor and smelled strongly of mildew. The only light came from a flickering candle jutting from a Chianti bottle perched atop a card table. The card table was situated against the far wall, alongside a small, narrow oaken door with old-fashioned hinges. Sitting behind the table was a huge figure dressed in the hooded robes of a monk.

The monk did not see us enter for his head was lowered, as if in prayer. The motion of his right arm, however, was far from sacred.

The sensitive snarled something in Italian and the monk pulled his hand free of his cassock. Pangloss's messenger made a withering remark, then gestured first to me, then to the door.

The monk got to his feet, the peak of his hood brushing the low ceiling. I bit my tongue to keep from gasping aloud, my heart banging against my ribs like a hammer. Whatever his religious beliefs and vices might be, it was obvious the monk who stood guard in that empty cellar was not human.

The ogre's lambent eyes glowered from under beetling brows, his nose wide and flat like a gorilla's. His jaw jutted strangely, as if the lower mandible did not match the rest of his skull. The skin was coarse and large-pored, with a grayish complexion that made him look like he needed a good dusting. He was massively built, his hands large enough to conceal a cured ham in each palm. I could tell he was bald underneath the hood he wore, and I caught a brief glimpse of pointed ears set flush against his head. The folds of his vestments camouflaged his twisted physique, although it accentuated the unnatural width of his shoulders.

The ogre studied me warily, then spoke to the sensitive, his voice a bass rumble that sounded like rocks being ground together; I saw rows of sharp, inward curving teeth, like little saracen blades, set in pink gums. While they were occupied, I looked at the book the ogre had left open on the table. It was a volume of nursery rhymes, lavishly illustrated with pictures of plump, apple-cheeked children dressed in sailor suits and pinafores jumping candlesticks, fetching pails of water, and going to bed with one shoe on. My gorge began to rise and I quickly averted my gaze. The ogre fondness for veal is well-known, but it seemed this one liked playing with his food.

The ogre monk produced an antique key fashioned of iron and unlocked the worm-scored door. The sensitive had to stoop in order to cross the threshold and I nearly banged my head on the lintel. The ogre grunted noncommittally and locked the door behind us.

I found myself in a narrow, sloping passageway lit by a string of low-wattage bulbs attached to the roof of the tunnel.

Most of the catacombs are located near the Appian Way, in what had once been the farthest reaches of the city. I was not aware of such extensive catacombs in that particular section of Rome.

We passed row upon row of *loculi*, the narrow shelf graves cut in the soft stone that house the bones of the poor. The surrounding rock formations were porous and there was little moisture found in the catacombs, the end result being that even the oldest bodies were surprisingly well-preserved. The dead, dressed in the remains of their winding-sheets, watched with empty sockets as we traveled deeper into their realm.

After walking for a half-hour and descending three levels, the corridor emptied into a *cubiculum*, one of the larger and more elaborate burial chambers reserved for the wealthy dead.

I stepped into the vaulted chamber, staring at its grisly decor. The *cubiculum* had been turned into a shrine of some kind, although I had a hard time imagining who might be so desperate as to seek solace in such a place.

The far wall was studded, from floor to ceiling, with human skulls embedded in its mortar. The skulls—all of them missing their lower mandibles—were stacked one atop another. The heads of adult males rested, upper plate to crown, alongside those of women and the unfinished craniums of infants.

The skulls surrounded a reliquary recessed into the wall. The reliquary's interior was composed of thousands upon thousands of painted tibia, finger, and toe bones fitted into a gruesome mosaic. Although the colors had faded over the centuries, I could still make out the figures of a man and a woman, one hand lifted in greeting while the other hid their genitals. A withered, mummified arm—whole from the shoulder—rested in the shrine, apparently fixed to the shelf by a large metal bolt in its palm. I was uncertain whether the relic was an obscure saint or an unlucky pilgrim.

Chandeliers made from bones and wire hung from the ceilings. Candles burned in upside-down skulls, casting warped shadows throughout the burial vault. The walls that weren't dedicated to the skull shrine were pocketed with larger versions of the shelf graves the poor had been unceremoniously dumped in, resembling bizarre multiple built-in bunk beds.

Mummified monks and priests, dressed in the rotting clerical garb of some long-forgotten religious order, stood eternal vigilance alongside their patrons' tombs; suspended by hooks set into the walls, their ancient skeletons were held together by wire and petrified ligaments. I was reminded of a brace of marionettes dangling from their strings.

Some of the dead holy men clutched the rusted remains of swords, while others fingered rosaries. I wondered if they were there to keep the occupants of the catacombs from being molested or escaping. Most of the dead sentinels possessed enough skin to cover their bones, although it was as stiff and yellow as parchment. Some seemed to laugh, others to cry, their black tongues exposed between toothless jaws. The ones who still had their faces were the worst, their lips twisted into parodies of a kiss.

One of the dead things stepped forward and fit an ebony cigarette holder between his grinning jaws. "Miss Blue. Delighted you could make it."

My vision wavered and the walking corpse became Dr. Pangloss, international scholar and *bon vivant*. Although he was dressed in the latest Italian fashion, his eyes obscured by Mastroianni-style sunglasses, he looked perfectly at home among the inhabitants of the catacombs.

The sensitive blurted something in Italian, his manner anxious. He dry-washed his hands, watching Pangloss expectantly.

"Yes, I can see that she's here," the vampire snapped in English. He said something more in Italian, then reached inside his breast pocket, producing a small packet of white powder.

The sensitive snatched the heroin from the vampire's hand, scurrying into the shadows.

"You must forgive Cesare," apologized Pangloss. "He is a telepath with no control over what he receives. Imagine having a radio in your head that you are helpless to turn off. He depends on me to provide him with the means to escape the voices, the poor lad."

"How humanitarian."

Pangloss arched an eyebrow. "Yes, isn't it." He brushed past me to perch on the edge of a sarcophagus. "This place"—he indicated our surroundings with a languid wave of the hand—"was forgotten by the Christians after the eighth century, *anno domini*, and has yet to be rediscovered by the human world. Pretenders, however, never forget. These catacombs are held sacred by the Pretending races. It is one of the few locations where we can meet without fear of vendetta. It is a neutral territory, so to speak. You need not fear violence from me while we are here. I trust I can expect the same from you?"

I nodded. Even though Pangloss was a monster that preyed on the weak and helpless, I had no reason to doubt his manners.

"Were you surprised to hear from me? Do say yes, it would flatter me so."

"Yes. I admit I was surprised. How did you know where I would be?"

"Do you think I would waltz away from our last encounter without bothering to keep myself informed as to your whereabouts? I know many things about you, my dear. I know you've taken up with that deluded old fool, and I know all about your 'hunting trips.' Who are you warring against?"

"What makes you think—"

"You must be warring against someone. Who is your brood master?"

"I don't have any idea what you're talking about."

"Surely you're not that ignorant! Who is responsible for you?"

"He called himself Sir Morgan."

Pangloss's mocking smile diminished. "You're operating under Morgan's orders?"

"His orders!" I didn't bother to restrain my burst of derisive laughter. "I'm looking to kill the motherfucker!"

Pangloss looked genuinely perplexed. He toyed with his cigarette holder and stared at his shoes. His voice was distant and detached, as if he was thinking aloud. "Morgan . . . I should have pegged you as one of his gets. All that anger and hate boiling away inside . . . I'm surprised. He must be getting forgetful in his old age. Foolish of him, really. Seeding a specimen like you . . ." He saw the confused look on my face, and the sardonic smile returned.

"What you must understand, my dear, is that we vampires are a prolific race. Like the Greek gods of Olympus, where falls our seed there is life. Or unlife. Every human we drain will rise again. Every schoolboy knows that. And since it wouldn't do to have too many undead running loose, we take matters into our own hands." He pantomimed wringing the neck of a chicken. "Most of us take birth control very seriously. That is not to say I don't have a brood of my own. You're looking confused again. Don't you know anything about . . . No, I guess you wouldn't.

"Anyway, every Noble has a brood, those vampires who owe their existence to him. You see, when Morgan took your blood he left some of himself behind— remaking you in his own image, shall we say? However, it is the strength of *your* will that decides if you will become a Noble. And we are usually very careful in our choice of prey. It wouldn't do to pick a victim who possesses a powerful will."

"Who needs the competition?"

"Correct! You do catch on quickly. The size and quality of a Noble's brood determines his or her social status. Don't look so surprised, child. Our lives are long. What else is there to fill them besides intrigue?

"There are periodic outbreaks of brood war, where rival nobles command their gets to attack one another in an attempt to rise in the social ranks. That is why we prefer to prey on humans with weak wills; they make compliant gets."

"Are you saying Morgan is my father?"

"In a way, yes. That is why I thought you were under orders. But I can see that you are something of a rogue, by our standards. It takes a vampire decades, if not centuries, to break free of his brood master and start thinking for himself. I've only had it happen to me once before. You see, my dear, Morgan was once one of my gets. I guess you could say I'm your grandfather."

"I'd rather not."

"Sarcasm suits you, my dear. Try to cultivate it. But this does put a new face on things. You see, your little 'hunting trips' have not gone unnoticed. I have remained silent up to now because it suited my purpose. You have, unwittingly, kindled a brood war between two highly placed nobles. Each has accused the other of participating in hostilities without a formal declaration of war. If things go any further, the entire pecking order will be restructured."

"And you want me to stop?"

"Nonsense, my dear! What made you think such a thing? No, feel free to continue what you're doing. By all means, be my guest! You see, my charming young one, by Noble standards I am quite puny. I don't even have a real title. I abhor blatant game-playing. I find it so debasing. No, I prefer biding my time, waiting for those brash fools above me to tear each other apart. My betters underestimate me, simply because I prefer to feast on lighter fare.

"I possess a discerning palate, my dear. I find rage, pain and fear far too overpowering. They lack subtlety. Where's the finesse in leeching off a Ku Klux Klan rally? While these emotions are, unquestionably, very potent, they lack focus. That is why I prefer the petty jealousies and backbiting found among art movements and intellectual societies. Shattered friendships, bitter denouements, ruined marriages, stormy personal relationships . . . Ahhh!" He smiled knowingly, like a chef reciting the ingredients for a prize-winning recipe.

"I've sampled them all, mind you, and I must say that the best still remains a toss-up between the modernists and the *fin-de-siècle* school. On one hand you had Pound, Picasso, Modigliani and Stein, but then there's Beardsley and Wilde. Although I must admit the Pre-Raphaelites were a tasty lot—Rossetti in particular, although his sister had her good points." Pangloss smacked his lips and rubbed his palms together, as if he was a wine connoisseur discussing his favorite vintage. "But I digress. When I sent Cesare looking for you, I'd originally planned to discover which Noble you were working for and plan my strategies accordingly. But now that I know that you're a free agent, I can offer you something far more profitable; I am willing to take you on as my pupil, seeing how grossly ignorant you are of the basic facts of unlife. You'll never learn anything from Ghilardi, that doddering old fool. You need me, my dear, if you wish to survive for long in the Real World."

"I have the *Aegrisomnia*."

Pangloss snorted. "Ah, yes, Ghilardi's holy writ. While it may prove useful now and again, I'm sure you've noticed that it's far from complete. Ghilardi knows nothing of its true origins. Its author was a brilliant fellow by the name of Palinurus. Lived in the thirteenth century, if I remember correctly. He composed the original text and illustrations while afflicted with a strange fever of the brain, dying a few days after its completion. Come now, do you suppose we'd allow something like that to fall into Ghilardi's hands if it were of any *real* use? It suits our purposes that he be ridiculed as a member of the lunatic fringe. We have long believed the best hiding place is directly under the human nose.

"There is so much I could show you, if only you'd put aside this irrational hatred of our species. You deny what you *are* by destroying that which is like you. It's a futile gesture, my dear. You seem to think that being human is something exalted, something to be proud of. As the years pass, you'll see them for what they really are: myopic little beasts intent on destroying their world. Why, if it weren't for us, the human race would have nuked itself out of existence nearly thirty years ago."

"You mean the fleas are keeping the dog alive?"

"If that's how you choose to see it. Humans are little more than cattle in a mad race to the slaughterhouse, and they don't care whom they stampede along with them! Must we stand by and watch as they destroy both their world and the Real one?"

"You make it sound so noble and self-effacing. I thought you enjoyed human pain and suffering?"

"That is true, in most cases. But where is the percentage in killing off the entire human race, just for the sake of a good dinner? Don't be naive. There is no atrocity mankind has perpetrated on itself that was the direct result of a Pretender command. In fact, up until this century we have remained fairly passive. It wasn't until humans stumbled across a means of destroying themselves en masse and forever that we felt compelled to intervene."

"I'm having difficulty picturing you as a protector of the human race."

Pangloss shrugged. " 'Husbander' would be a better word. Would a farmer stand idly by and watch his herd die of hoof-and-mouth? No! It is in *our* best interests that the human race continue. Of course, that doesn't mean their future will be a pleasant one. You're avoiding answering my proposal. Will you join me?"

"And what do you expect from me in exchange for learning at your feet?"

"What you're already doing."

"Except that I leave your gets alone."

"Precisely. Think about it, my dear. I'm offering you a chance for a title. You could become a *marchesa*, perhaps even a duchess!"

"You might as well bribe me with Monopoly money."

A look of incomprehension flickered across Pangloss's face. It was unnatural for a Noble to turn down a chance at advancing in social position. "Extraordinary," he murmured. "I can lead you to Morgan."

My heart jumped at the idea and I began to sweat. It was tempting . . . very tempting. There was nothing I wanted more than the opportunity to tear Morgan to shreds with my bare hands. And Pangloss was offering to take me to him. If . . .

The Other was eager to accept his invitation. *You'd be among your own kind. You wouldn't have to worry about being on the outside, of being a freak. You would be accepted for what you are.*

I looked at Pangloss, dressed in his fancy silk shirt and fashionable trousers. I looked at his finely manicured hands and carefully coiffured hair. I looked at him and saw a wizened, mummified dead man with no lips and skin the color of rancid tallow.

Among your own kind . . .

"Go to hell."

"My child, most of my closest friends are from there." Pangloss sighed. "I'd hoped you would be cooperative, but I can see there is too much of Morgan in you. Very well. I'll have Cesare escort you back the way you came." He called for the sensitive. "Cesare!" There was no response. "Cesare!" Pangloss's shout rattled the bones of the forgotten dead.

Cursing under his breath, Pangloss brushed past me to investigate the corner where his flunky had crawled to do his fix.

Cesare squatted on his haunches, propped against one of the lower death shelves. The candle and spoon he'd used to cook his fix lay at his feet, along with a spilled flask of mineral water. The candle had burned itself out, snuffed by a pool of its own wax. The bottom of the spoon was black with carbon from the flame. The rubber tubing was still knotted above the youth's elbow, the empty syringe dangling from his forearm by its needle. Vomit dripped slowly from the corner of his mouth.

"I'm afraid that was a little too pure for the poor boy. Humans are so fragile." Pangloss sounded like a housewife trying to estimate the correct patent medicine dosage for the family pet.

I turned away from the tableau; the sight of a fresh corpse among the ancient dead was oddly disconcerting. There would be no more voices for Cesare. A chill worked its way through my body; the youth had died while Pangloss discoursed on Pretender sociology. Had he known all along that the heroin he'd given his servant was uncut? The more I thought about it, the more I wanted to be free of the subterranean maze of vaults and dead things.

"Bother. I guess this means I must escort you back myself," sniffed Pangloss, heading toward one of the narrow passageways that opened onto the *cubiculum*.

"Wait! What about him?" I pointed to Cesare's body, crouched in a rough semblance of devotion.

Pangloss glanced around the burial chamber, then shrugged. "He's in good company."

The passageway was close and dark and smelled of dust and cobwebs. Pangloss walked just ahead of me, keeping up a constant chatter about the foibles and vices of famous dead people. I found being in such close quarters with the leering vampire unpleasant, but I was dependent on him to lead me out of the catacombs.

After we had been walking for some time, Pangloss stopped and turned to face me, his tone conversational.

"Do you remember when I told you that the catacombs are sacred neutral ground? Well, we're no longer within its jurisdiction."

The low-wattage bulbs strung along the ceiling suddenly surged, burning at three times their strength before bursting in a chain reaction of *pops!*

Pangloss was on top of me, his fingers closing around my neck like steel bands. I could see his eyes, glowing like a rat's in the pitch black as I drove my knife into the good doctor's chest. Pangloss howled as the silver blade sank deep into his flesh and the surrounding dead trembled at the sound. I slashed again, but Pangloss was gone.

I got to my feet, panting and shuddering like a winded racehorse. There was blood on my shoulder. I'd been bitten. I heard something that sounded like a cat in heat, shrieking and cursing from one of the myriad galleries that extended from the main corridor. I must have wounded Pangloss more than I thought. Holding my knife at the ready, I proceeded through the catacombs, following the lightbulb shards. I felt like Hansel or Gretel, following the trail of bread crusts after the evil stepmother left them in the woods to starve. I thought about the ogre waiting on the other side of the door and began to giggle.

I was alternately freezing and sweating; my joints ached horribly and my head felt like it was coming apart at the seams. Had Pangloss infected me with some kind of poison? I remembered what he'd said about vampires injecting part of themselves into their victims. Maybe the Morgan inside of me was battling with Pangloss for possession. I had a vision of them locked in mortal combat deep within my stomach, aristocratic jet-setter versus effete intellectual.

I don't know how long I wandered the catacombs in a delirious stupor, but I managed to stay in the right passageway. I stared at the heavy door for several minutes before recognizing it as the end of my journey. The hinges were on the outside and there was no handle on the inside, only a keyhole.

Beyond caring whether the ogre heard me, I used my knife to pick the lock from my side of the door. It wasn't very difficult; the door was very old and the locking mechanism crude by today's standards.

I opened the door slowly, knowing at any minute the ogre would reach out and snare me by my hair. I experienced a vivid image of myself being held aloft by my ankles and lowered, headfirst, into the creature's waiting jaws. I shook off the vision and peeked into the basement, only to find it empty. The ogre's place beside the door stood deserted.

Relieved, but still cautious, I pushed open the door and entered the basement. Judging by the light angling through the windows set at ground level, it was late afternoon. I hurried up the stairs, unmindful of their creaks and groans. I had to get out of there before the ogre came back.

I was on the deserted first floor, at the foot of the crumbling remains of a curved staircase, when I caught sight of the open door at the top of the stairs. It had been closed when Cesare first escorted me through the old villa. Even though I was weakened by fever and my bones felt like they had been hollowed out and filled with lead, something in me had to investigate the room at the top of the stairs.

I was being dragged up the stairs by a force I was helpless to resist or comprehend, like the toy skaters that pirouette atop their mirror lakes. I did not want to see what was in the room. I wanted to escape the villa and its monstrous guard, but I mounted the stairs one by one, my eyes focused on the half-open door.

Back when the villa was alive, the room had been a nursery. It was light and airy and I could still make out the fairy-tale characters that decorated the molding near the ceiling. There was no furniture except for a soiled mattress in one corner covered with filthy blankets. The room smelled like a lion's cage. There were urine stains on the wall at the height of a man's head.

There were toys scattered throughout the nursery, some new, others antique, all of them broken. An Edwardian rocking horse, its back broken and saddle askew, stared at me from the gathering shadows.

I crossed the threshold, stepping across a battalion of painted lead soldiers bent into clothespins. The walls near the ogre's bed were decorated with illustrations torn from children's books. My foot nudged something. It was a large Raggedy Ann doll, its red yarn hair askew and missing one shoe-button eye. Stuffing dribbled from the gaping hole between its candy-striped legs. Grunting in disgust, I turned to leave the monster's boudoir. I looked down and saw what looked to be the dislocated arm of a baby doll. Then I saw the knob of bone that had once fit into the shoulder socket. No. Not a doll.

I vomited loudly and copiously, ridding myself of Pangloss's contagion. I was so centered on my purging I didn't hear the monster come home. There was something like a cross between a panther's snarl and the shriek of a bat from downstairs, then the villa began to shake as the ogre stormed up the stairs.

The door flew open, smashing into the wall so hard it sagged on its hinges. The ogre filled the threshold, his monk's hood pushed back to reveal his hideous, inhuman face. He glared at me, his gorilloid nostrils flaring, and a dim flicker of recognition sparked deep within his eyes. Then he charged, hands outstretched, bellowing at the top of his lungs.

I sidestepped five hundred pounds of enraged ogre as he crashed into the nursery wall hard enough to shake the house. Rotting plaster fell from the ceiling and a huge crack marked where he'd collided with the wall. The ogre spat out a curved tooth, ignoring the trickle of blood seeping from his nose.

There was no way I could go toe to toe with such a monster. I wasn't even sure if ogres *had* weak spots. My back was to a double casement that faced the back of the house. Without bothering to see where I might be landing, I smashed through the windows and plummeted into the unknown.

I came to in a nearby alley with a broken arm and some busted ribs. I'd landed in the overgrown garden attached to the villa and somehow succeeded in scaling the wall before the ogre located me. I still felt like shit and it took several days to fully recover from the effects of Pangloss's bite. At one time I distinctly heard him talking to me inside my head, telling me to join him. But it might have been an auditory hallucination.

I returned to Geneva, but I could not bring myself to tell Ghilardi of my encounter with Pangloss and the revelations he'd made. It would have ruined his book.

1978: Ghilardi suffered a massive stroke while trying to find a publisher for his new work. I curtailed my hunting expeditions and remained in Geneva. When I first met Ghilardi, his eyes were blue fire, the color of sapphires held to the light. After the stroke they started to fade, growing paler every day. It was hard to watch him die like that, knowing the vitality he'd once had, but I was equally curious. I had never participated in a natural death before.

He died June 2, 1978. I was with him when it happened. By that time his eyes were so pale a blue they were without color, like those of a child fresh from the womb. The left side of his face was slack and his left hand a useless snarl of meat and bone.

"Sssonja . . ." he slurred. He seemed more alert than usual that day. "Do you see it?"

I scanned the bedroom on all levels; and as far as I could see, we were alone. "See what, Erich?" I turned around in time to watch his eyes close. I didn't need to touch him to know he was dead. I sat there for a long moment, my sense of loss so overwhelming it couldn't register as an emotion, and stared at what was left of my friend and tutor.

I was named Ghilardi's principal heir and executor of his will. I inherited the house, the grounds, the family fortune and a professionally forged set of documents that provided Sonja Blue with a recorded past.

I also inherited Ghilardi's notebooks and the typewritten manuscript concerning his greatest discovery: me. This was the book that would lay to rest the idea that Erich Ghilardi was a kook. I burned every last page in the central hall's marble fireplace.

After I'd consigned Ghilardi's reputation to the flames, I drove my Jaguar to Geneva. After wandering the streets for several hours, I found myself standing on the shores of Lake Geneva. I stared at the same lake on which Jean-Jacques went boating with his beloved dullard, Marie-Thérèse, and where, fifty years later, a poet's wife gave birth to a monster.

I was certain I would not find my answers in Europe. I rang Ghilardi's solicitors and liquidated my entire inheritance, except for two books, and bought a one-way ticket to the Orient.

I went to Japan, hoping its saffron-robed holy men and black-garbed assassin priests might know more of the Real World than the scientists and occult investigators of the West.

While waiting for the bullet train that would take me into Tokyo from the airport, I noticed a young girl dressed in the drab uniform the Nippon educational system had copied from German private schools earlier in the century. She looked to be no more than twelve or thirteen, although the roundness of her face made her seem even younger.

She was chewing gum and paging through a comic book the size of a telephone directory. I glimpsed a woman, naked except for strategic shadows, cowering before a hulking giant. The giant was covered with scars and tattoos. A poisonous snake with dripping fangs was wrapped around the monster's erect penis; rather, it was wrapped around where the giant's erect penis *would* have been, if the censors hadn't airbrushed it out.

The schoolgirl extruded a bubble the color of flesh, flipped the page, and continued reading. The giant pressed his thumbs into his protesting victim's eyes. I realized that finding answers here would not be as easy as I'd thought.

I soon discovered that coming to Japan had been a mistake. I stalked the human beehives of Tokyo, frustrated in my search for Pretenders. Everyone in the city wore a mask; it is a part of their culture. Pretending to be something they're not is second nature to the Japanese. Their thoughts formed an impenetrable wall I was neither skilled enough nor ready to understand. I felt even more alienated than I had in Europe.

Still, it wasn't a complete loss on my part. I was in a mammoth downtown Tokyo department store; it was a busy afternoon and it seemed as if the entire country had picked that day to come and shop. Despite the crowds, I was able to maintain suitable personal space. I was unsure whether their reluctance to come too close had to do with my being *gaijin* or Pretender.

Either way, I followed the path of least resistance, allowing myself to be buoyed along in the general direction of the shoppers. The Japanese equivalent of canned music blared from hidden speakers, mixing with the roar of a thousand alien voices.

I found myself standing near a bank of elevators. There were two young Japanese girls dressed in feminine versions of the department store uniform posted outside the lifts. Both wore spotless white gloves and spoke in artificial falsetto voices like cartoon mice. The elevator girls smiled fixedly, bowing to the customers with machinelike precision and made what looked like ritual hand gestures. Their arms rocked back and forth like metronomes, indicating which lifts went to which departments. I watched the puppet women as they repeated their robotic gestures over and over for an endless stream of shoppers, their smiles never faltering. I was suddenly overcome by the need to cry. Strange. I didn't weep at Ghilardi's death.

I was surprised to see a small, bowed man with the wrinkled face of a sacred ape looking up at me. At first I thought I was being accosted by some exotic variation of Pretender. Then I realized I was looking at a *very* old man.

"You come away from this," he said in English. "No place for you." He gestured with a crooked finger and began threading his way through the dense packing of consumers. Intrigued, I followed him. The old man's aura was roseate, but I could not divine if he was of Pretender origin.

The bent old man led me to a traditional Japanese house, sequestered from the bustle of the street by ancient stone walls. He showed me his garden, with its intricate patterns raked in the sand and shared tea with me.

His name was Hokusai, and he was a descendant of Shinto wizards and samurai swordsmiths. He had been trained in the art of "seeing beyond" by his grandfather and was adept at identifying people and places of power.

"You shine very strong. Maybe too strong. And sometime there is darkness at the edge of the bright." He frowned, unable to fully explain himself in English.

I suspected that even if I spoke fluent Japanese he would still have trouble finding the right words. "Why did you ask me to follow you here?"

"I watch you watch elevator girls. The dark was eating the bright."

I nodded that I understood and the wrinkled monkey face beamed happily. For the first time since Ghilardi's death, I found myself at ease in another's presence.

The old gentleman told me that as a child his grandfather filled him with stories of the elemental spirits that had once ruled the island kingdom before the days of the first emperor. The old wizard had been adamant that the spirits would return within his grandson's lifetime and wished that Hokusai be trained in recognizing their signs. Now it seemed his grandfather's predictions had come true.

I was humbled by the old man's hospitality and what I knew to be uncharacteristic openness to a foreigner. I didn't have the heart to tell him he was sharing tea with a monster. It was Hokusai who reforged the silver dagger Ghilardi had given me years ago, transforming it into a handsomely mounted switchblade. The handle was fashioned of teak and the inlaid dragon adorning it from gold leaf. The small ruby that was the dragon's eye also served as the triggering stud. Hokusai refused payment, claiming that he owed it to the ghost of his grandfather.

I left Japan after a month's stay. My next port of call was Hong Kong. I never saw or heard from Hokusai again.

What occurred in Hong Kong was bound to happen, eventually. I'd succeeded in forestalling the inevitable for years. Hong Kong is so alien a place for Westerners, even inhuman ones, that it's easy to forget your past and your future. There is only now in Hong Kong and that is, in itself, timeless.

I found myself in one of the city's huge open-air bazaars, if you consider a street jammed with fish peddlers open air. The noise was terrific, hundreds of voices yelling, haggling and arguing in as many dialects. Street urchins of indeterminate sex and age waved chintzy, mass-produced gewgaws in my face, shrilling "Yankee! Cheap! You buy!" After my failure in Tokyo, I limited my mind scan to random samplings of the crowd. Then I saw him.

He was an elderly priest, dressed in the saffron robes of a Buddhist monk, a neat smear of red on his shaven brow. Though he hobbled with the aid of a gnarled stick, his power was evident to those who could see. The monk paused in his journey and glanced in my direction. His placid, moon-round face was replaced by the features of a fox. I tried to go after him but a group of housewives, haggling over the price of snake, blocked my path. By the time I reached the spot I'd last seen him, the monk was nowhere to be found.

"You look somebody?"

It was a long-haired, seedy Chinese male in his late twenties who'd spoken. He lounged against a nearby doorway, arms folded across his chest. He wore a pair of much-mended American jeans and a faded T-shirt bearing the logo BRUCE LEE LIVES.

"Yes. There was a monk here just a second ago. Did you see where he went?"

The man nodded. "I see. I know priest. Show you where he go. Ten dollar."

Too eager to be cautious, I shoved a note in his hand. He smiled broadly, revealing crooked teeth the color of wild rice. He led me through a series of narrow streets that took us away from the main thoroughfares, emptying into a squalid, dimly lit alley.

"Priest live here. Very holy man. Very poor," explained my guide.

I was dubious of his claim, and I knew what was going to happen, but I couldn't risk the chance that he was telling me the truth. I took a hesitant step into the alley. "Are you sure this is where—"

I never finished the sentence. There was a sharp blow on the back of my skull and the pavement tilted up to greet me. Stupid. My guide's hands were on me, searching my pockets with the speed and skill of a professional mugger. He found the switchblade and paused to admire the craftsmanship. His thumb brushed the tiny ruby dragon's eye and the knife revealed itself. He knelt and pressed the tip of the switchblade against the hollow of my throat, teasing a drop of blood from my skin.

"Good knife. You got money, Yankee? Dollar? Traveler check? What you got for me? Huh? What you got?"

He didn't like my answer.

My right hand clamped around his throat and I saw his eyes bulge inside their epicanthic folds. He forgot about slicing my throat and tried to pull my hand away from his windpipe. I felt his larynx turn to pulp. I got back on my feet, keeping my erstwhile guide at arm's length. Normally I would have snapped his neck and let it go at that, but I was in a foul mood. I had come close—so close—to finding what I was looking for, only to have this geek throw me off the scent.

My attacker was turning colors, his tongue so swollen he'd bitten halfway through it. He made a noise like mice trapped in a shoe box. Vaguely curious, I looked inside his head to see what his thoughts might be, now that he faced death.

I found an open sewer. My guide was a nasty piece of work, as humans go. He'd spent several years in Vietnam buying children orphaned by the war and selling them to brothels in Hong Kong, Tokyo, Seoul and Manila. When that no longer proved profitable, he sold junk to the Yankee GIs until the South Vietnamese bureaucracy chased him out of Saigon for failure to pay bribes on time. Now he lured Anglos into dark alleyways under pretenses of sightseeing or sex, murdering for the contents of their wallets or a wristwatch. It was safer and easier than dealing with the Yakuza or the Triad, and he had a low overhead.

I withdrew, disgusted by my victim's lack of humanity.

Who's the monster, Sonja? You or him?

I flinched. I wasn't used to the Other speaking directly to me. The strangling man at the end of my arm looked like a perverse hand puppet. Spittle, blood, and foam flecked the corners of his mouth. His tongue was the size and color of a black pudding.

"Monster" is such an unfair word, don't you agree?

I was aware of the hunger building inside of me. A cold sweat broke across my brow and I began to tremble.

What makes the word "human" so damned wonderful? You're always mourning your humanity, denying yourself the power and privilege that are yours by right for fear of becoming inhuman. You fight to keep from doing what is natural for you, simply because you pride yourself on being human. What is being human? Is it being like him? Why don't you put him to some use, eh? You'll be doing society a favor . . .

I was standing on the mountaintop with Satan whispering in my ear. And I was weak.

He was so close to death when I took him there was no real fear left in him, only resignation. The flesh of his throat was unwashed and tasted of sweat and dirt. The faint odor of ginger clung to him.

I trembled as if caught in the heat of erotic passion. His skin was taut and soft under my lips as I felt his weakened pulse throb against the points of my fangs, inviting penetration.

"No. I can't do this, even if he is murdering scum. I didn't come all this way. . . not for *this*."

Didn't you? You knew what his intentions were the moment you saw the alley. You knew but you went ahead. Why? Hasn't it been leading up to this ever since you first tasted human blood and found it good?

"No! I can buy blood on the black market. Not like this . . ."

Ah, yes. The blood in the bottles. Sterilized for your protection. How fucking bland. You really do disappoint me, Sonja . . . Or do you?

The hunger was a dark bubble in my gut. I could *smell* the bastard's blood waiting for me on the other side of his skin. I couldn't do it. I *wouldn't* do it. But I did.

The man jerked as my fangs entered the warmth of his jugular. It was so sweet. I realized how bland and characterless the bottled blood really was. The Other was right: nothing can compare to the taste of blood stolen fresh from the vein. It was the difference between beer and a fine champagne. It felt so natural to have hot, fresh human blood squirting into my mouth. I drank like a woman rescued from the desert, afraid of wasting a single drop. Wave after wave of pleasure washed over me. I had been a prostitute for five years, but that was the first time I experienced orgasm.

By the time I was finished, my would-be murderer was very pale and very dead. I left him in the nameless alley, along with my humanity.

More disturbed than enlightened by my sojourns in the East, I decided to visit the scene of the crime: London. It seemed the logical place to start if I was going to track down Morgan. It was 1979, ten years after Denise Thorne's mysterious disappearance and my secret birth.

Things were very different from the last time I was in town; the punk music scene was building up the PR to jump the Atlantic. The hippie sentiments of peace and love had curdled into bitterness and resentment. Yet, in their own way, some things were the same.

The Apple Cart Discotheque had mutated over the past decade and turned into Fugg's. Fat tarts in cheap wigs and cheaper makeup did the bump-and-grind down a runway for the edification of a handful of hard-core rummies. The dancers chewed gum and made crude fuck-motions with their hips. The men scattered up and down the runway looked about as aroused as dead newts.

I crossed to the bar, my memory decorating the dive with phantom go-go girls and jet-setters in paisley-print shirts.

The bartender gave me a sour look. "Ain't hirin'. Business is bleedin' awful."

"I'm not looking for a job. Do you know a man called Morgan? Claims to be a peer." I handed him a fiver.

The bartender shrugged. "Mebbe. Think that's what he calls hisself. Used to, rather. Ain't been around in a while."

"How long?"

"Year. Mebbe two. Suits me if th' bleeder never shows his face again. Every time he comes 'round, one of me best girls ups and quits. Never fails. They go packin' off with him without givin' proper notice and I never see hide nor hair of 'em again." He shook his head. "Just can't figure it. What would a toff like him want with birds like that? Me, I met the wife at a church social."

Everywhere I went, the story was the same: yes, they knew Morgan, no, they couldn't say when he might show up again and could care less if he did.

Morgan kept to a schedule, at least in London, and I was unlucky enough to have returned during his off-season. I realized it might be another ten years before he made the circuit again, since time means little to Pretenders. The idea of waiting chafed. I wanted to have my revenge while I could still *feel* it.

I consoled myself by cleansing London and its neighboring districts of undead.

Clearing out the revenants was easy enough, although the vampires—the ones with enough skill and brains to pass for human—proved to be a different matter. Most of them posed as nondescript shopgirls and junior bank clerks—no one you'd look at twice. Although I had no trouble locating them, they usually succeeded in giving me the slip.

I was in a small pub near the East End when I spotted a pale young woman nursing a pint at one of the back tables. She was dressed dowdily and was rather unremarkable in appearance. Just another lower-middle-class working girl out for her weekly glass of stout. But there was something odd about the way she brought the glass to her lips and how the amount of ale stayed the same. I shifted my vision to see what she looked like in the Real World.

An ancient crone was seated where the girl had been, her face hideously wrinkled. When she noticed me watching her, she put down her drink and left the pub. I hurried after her. The hag moved faster than I'd expected and was already a block ahead of me. I saw her dodge into one of the mews that riddled the district. I followed, switchblade in hand and eager for confrontation. Instead, I found nothing. Not a trace. But how did she know?

"That you were goin' t' kill her? Have y' tried lookin' in th' mirror lately, pet? You got 'big-time predator' writ all over!"

He emerged from the fog, dressed in a silk suit the color of reptiles, a foul-smelling French cigarette hanging from his lower lip. I grabbed him by his narrow lapels. He looked a bit nonplussed, but there was no fear in his voice.

"Here now! Don't go wrinklin' th' material, luv."

"Who are you? How'd you—"

"Know what you were thinkin'? It's me job, ducks."

Something dark and fast with sharp edges scampered through my mind. I grunted and let go of him.

He carefully rearranged his clothing. "I'm human, don't you worry. As if that bleedin' means anything. I know some things. I know yer not human, but y' ain't one of *them*, either."

"You . . . you can see them? You see the Real World?"

"If that's what y'call it . . . Yeah, I see shit. Used t'think mum was balmy, rattlin' on about th' old lady down th' row bein' a werewolf. Until I started seein' things, too." He grinned, revealing National Health teeth.

I didn't like standing in the open discussing the Real World, and I especially didn't like the leering youth who'd come out of nowhere, claiming to know my secrets. The Other whispered that there was a quick and bloody solution to my problem.

Fear flickered across his face, only to be replaced by a crafty grin. "Yer lookin' t' kill them beasties, ain'tcha? I mean, th' very sight of 'em makes you want to heave, right? But y' got way too much mojo, luv. They can spot y' half a mile off. See?" He produced a small pocket mirror from inside his jacket and held it so I could glimpse my reflection. I'd avoided looking in mirrors ever since the night my reflection had taken a life of its own. I realized it'd been a mistake.

I was surrounded by a crimson nimbus that strobed and pulsed with my heartbeat, like an Eastern Orthodox saint. "That's why th' minute you show yer lovely face, they split. What you need is a judas goat, see? Someone t' lure 'em away and set it up so you could snuff 'em easy, eh?"

"Go on. What would you get out of this? Besides money?"

He grinned and I was suddenly aware that he was an extraordinarily handsome man. "Y' got a good head f' business, luv. First rate. Let's just say I'm in th' market for a wee bit of protection. There's this bloke—couple of them, really—that's hot for me. Think I burned 'em on a business deal. They're wrong, of course."

"Of course," I echoed, retracing my steps out of the mews. My companion fell in beside me, still talking.

"I've checked y' out. Yer good. Real good. So what d' ya say, luv?"

"My name is not luv."

"Fair enough, luv. So what's it gonna be? We gotta deal?"

"What's your name?"

He came to a stop and scowled, his eyes fixed on something in the fog.

"Bloody hell!" He turned to flee back into the mews. The toughs emerged from the fog, as swift and silent as sharks. They were husky skinheads, dressed in the tatters of American denim jackets and leather pants. Their wrists bristled with chrome-studded black leather.

"Y'ain't gettin' away from us this time, y' lit'l soddin' queer," growled one of the skinheads as he snagged a handful of lizard-green jacket. "Stig, take care of th' bird."

"Like hell you will!" I grabbed the one called Stig, twisting his arm in a way it was not meant to go. His scream revealed him to be younger than he looked.

The first punk was pounding my newfound partner's head into the pavement. Since he didn't have any hair, I grabbed his ears. One of them came off in my hand; just don't make 'em like they used to, I guess.

Blood leaked from the sensitive's nostrils and his left eye was swollen shut. I lifted him in a fireman's carry and headed for my digs at a dead run. I could hear the shrill cry of a bobby's whistle from somewhere close by.

"Now, as I was saying before we were so rudely interrupted, what's your name?"

"Geoffrey Chastain . . . Look, call me Chaz, okay?"

The seven years I spent in the company of Chaz, waiting for Morgan to resurface, were . . . educational. I got to know every lowlife dive and sleazy after-hours club in the kingdoms, associating with the trashiest bastards ever to draw the dole. Don't get me wrong; I learned a lot from Chaz.

Although his telepathic abilities weren't up to Pretender standards, he'd mastered them to an amazing degree. He knew how to dampen his reception so he wouldn't be "on" twenty-four hours a day, and claimed that half the schizophrenics walking around complaining of "voices" in their heads were sensitives unable to turn down the volume. He also knew how to shield himself from other sensitives. Bright boy. A complete and utter prick, but still a bright boy. He was my only friend.

I hadn't realized how much I missed having someone to talk to, someone I didn't have to Pretend with. Chaz was my friend and confidant—and, at times, my lover.

He peddled dope on the side—"I *know* what you need" was his favorite come-on with the junkies—without fear of reprisals from disgruntled customers or rival dealers. Word on the street had it that Chaz was under the protection of someone—or something—mean enough to shit plutonium.

He relied on me to save his ass whenever he got in trouble, which proved to be a regular occurrence. In '83 he nearly got us both killed, thanks to his involvement with a Scottish gangster named Edward "Thick Eddie" Magruder.

Thick Eddie was famous for his brutality and intolerance of betrayal. Chaz had skimmed several hundred quids-worth of cocaine during a deal he'd set up for the mob boss, and Thick Eddie wasn't about to let Chaz go around bragging about it.

Thick Eddie sent the prerequisite goons around to rough up Chaz. They were large, squarish men dressed in cheap suits. I had no intention of letting Chaz be hurt, but I'd grown somewhat weary of his reliance on me. Chaz's tendency toward self-destruction showed in his taste for rough trade and the habit of making enemies of the wrong people. So I took my time before rescuing my judas goat from Magruder's agents.

Since Magruder had a legitimate grievance, I let his men off easy with a broken arm apiece. Magruder didn't see it that way and within twenty-four hours there were two more chunks in cheap suits coming around Chaz's digs, only this time they were armed.

One of the hit men ended up in the hospital with a fractured skull, two broken arms and a ruptured spleen. The second was dumped in front of Magruder's "legitimate" business, which happened to be wholesale carpeting. I should say the Other dumped the body there, for she was the one who killed him.

I remember nothing of my second confrontation with Thick Eddie's men beyond one of the squarish men pulling his gun on me. I regained my senses hours later, only to find myself miles from where I last remembered being, soaked in blood and aching from broken bones and internal injuries. My right shoulder throbbed fiercely, meaning I'd taken a bullet.

I found Chaz at my flat. He'd fled his own digs when Thick Eddie's men jumped us the night before. We both knew Magruder wasn't the type who'd take kindly to having his employees murdered. I suggested that Chaz give Thick Eddie restitution for the cocaine he'd stolen. Chaz wasn't thrilled with the idea, but finally agreed to do it under the condition that I accompany him.

Using underworld channels, Chaz sent his proposal to Thick Eddie, stating that he would meet him if he came alone. Magruder refused to meet anyone, including his own mother, alone, so Chaz grudgingly agreed to the presence of a "personal bodyguard."

The rendezvous point was an old warehouse facing the Thames. The place stank of dead fish and less wholesome flotsam. Magruder was already there by the time we arrived. He sat on an old shipping crate, smoking a smelly cigar and reading the evening paper. The headline read BOY TRAPPED IN REFRIGERATOR EATS OWN FOOT.

Thick Eddie glanced over the top of the paper at us, chewing his cigar speculatively. "I dinna believe th' lads a' first, when they told me 'twas a lassie. Me lads are brave 'uns. Not th' kind t' run scared an' tell wild tales, they are." Magruder fixed his eyes on me. "Then, things 'tain't always what they seem, eh? Me gran, she were allus sayin' that."

Of all the people in the United Kingdom he could choose from, Chaz *would* have to pick a Pretender crime boss to piss off! Actually, Thick Eddie was only part Pretender. Although his ogrish heritage was evident in his heavyset frame and coarse features, he was, essentially, human.

"Why didn't you tell me Magruder was part ogre?" I hissed into Chaz's ear.

"I didn't know! I've never seen him in person before." For once I had no reason not to believe Chaz's excuse.

Chaz cleared his throat and stepped forward. "I, uh, got yer money right here, Eddie." He hoisted a small overnight bag as proof. "I hope yer'll, uh, see fit t' let bygones be, uh, bygones, eh? It were all a misunderstandin'."

Thick Eddie stared at the proffered bag, his heavy-lidded eyes resembling those of a basking lizard. "Yew know I make more'n that every hour, lad. 'Tain't th' money that's important. Nay, 'tis th' principle o' th' thing. If I let yew go now, every punk in London'll be thinkin' he can pull a fast'un on Eddie Magruder. That's why I decided t' call in some help." Magruder motioned with his cigar, and a chunk of shadow separated itself from the darkness of the warehouse. "I'd like yew t' meet me cousin, Jo'die."

The ogre towered over his mongrel kinsman. Despite the differences in their heights and builds, there was a marked family resemblance. The ogre growled something in his native tongue and Magruder lifted an eyebrow.

"Aye, now? It seems Jo'die finds yer lady friend a wee bit familiar."

The ogre pushed the brim of his hat back with a taloned finger the size of a small sausage, his brow furrowed by unaccustomed brainwork. It was the ogre monk.

"Fuck this!" shrilled Chaz, hurling the bag of money at Magruder and fleeing in the direction of the exit.

The ogre roared like a lion and bounded after Chaz. It only took three strides of his long, oaklike legs for Jordie to catch up.

Chaz shrieked as the ogre grabbed him by the back of the neck, dangling him like a puppy.

"I'd see aboot that, if I were yew, lass," suggested Thick Eddie as he bent to retrieve the bag Chaz had abandoned. "Jo'die may just be a wee bit peckish right now."

Cursing the ogre and the northern climes that produced such changeling bastards as Thick Eddie Magruder, I sprinted to Chaz's rescue.

Jordie had reversed his grip and was now holding Chaz by his ankles. I slammed into the ogre just as he began to lift his apelike arms. Ogres like to eat their prey headfirst. I don't know why, they just do. Jordie let go of Chaz and swatted me with a hand the size of a telephone directory. Chaz didn't waste any time getting to his feet and leaving me alone with Magruder's cousin. Jordie, seeing his prey making its getaway, moved to follow.

"Jordie!" The ogre's huge, hairless head swung toward me, momentarily distracted from its victim. "Remember me, Jordie? In Rome? At the villa?"

I could almost hear the cogs turning in the bullet-shaped head as his brows furrowed and unfurrowed. Comprehension dawned in his orangish-brown eyes, and his lips pulled back to expose a mouthful of knives.

I leapt to meet his charge, moving inside his reach in order to drive my knife deep into his side. The blade tore through the ogre's outer garments. However, it slid along the monster's ribs as if his skin were made of rubber. Not even a scratch!

Jordie bellowed his hunting cry, his throat sacs swelling like a howler monkey's. He locked me in a simian embrace and began to squeeze. His brutish face was inches from mine as he crushed my bones. Black sunbursts filled my eyesight as the ogre laughed, exhaling a fetid breath that was like standing downwind of a slaughterhouse on a hot August day.

I was still clutching my knife, although my arm was pinned to my side. I squirmed frantically in his grip, trying to work my knife hand free. This seemed to amuse and excite the ogre, and he licked my face with a long, rasplike tongue. I received an explicit mental image of myself being ravaged, then devoured. He was still trying to decide whether to kill me before or after the rape.

I voiced my disgust with ogrish courting techniques by wrenching my arm free and driving my switchblade to the hilt in his right ear. It slid in beautifully, like they were made for each other.

The ogre yowled, dropping me in favor of clawing at the weapon embedded in his brain. I assessed my damage: only a few broken ribs and a dislocated shoulder. Jordie crashed about, flailing his arms and squealing like a frightened sow before finally collapsing face forward, his cries halted in midsqueal. Blood seeped from his nose, mouth, and ear. I retrieved my blade, making sure to give it an extra twist, just in case, and hurried away before Thick Eddie came looking for his kin.

Luckily, Eddie Magruder didn't have time to send for any more of his family. For reasons unknown, his car mysteriously exploded two days after our "business transaction" in the warehouse. The wholesale carpeting business can be very cutthroat at times.

That's funny. I'm having trouble visualizing Chaz. The face is there, but it's blurred, like an old movie that's jumped its sprockets. Everything's jerky . . .

I remember the last vampire I killed in London. Chaz went to a gay bar in one of the seedier districts. There were always plenty of vampires to be found in the bars, not to mention *vargr* and incubi. True predators, they found those living on the periphery of human society the perfect victims: homosexuals, prostitutes, junkies and the homeless make up the Pretenders' staple diet.

Chaz had picked up a handsome young man dressed in exquisitely pressed chinos with neatly rolled cuffs and a tight-fitting white T-shirt. Chaz led the vampire into an abandoned house; the place was partially demolished and there was a gaping hole where the first-floor ceiling should have been. I crouched upstairs, watching my judas goat as he lured the sacrificial victim deeper into the trap.

I jumped, savoring the split second of free-fall before I crashed on top of the startled vampire. I pinned him to the floor, straddling his chest.

He was a strong one, and as vicious as a rutting tiger. I managed to stick him once, twice. Then he rolled over and I saw his face for the first time. I froze, the knife poised for the killing thrust.

Chaz was shrilling, "Kill him! Kill him! Fer Chrissakes, kill him!" But I couldn't. I was paralyzed. I *knew* the bastard!

The vampire writhed under me, spitting and clawing like a rabid cat, but I couldn't drive the blade home. The last time I'd seen him, he'd been behind the wheel of a Rolls Royce the color of smoke, dressed in the livery of a chauffeur.

"Where is he? Where *is* he?" I didn't recognize the voice as my own. I tasted bile and blood rising in my throat. My rage bordered on euphoria. "Where is he? I know you're one of his gets. I saw you with him!"

The vampire twisted his head from side to side, babbling incoherently. My paralysis ended and I smashed my fist into his mouth. I didn't feel his fangs as they shredded my knuckles. His blood was thick and dark, like dirty motor oil. All I could see was his demonic leer as Denise beat on the glass partition in the back of the Rolls. I brought the switchblade across his face, laying his handsome features open to the bone.

The vampire chauffeur screamed and put his hands to his ruined face, pushing me off his chest.

Chaz was shouting at me to stop him before he escaped as the vampire staggered toward the front door.

Blind in one eye, he tumbled down the front steps and landed on the street. There were viscous smears on the steps and his white shirt was the color of old ketchup. The vampire got to his feet, clinging to a nearby streetlight for support. He looked like a music-hall drunk.

I charged out of the building, Chaz on my heels. I had every intention of dragging the thing back inside and finishing my interrogation, even if it meant skinning him layer by layer.

The knife had sliced away the vampire's upper lip and left cheek, exposing his teeth and upper jaw. He looked like he was leering at me again. Maybe that's what made me lose control.

The vampire raised his hand in a feeble attempt to deflect the next blow and said "No . . ."

Perhaps he was trying to tell me he didn't know Morgan's whereabouts. Maybe not. I'm no longer sure. I was beyond caring. I was in the backseat of a Rolls Royce with a chauffeur whose grin was impossibly sharp. The switchblade impaled his right eye, burying itself in the spongy softness of the frontal lobes, severing left brain from right. I made sure to twist the knife.

The vampire slid off the blade and lay sprawled in the gutter under the streetlight. I felt as if I was emerging from heavy sedation. I was vaguely aware I was standing on a London sidewalk with a rapidly bloating corpse at my feet. Blanched faces watched me from behind the curtains of a dozen windows.

Chaz tugged on my sleeve, his voice urgent. "C'mon, Sonja! What's wrong with you? Cor, y' really fucked it this time!"

That's how I returned to the land of my birth. The last time I was in America I'd been a pampered rich kid with her whole life laid out for her like a party frock draped across the foot of her bed. Now I wasn't even me anymore.

Socialite, hooker, vampire hunter and vampire—no one could accuse me of leading a dull life.

Chaz came along at the last minute. Turned out to be a mistake. The scuzziest down-and-out dive on Skid Row was too wholesome for him. No sense of history. All he did was bitch about how much he missed the clubs in Soho. He was the one who brought Catherine Wheele to my attention.

Shit! What's wrong? Everything's jumping and rolling like the picture on a cheap TV set. The weird part is that it's so familiar . . . like it's *supposed* to do that. I can't even *think* about Catherine Wheele without the signal trying to scramble.

We control the horizontal. We control the vertical.

Like fuck you do! What's going on here? Damnit, if this is your doing . . .

*Me? Why should I keep you from continuing your boring little monologue?
I've only heard it every sleep for the past six months. "Poor pitiful me, I've become
a big bad monster." Give me a break! No, as much as I'd love to change channels,
I'm not the one behind your technical difficulties. You gotta dig deeper.*

Deeper?

Just tell your story. You'll find out.

Chaz showed me the article in a cheesy supermarket tabloid he'd brought
home. It had Sister Catherine Wheele, dressed in a red-white-and-blue
spangled jumpsuit, holding a microphone. Her makeup was running. A smaller
photo was cropped and inserted into the lower right-hand corner. The photo
was of Shirley Thorne, wife of industrialist Jacob Thorne and mother of missing
heiress Denise Thorne. The article claimed Mrs. Thorne was funneling a
small fortune into the Wheele ministry in an attempt to contact her long-
lost daughter.

I sent Chaz to scout out Wheele, to see if there was any truth to the
rumors behind her being a wild talent. He was gone a long time. It's getting
hard to think.

Tell the story.

Meet me . . . He was going to meet me at the playground after midnight.
He was standing by the basketball goal. Why is this so *difficult?* I walked up
behind him. He turned. He was smiling. As usual. Before I could question
him about Wheele, he kissed me. Didn't say a word, just kissed me. And fired
point-blank into my gut. Knocked . . . knocked me down. He ran away, didn't
look back. Smart boy, knew better than to hang around. There was a flechette
lodged in my belly. Tranquilizer of some kind . . .

Hands. Hands all over me. Set me up. Little shit. Set me up. But he didn't
tell them the truth. Not the whole truth. The pain and rage made it so hard
to keep control, the Other emerged. Men were screaming. Blood in me and
on me. Someone chanting "Antichrist" like a mantra. And then . . . then . . .

Aw, don't tell me you're not going to finish this exciting episode.

Can't. Nothing but static, white noise, hurts when I try to remember . . .

*What a wimp! You're real good at slam-dunking bad-ass bikers into trash cans,
but come the first aversion barrier and you're whining like a goddamn baby!*

What are you blathering about?

*Look, bright girl, you've been running the same damn autobiographical saga
every sleep for the past six months and you never get past the first barrier. Never.
I've let you slide because . . . well, because it suited me. But it's time for you to
finish the story, Sonja.*

No.

You don't have much to say about it.

No. You're lying. There's nothing there. You can't fool me into looking.

Whatever you say, luv.

The barrier is gone and white-hot static fills my head and I try to yell and tell it to stop, but the noiseless noise fills my mouth and nostrils. I'm drowning in emptiness.

Something clicks inside my skull. I feel as if a searchlight has been trained on my brain. Something's in there. Something big and powerful and mean. Fingers of laser light probe the contours of my frontal lobes. I can't move. I can't think. I can't breathe. The intruder isn't a nimble sneak thief like Chaz, but a vandal intent on ransacking everything, unmindful of the damage. My memory is ruptured and the past spills out, filling my head with a thousand simultaneous emotions. I imagine synapses burning, fuses blowing. The creature in my head hits bottom, but that's not good enough for it. It worries at the capstone separating my mind from that of the Other's. I can feel it tugging inside my skull, like pliers on a bad tooth. Then all hell breaks loose.

I can't! I can't! Don't make me, please, don't make me.

Don't make you do what?

Look. Don't make me. Can't make me. She won't let me.

Who won't let you?

She won't!

What are you so scared of? What could possibly frighten you so badly you'd rather go mad than look at it? What is it Sonja?

Shut up! Shut up! I won't look. I refuse to listen to you.

Who erected that barrier, Sonja? Was it Wheele? No, Catherine Wheele is expert at knocking down walls, but I doubt if she knows the first thing about building them. No, Sonja, I think you know who built that wall. It was Denise, wasn't it?

Denise is dead.

Is she? Why won't you look?

Liar. Liar. Liar.

What is Denise afraid of? Finish the story, Sonja. What is Denise afraid of?

You.

Me?

She's afraid you're not what Ghilardi thought you were. That he was wrong. That you're *not* a demon from hell. That there's no Other and no Sonja Blue, only Denise.

Now, was that so bad? The last time you wimped out and went nuts rather than consider that possibility. And look where it got you! You and your humanity hang-up! You provided Wheele with a loaded pistol and invited her to fire it point-blank!

Is it true?

Hmmmm?

Is it true that you and I aren't real? That we're just parts of Denise Thorne's imagination?

You got me. Even if I did know, would you believe me if I told you?

But if it *is* true, then I don't exist. Neither do you. Doesn't that bother you?

Maybe. We're still here, aren't we?

But . . .

Time to wake up.

Claude bent over the motionless body on the futon. He'd found her earlier that afternoon, fully dressed, right down to her ubiquitous sunglasses. At first she didn't seem to be breathing and her pulse was abnormally slow. Was she asleep or languishing in a coma?

He'd spent the rest of the day crouched beside the pallet, watching his captor for signs of life. He'd dosed off once or twice, only to be awakened by vivid images of a man being beaten to death with a cane and a moldering, sharp-toothed thing wearing tinted glasses. He tried reading the old leather-bound book in order to pass the time, but the text was indecipherable and half the pages were covered with baroque geometric patterns. The only other book in the loft was a slender volume in German, so Claude leafed through *The Vanishing Heiress* staring at the photos of Denise Thorne.

The funny thing was—at least Claude thought it was funny—was that he could have escaped. But he'd decided not to. There was too much he didn't know, and like it or not, Sonja Blue was the only way he'd ever find any of the answers.

The shadows in the loft had lengthened into early evening when the muscles in her arms, legs and face began to contract and relax. He was reminded of the dead frog he'd hooked up to a dry-cell battery back in high-school biology class.

Her abdomen hitched sharply as her lungs shifted back into gear. The fingers of her hands, folded flat over her rib cage, stretched themselves backward, the joints crackling like dry leaves.

"Are you, all right? I thought you were sick or something."

The first thing she thought as she surfaced was, *I'm going to kill that bitch.* But what she said was, "Yeah. I feel fine."

THE REAL WORLD

"He's as blind as he can be, Just sees what he wants to see.
Nowhere Man, can you see me at all?"
*   --Nowhere Man*, Lennon & McCartney/Northern Songs

Catherine Wheele stood at the bedroom window and watched the night arrive. She wore the peach-colored negligee from the day before, her wig resting atop a Styrofoam skull on the night table. She fingered a strand of her real hair as she sipped her highball.

She remembered the day Zeb informed her that the wives of prophets and power brokers didn't have hair the color of mice. The wig had been Zeb's idea, like so many other things. He claimed the congregation wouldn't sit still for a dye job, but a wig . . . Hell, their mamas wore wigs. And he'd been right. As always . . .

Well, almost always.

She watched her ghost image in the window. Without her wig and makeup she looked a lot like her mother. The thought made her scowl; that made the resemblance all the more telling. Now she looked *exactly* like her mother.

She didn't like thinking about her family. Whenever she let her mind wander back to North Carolina, it triggered the things lurking at the corners of her eyes.

The flickering shadows had been there as far back as she cared to remember. But now . . . now they seemed to have mass and substance and definite shapes and sizes and recognizable features. She wondered about her sanity; maybe she was going mad. What worried her was the possibility she *wasn't* losing her mind.

A sodden groan emerged from the heart-shaped bed dominating her boudoir. She glanced at a pile of bedclothes the color of cotton candy. The shadows capering at the edges of her vision turned into mist.

Wexler. She'd almost forgotten about him.

The bedclothes stirred fitfully, then were still. She snorted derisively as she finished her drink. Wexler! What a disappointment. How could she have deluded herself into thinking he was worthy as a consort?

Oh, he was adequate enough between the sheets. But he lacked Zeb's savvy and Ezra's selfless devotion. She needed those a hell of a lot more than she needed his spurting member. How could she have been so blind as to trust him with something as delicate and potentially dangerous as the Blue woman? Ezra would have seen through Wexler's media-celeb glamour within seconds. But Ezra was dead by the time she'd been forced to coopt Wexler and his sanitarium into her plans. He'd been killed—murdered!—by the same abomination Wexler, the damned fool, allowed to escape. She projected a splinter of anger at the bed, smiling as Wexler whimpered like a drowsy child.

She returned her attention to the nightfall outside her window. The photosensitive burglar lights, set flush in the ground and nesting in the branches of the trees, switched on one by one as the shadows lengthened.

She watched her employees, dressed in their identical dark suits and narrow ties, as they patrolled the perimeters of the estate. Most of them were her own elite guards, the ones Ezra had dubbed "Wheelers." They were loyal to her, and she'd made sure their devotion contained the proper synthesis of religious awe and pit-bull savagery. They'd gladly lie, cheat, steal or murder for her—and often did.

Ezra hadn't approved of her method of conditioning the Wheelers. Poor old-fashioned, possessive Ezra.

"If it wasn't necessary when Zebulon was alive, why is it so damned important now?"

"A lot of things weren't necessary when Zeb was alive. Paying them isn't enough, Ezra. I want to make damned sure no one turns Judas and gives state's evidence. Is that clear, Ezra? It's to protect the ministry!"

He didn't really believe what she'd told him, but he never forbade it. Would she have stopped if he'd really put his foot down? No. Although she'd loved Ezra, he'd never been capable of inspiring fear like Zeb.

One of the guards patrolling the garden terrace below halted, having spotted her in the window. Who—or what—was he associating her with? She tried to place the Wheeler and his pet obsession. So many of them were fixated on their mothers . . . Ah, yes, Dennings. His heart's desire had been Sophia Loren, circa 1962. She moved away from the window. Dennings shivered as if seized by a sudden chill, then continued on his rounds.

Spurring unquestioning loyalty among her Wheelers was absurdly simple. All it involved was tapping into the right fantasy and constructing the proper illusion. She called her personal form of conditioning "Heart's Desire." And the best time for brainwashing was during sex.

She enjoyed the looks on their faces as they humped famous movie stars, heads of state or professional athletes, although nothing could compare to the horrified pleasure-guilt of those who found themselves erupting inside their mothers.

The Oedipal desire was, by far, the most common, although there could be nasty backlashes if not handled carefully. Like the boy who'd put his thumbs in his eyes. That had been most unfortunate. But most of her "recruits" were men of questionable moral fiber to begin with, and being a motherfucker was nothing new to them.

Her Wheelers served her without question or qualm, eager for a replay of their ultimate fantasy. While she had no intention of ever permitting an encore, she encouraged the belief that repeat performances were possible. Her punishments, however, proved to be far more frequent.

She moved to her combination wet bar and vanity table, pouring herself another Wild Turkey from the commemorative Elvis decanter. A larger-than-life oil portrait of her late husband grinned down at her from over the bar.

She'd come into the world squalling white trash, the daughter of Jeremiah and Hannah Skaggs, the third of eight children. She wasn't Catherine back then. Her mama had named her Kathy-Mae, and she was just another snot-nosed, scabby-kneed, malnourished yard ape destined to grow up hard and ignorant in the Carolina hills.

Jeremiah Skaggs worked at the sawmill, when he could get the work. Papa liked to get a belly full of liquor and Jesus, and when he was like that, he wasn't very careful.

"God looks after His children," he used to say. God must have been looking the other way when Papa lost his left pinkie, then the first joint on his right pointer. The sawmill boss refused to hire him again after he buzzed his left ring finger up to the second knuckle. Papa accused him of being a communist devil-worshiper.

Mama took in laundry. Catherine could not remember her mother smiling or laughing. Mama's voice, when she bothered to speak, was a nasal whine, like the droning of a giant mosquito. She was ten years younger than Papa, although you couldn't tell it by looking at her. Both her parents seemed ancient, their faces seamed and pitted by years of deprivation. They looked like the apple dolls Granny Teasdale sold to the Yankee tourists during the summer.

Her childhood consisted of dirt, hunger, backbreaking labor and fear. Violence, in the form of her father's drunken tirades, was a daily occurrence— like breakfast and dinner, only far more reliable.

She didn't have much to do with her siblings, but she thought it was because she was her mother's first girl child and the only one she'd named herself. Papa had been on a bender when she'd delivered. He'd been scandalized when he found out she hadn't picked a biblical name.

She never played games with her brothers and sisters, preferring the company of an imaginary friend called Sally. When she was involved in her make-believe games, pretending she was rich and living in a big house with running water and electricity, was the closest she ever came to experiencing childhood.

When Papa found out she was holding conversations with an invisible friend, he hit the ceiling and her as well. She was possessed and needed the devil beat out of her or she'd be sentenced to eternal damnation. Papa took her to a backwoods preacher called Deacon Jonas so she could be saved proper.

Deacon Jonas was a big fat man with white hair and a lumpy red nose the size of a potato. He listened to Papa describe her relationship with Sally, nodding and grunting and looking at Kathy-Mae with watery eyes. He told Papa that he wanted to pray over her and that Papa would have to wait outside until it was done.

After Papa had left, Deacon Jonas opened his pants and showed Kathy-Mae his thing. Even though she was only six, Kathy-Mae had already seen several of them and was not particularly scared or impressed by the deacon's. The deacon buttoned himself back up, then said the Lord's Prayer.

Sally stopped coming to visit her and after a while Kathy-Mae forgot about her imaginary friend. There was too much work to be done for her to waste time on such foolishness. She helped her mother take care of the house and look after the little ones, who tended to blur into an amorphous, nameless face with dull eyes and an upper lip caked with dirt and dried snot.

Her life in the Skaggs household had never been great, but things started to get really bad after she turned twelve. When she'd started her monthlies, she noticed Mama looking at her funny. Papa was doing it too, but in a different way. He looked at her the same way Deacon Jonas had when he'd prayed over her, only not so timid.

Sometimes he'd come home liquored up and Mama would meet him on the porch and they'd get to arguing and then he'd use his fists. He'd be too exhausted after he finished beating her to do more than sleep it off, so Mama'd get in bed with Kathy-Mae. They both knew it wouldn't be long before Papa got what he wanted, but it was a ritual Mama felt obliged to perform.

Maybe that's why she confessed. Perhaps she thought it would take the edge off what was to follow.

Mama told Papa that he wasn't Kathy-Mae's real father.

Thirteen years ago, when Mama was young and only had two children, a stranger came to the house. Papa was working at the sawmill and Mama was in the dooryard, scrubbing clothes in the big washtub, when the stranger walked up from nowhere and asked for a drink of water. He didn't look like anyone in particular, just another raggedy man wandering the countryside, looking for a handout. But his eyes . . . The next thing Mama knew she had her skirts up and the raggedy man was humping her on the front porch in broad daylight. She couldn't remember if she'd agreed to it or not. In fact, she couldn't remember if the stranger was short or tall, fat or thin, dark or fair. It didn't take him very long, even by Papa's standards, and as soon as he'd finished, he was gone. Not even a "thankee kindly, ma'am." Mama passed it off as a particularly vivid dream . . . until she saw her newborn daughter. Kathy-Mae had her daddy's eyes.

Papa repaid Mama for cuckolding him with two black eyes and a busted lip before turning his attention to Kathy-Mae. Kathy-Mae tried to run, which only made him madder. The sight of blood geysering from her nose excited Papa to something more than physical abuse. He dragged her out to the toolshed behind the house and raped her on the rough plank floor until her buttocks were full of splinters. He left her huddled atop a pile of old burlap sacks, her eyes swollen and crotch bleeding. He informed her, through the locked door, that he didn't want her "polluting" his *real* children and that he meant to keep her in the toolshed for the rest of her life. Or until he got tired of her.

At first she couldn't think. Her brain was a lump of cold, insensate clay. She hoped it would stay like that forever, but knew it was too good to last. Although ravenously hungry, she managed to cry herself to sleep.

She had a strange dream that night.

She dreamed Sally came back to visit her. She couldn't see Sally very clearly, but she could hear her voice inside her head.

"Do you want out of here? I can take you away from the pain and the bad things. If you agree to that, it's a bargain. I'll always be here and you'll never be able to leave me. Do you want that?"

"Yes."

Sally rushed forward, her arms open to embrace Kathy-Mae, and for one brief moment she could see Sally clearly. She tried to cry out, to renege on her bargain, but it was too late. Sally's arms closed about her shoulders and she seemed to sink into her, like a snowflake melting on her tongue, then Sally was gone. Or was she?

She dreamed she could see inside the house, even though she was locked in the shed. She saw Mama and Papa sleeping side by side in the old wrought-iron bed. Mama had the littlest one in the bed with her, cradled in the warm hollow between her right arm and breast. Somehow, she knew it was Sally who was showing her these things. Kathy-Mae dreamed Sally told her Mama to get out of bed. Mama got out of bed. Then she dreamed Sally told Mama to go to the kitchen and fetch the butcher knife. It was a big, ugly and very sharp piece of cutlery.

Sally told Mama to slit Papa's throat. Since he was full of squeeze and exhausted by his earlier activities, it was pretty easy. The blood escaping his throat formed a sodden halo around his head.

Sally told Mama to go and visit each of the sleeping children and make sure their dreams never ended. The baby was the only one who woke up; it whimpered as Mama slit its tiny throat from ear from ear. Mama had butchering piglets down to an art.

In her dream, Sally told Mama to unlock the shed. Funny how real it seemed, not at all like a proper dream. Kathy-Mae could feel the dew on the grass as she walked alongside her mother. Sally was walking on the other side, but Kathy-Mae couldn't really focus on her. Shadows seemed to crowd the corners of her eyes, obscuring her view. It was a dream, wasn't it?

Mama looked funny in the moonlight. She wore her old flannel nightgown, but the blood made it look different. She still clutched the dripping butcher knife in one hand. Her eyes were blank and glassy, but her cheeks were wet with tears and nervous tics twisted her features into a rictus grin. That scared Kathy-Mae, but not enough to make her stop dreaming.

Sally climbed into the bed of Papa's pick'em-up truck and handed the can of gasoline to Kathy-Mae's mother. No words passed between them. In Kathy-Mae's dream, Mama knew what to do.

The gasoline fumes made Mama's eyes water even more as she doused her nuptial bed. Then Mama got back into bed and lay down beside her butchered husband. She cuddled the dead baby to her breast as she struck the match.

Kathy-Mae experienced only the slightest twinge of guilt as she watched her home go up in flames. After all, it was only a dream, wasn't it? Not even a nightmare, really. Besides, Sally was the one responsible, not her.

When she woke that morning, she found herself shivering on the front lawn. The three-room shack that had served as the Skaggs' home was a jumble of charred timber and smoking brick. Kathy-Mae knew she should scream or cry, but there was nothing inside her. At least nothing that was sad.

The nearest neighbors were the Wellmans, three miles up the road. She figured she could work up some passable tears by the time she got there.

Despite her claim that she'd never leave, Kathy-Mae could not find any evidence of Sally's presence. She *did* feel kind of different, as if there was something glowing in her belly, sometimes. Kathy-Mae didn't think it was Sally. During the months following the fire, Kathy-Mae gradually forgot Sally's oath and convinced herself that the reason she alone had escaped the horrible blaze that had claimed her family was that she'd chosen to sleep on the porch that night.

Being an orphan wasn't too different from the life she'd known before her family was destroyed. The state put her in a succession of foster homes, where she was mistreated and malnourished, until she ran away for good at the age of fourteen. She doubted her "parents" would bother to inform the state, since that meant they'd stop receiving maintenance checks.

She hooked up with a passing carnival and since she could pass for sixteen and lie about being eighteen, ended up working one of the shill booths during the day and dancing the hoochie-coo at night. Sometimes she sat in for the Gypsy Witch, reading the fortunes of popcorn-munching, goggle-eyed fish. That's how she met Zebulon.

He called himself Zebbo the Great and dressed like a third-rate Mandrake the Magician, right down to the patent-leather hair and pencil mustache. Kathy-Mae thought he was the most debonair man she'd ever seen outside the movies.

Everyday she watched him from her place behind the Hit-the-Cats booth, too terrified to even talk to him. She was afraid she'd come across as a crude, unschooled hick, so she kept her adoration to herself. She didn't have to suffer unrequited love for long, since Zebbo the Great could read minds.

Oh, he was nowhere as powerful as she would eventually become, or even as facile as that sleazy Brit. Zebulon had a gift, and that gift happened to be low-wattage psychic receptivity. If someone thought about something fairly simple—like a color or a face card—Zebbo the Great could pick up that thought with minimum effort. Telephone numbers, street addresses, and the like were beyond his limited retrieval methods.

Kathy-Mae was astonished and incredibly flattered when Zebbo the Great started paying attention to her. Zebbo was as dashing and romantic a figure to be found on the midway, and he could be relied on to say things like "your love called to me with the voice of angels. We were meant for each other."

She was fifteen, Zebulon thirty-two, when they got married.

They hadn't been married two days before Zebulon started talking about her gift and all the things they could do together.

Kathy-Mae wasn't too sure about whether her gift was real or not, since it was tied to Sally and her dream and she didn't like thinking about *that* at all. Zebulon was insistent. She knew the power was still inside her, that it hadn't gone away, but she was afraid of it. What if it got away from her and she ended up hurting Zebulon? She tried to explain her fears to her husband, but he couldn't understand her hesitancy. She'd never been able to bring herself to tell him about what happened the night her family died. Maybe if she'd broken down and told him, maybe things would have worked out differently. Knowing Zebulon, probably not.

Zeb finally coerced his bride into serving as a "psychic transmitter" in his act. The marks filled out index cards, listing their addresses and the names and ages of their next of kin, then handed them to Catherine—Zebulon renamed her on their honeymoon —who "broadcast" the information to her blindfolded husband on stage. On the occasions when she attempted to dip into the minds of the audience for additional, unsolicited information, she unwittingly triggered epileptic fits or temporary paralysis among the rubes. Zebulon insisted she stick to the note cards.

Their act was successful, but Zebulon wanted more than top billing at the state fair's sideshow. In 1960, two years into their marriage, he hit on the idea of becoming an evangelist.

"Honey, this racket's perfect for us! All we need is a tent, some folding chairs, a podium, and a secondhand pickup truck. We'll have flocks of suckers lined up, practically begging us to take their money! What do you say, sweetie? You think it's okay?"

Of course it was okay. Anything Zeb wanted was okay.

The early days were the hardest. There was hardly enough money to feed them, much less pay for the gasoline to get them from town to town. When it was hot and the tent was full of sweaty, reeking crackers and Zebulon's voice boomed on about damnation and the sins of the flesh, Catherine thought she could see Papa sitting in the audience, his eyes full of whiskey and the Lord and his throat a ragged, blood-caked mess. Sometimes Mama was there, cradling a butchered infant to her blackened breast as she rocked in time to the gospel music. That's when Catherine took to drinking. Zebulon disapproved at first, although he never went so far as to actually forbid it. Maybe he was afraid she'd cut off his "pipeline to the Lord."

During their second year on the hallelujah trail, Catherine became pregnant. Zebulon was less than thrilled. A baby meant added distractions and hassles. Catherine was convinced that once it was born, Zebulon would change his mind. The miscarriage occurred in her second trimester, triggered by stress and drinking. Zebulon refused to take her to a hospital. It wouldn't look right for a miracle man to have to take his wife to an emergency room. Instead, he fed her handfuls of aspirin and wrapped her belly in warm towels.

After their third year as the Wheeles of God, things began to change. Zebulon's reputation grew, thanks to his ability to "call out" the faithful. Believers flocked to their tent shows, eager to witness even the tattiest of miracles. Professional debunkers would occasionally sit in on the services and observe Catherine as she distributed "healing cards" among the congregation, telling them to write down their specific "prayer needs," as well as names and addresses. She enjoyed the look of confusion on the unbelievers' faces when she did not take the cards backstage or make hand signals to her husband while he was on stage.

Zebulon's healing gift, however, was a product of his years as a stage magician. His greatest success was a variation of the old man-who-grows carny trick. In order to heal someone with a short leg, all he had to do was find an appropriate mark with loose shoes, place his hand beneath the mark's feet when they sat down, and twist his hand so that the shoe on the farthest foot was pulled slightly off and the shoe on the nearer foot was pressed tightly against the sole. Then, by reversing the twist, the farther shoe was pushed on against that sole, giving the appearance that the two shoes—and, more important, the feet inside them—were the same length. The marks hobbled away, convinced they were cured, and the love offerings doubled with each show.

Catherine was amazed at how little was needed for the faithful to justify their belief in Zebulon's claim that he was a conduit to God. Most of the time there was no need for sleight of hand or carny scams. Zebulon simply bullied them into thinking they were healed. The people who attended their revivals weren't humans; they were sheep. Sheep to be herded in and fleeced as quickly and as efficiently as possible. By the time the Wheeles of God came back through town again, everyone would have forgotten how they'd kept their arthritis but lost their savings.

The radio ministry came in '64, just in time for Zebulon to rant over the air about the Communist/Jewish conspiracy orchestrating Kennedy's assassination and allowing four long-haired, homosexual foreigners to pollute America's youth.

Their first real church—with solid wood floors and walls made of something besides canvas—materialized in '66. This gave Zebulon a bit more respectability among the evangelical crowd and enabled him to ally himself with a loose coalition of fundamentalist churches somewhere to the right of hard-shell Baptists and Seventh-Day Adventists. Zebulon was forty and Catherine twenty-three when they bought their first Coupe de Ville.

The years became an endless succession of radio appearances, revival tours held inside air-conditioned public auditoriums instead of tents and incoming checks and money orders made out to their home ministry. Zebulon already had hopes of expanding into television and broadening the church's power base.

During those years Catherine's understanding of her powers grew. Zebulon didn't approve of her using her gift outside the routine, and she knew better than to displease him. Zebulon's wrath was frightening and his healer's hands could be cruel. So her drinking grew heavier in order to keep the power inside her damped. It didn't work too well.

If she looked at the sheep too long she could see what was wrong with them: lungs the color of soot and sticky as fresh asphalt, tumors buried deep inside the folds of the brain like malignant pearls, cancer creeping like kudzu, bones twisted by arthritis into abstract sculpture . . . Well, at least her parents no longer made appearances during services.

Her feeling for Zebulon had always involved awe and fear; he was an emotional man, prone to acts of extreme temper, although he learned to control it in front of the cameras. As the years passed, the love she'd once felt for him was replaced by respect for his canniness. Although Zeb never got beyond eighth grade, he had an innate understanding of the best way to bilk a sucker.

Since his acceptance as a messiah figure, he'd revised his past so it would better fit God's gift to a suffering world. He'd received his calling as a barefoot, dirty-faced boy in rural Arkansas. No mention was made of his years on the carny circuit as Zebbo the Great. He'd somehow grown a war record, acquiring two Purple Hearts and a Bronze Star, even though he was only fifteen when World War Two was declared. He also managed to squeeze some missionary work in an obscure China province into his résumé. Catherine's past also underwent radical fictionalization: she'd somehow become the eldest daughter of one of the oldest and most respected Tidewater families.

Their life-style was far from ascetic; by the mid-'70s there were no fewer than six cars in the Wheeles' personal possession, the most humble being the Coupe de Ville. Catherine owned five fur coats and Zeb's wardrobe boasted dozens of expensive silk suits, although he always made sure he was photographed in the powder-blue three-piece polyester outfit that had become his trademark.

Their last sexual act, as man and wife, occurred sometime in 1971. Although she knew he was sating his carnal desires with a succession of sweet young things culled from the secretarial pool, Catherine wasn't concerned about losing her husband. By her parents' standards, their marriage was perfect.

In 1973 Zebulon introduced Ezra into the entourage. Ezra was everything Zebulon wasn't: formally educated, from a good family, and adept at handling the business needs of a rapidly growing television ministry. He became her lover a year later.

It was Ezra who talked her into trying to control and fully exploit her powers. She openly confided in him, revealing the secret of Zebulon's "gift of knowledge" in blatant disregard of her husband's orders.

Acting under Ezra's advice, Catherine tried dipping into the minds of the audience for the first time since the carnival days. She discovered that if she pushed too hard she ran the risk of triggering convulsions. Skimming the upper layers of conscious thought proved fairly easy, as long as the sheep had their attention focused on Zebulon. The names of doctors, medicines, and hospitals were quickly snagged and broadcast to Zebulon for use in the act.

When Zebulon realized what she was doing, he was very upset.

"I told you to stick to the script! No freelancing. You want to blow it for us now? After we've come so far and have so much to lose?" He raised his hand, and, out of habit, Catherine cringed, but her voice remained defiant.

"What are you making such a fuss about? Nothing went wrong, did it? Hell, the arena's full of old geezers with heart problems, so what's so unusual about one or two of them having fits? Most of them think they're experiencing some kind of religious ecstasy, for Pete's sake! *You're* the one that comes off looking like God's gift to backwoods hicks, so what are you bitchin' about?"

The hand wavered but did not fall. For the first time in their relationship, something akin to uncertainty flickered in Zebulon's eyes. Uncertainty . . . and fear.

That's when she felt the balance of power first shift in her direction. It wasn't long before things began to change between the two of them . . . and inside them as well.

The truce between the Wheeles was uneasy. Zeb didn't like being reminded that without his wife he'd still be doing a bottom-of-the-barrel mentalist act in some godforsaken carny. And he especially didn't like the idea of Catherine using her gift whenever and however she liked.

Catherine reveled in his fear. It made her feel good. So good, in fact, she almost didn't mind it when her parents reappeared, although she was dismayed by the fact they'd brought the rest of the family with them.

Zebulon's miraculous new ability to divine the nature of a supplicant's illness simply by looking at them drew more and more followers. Their television ratings soared. The other televangelists considered the Wheeles beneath their dignity and dismissed them as "tasteless." Zebulon said they were jealous of his ratings share.

Catherine's drinking problem reached chronic proportions. Ezra begged her to stop, but she couldn't. He didn't understand. The alcohol kept the things at the edge of her vision safely blurred. After a couple of years, the sexual side of her relationship with Ezra sputtered out, although he remained devoted to her. Bored, she began seducing the hired hands and, by accident, discovered the process she later developed into Heart's Desire.

His name was Joe. She couldn't remember his last name, not that it mattered. He was Joe, and that was enough. He was one of Ezra's underlings, handpicked by her former lover as a suitable proxy. Everyone in the organization knew that Ezra served as her panderer and that spending a few hours in "private meditation" with Mrs. Wheele often proved financially rewarding.

Nothing seemed out of the ordinary that night. They engaged in ritual small talk while enjoying a drink together. Joe knew what was expected of him; he was to play the adoring servant, confessing his long-denied passion to the lady of the house. The seduction occurred with clockwork precision.

He was in the saddle, grunting and sweating his way through a workmanlike act of coitus, when something inside Catherine's head reached out on its own volition and snared Joe's mind. His eyes glazed and his face went slack, yet his pelvis picked up its rocking-horse pace and his grunts became rougher. A weird moan escaped him as orgasm took him. After a few seconds the glassiness left his eyes, to be replaced by an expression of extreme revulsion.

Joe pulled himself from her, his face twisted into a horrified grimace, and stumbled into the bathroom, where he was noisily sick. More intrigued than offended by her partner's attitude, Catherine peeked into his mind.

(*I could have sworn she was Carolyn . . . just for a minute, that's all. That Carolyn's eyes were looking at me while I . . .*) Another spasm of nausea overcame him and she lost the thread of his thought.

Later that evening she ordered Ezra to bring her Joe's personnel file. In it she discovered that Joe's younger sister had been named Carolyn and that she'd died of leukemia at the age of thirteen. Understanding and exploiting this newly discovered power soon became her favorite hobby.

She and Zebulon seldom spoke anymore, outside of their folksy scripted banter in front of the cameras. Catherine had become so adept at maintaining the facade of the constantly cheerful, sloppily sentimental and unswervingly loyal country preacher's wife that crying and laughing on cue was instinctual behavior for her.

Zebulon was a great believer in playing every angle, but the Heavenly Contact scam was a big mistake. If his congregation had ever gotten wind of what he was doing, it would have ruined the ministry for good. Zebulon's sense of self-preservation was very acute, but on this occasion his greed was stronger.

Since he'd been raised ignorant of the Gospel, he had no idea how the faithful might react to the news that their beloved minister was holding seances, a form of witchcraft condemned in the Bible.

Although he might have been foolhardy, he certainly wasn't stupid. The Heavenly Contacts were never mentioned, much less discussed, in the computer-generated "personal letters" to his followers. Only select members of the Wheeles' Hub Brotherhood—those who'd donated over five thousand dollars at one time—were extended the offer of relaying personal messages to their dearly departed through the powers of the Reverend Wheele. All Catherine had to do was lift enough personal data from the minds of those present to convince the sheep that Zebulon was in touch with the correct spirit.

Zebulon decided to put an end to the Heavenly Contacts when Catherine started producing ectoplasm during a contact with the ten-year-old daughter of a well-to-do furniture-store owner. Zebulon leapt out of his chair, turning over the table, and the ectoplasm disappeared. At first she thought he was actually concerned for her personal safety, then she realized he resented her stealing the show. After all, *he* was supposed to be the pipeline to Heaven.

They had a big fight over whether to discontinue the Contacts, and to her surprise Zebulon agreed to back down. It was a good thing, too, because the Contacts scam ended up netting them their biggest sucker ever.

Shirley Thorne, the wife of the millionaire industrialist, contacted the Wheeles and begged them to conduct a Contact for her. She was desperate to find out if her missing daughter was among the divine choir. She'd hired dozens of psychics, parapsychologists, spiritualists, and mediums over the years, scouring the afterlife for hints concerning the whereabouts of her only child and had yet to come up with a suitable answer. She'd heard positive things about the Contacts and was willing to pay whatever they asked.

Mrs. Thorne soon became the Wheeles' sole Contact patron. Catherine discovered it was fairly easy to sculpt the greenish-white ectoplasm she exuded into a crude semblance of the lost heiress. In fact, the hardest thing she had to do was keep from laughing out loud whenever Mrs. Thorne, weeping and babbling endearments, tried to touch the weird puppet bobbing over the tabletop.

Mr. Thorne was not pleased by his wife's insistence on pumping money into what he considered a two-bit scam, and he was especially outraged to find his wife's name associated with the Wheeles in the pages of supermarket tabloids. Despite his opinion of the Wheeles, he never threatened to expose them.

Zebulon was sixty, Catherine forty-four; they'd been married twenty-eight years. They had a house in Palm Springs, a mansion in Beverly Hills and a holiday bungalow in Belize. They owned two dozen automobiles, not counting the Coupe de Ville. They had their own mobile video unit and a state-of-the-art television studio. Zebulon's voice was heard on over one hundred radio stations in the continental United States and the syndicated *Wheeles of God Show* was seen by an estimated 2.5 million viewers every week. Their ministry boasted 150 paid employees. Zebulon was in constant demand as a lecturer at conservative Christian rallies, and there were numerous photographs of him in the company of politicians, movie stars, ex-presidents and dictators adorning his office.

They had it all, with no end in sight for the foreseeable future. So it came as something of a surprise when her husband told her he wanted a divorce.

"Are you crazy? Do you honestly think the rubes who watch our show instead of going to church are going to stand for you divorcing me? The ratings—not to mention the love offerings—would fall through the floor! And why *now*, for the love of Pete? We haven't lived as husband and wife for close to fifteen years. What's the rush?"

"I'm in love, Kathy-Mae. For the first time in my life."

She winced when he said that. She'd always suspected Zebulon's interest in her had more to do with her gift than her self, but that didn't mean she enjoyed having it rubbed in her face. She also disliked it when he called her by her real name. It usually meant trouble.

"What is it? Have you knocked up another one of your precious little secretaries? Which one is it this time?"

Zeb's face paled. "What are you going to do?"

She folded her arms, looking at him with new interest. "If I didn't know better, Zeb, I'd swear you were serious about this one. It sure as hell never bothered you when I fixed up the others with that quack in Tijuana."

"That was different, Kathy-Mae. I'm not as young as I used to be. A man wants to leave something of himself behind. It's only natural."

"You didn't feel that way when I had the miscarriage." Her voice was very still. She remembered the contractions she'd suffered in the back of the old converted school bus that had been their home during their early days on the road, and how he'd refused to take her to the hospital. "You said it'd be in the way. Hold us back."

"Things have changed, Kathy-Mae."

"You're damn *right* they've changed! You're Zebulon Wheele, God's gift to modern man! Champion of the Lord's will and hero to thousands of ignorant shit-kickers all over this grand nation! You're no more free to run off and marry some little slut you've been screwing between the filing cabinets than the president is to take a shit on the White House lawn!"

Zebulon's anger overcame his fear. He grabbed her by the wrist and pulled her to him. He was madder than she'd ever seen him. She felt a sick thrill of lust build inside her. It was their first unrehearsed physical contact in years.

"You're a goddamn *freak*. You don't belong with decent folk! You've got no heart, no love in you! You're some kind of monster pretending at being human. I'm not letting you spoil this for me!"

"You're right, Zeb. I don't belong with decent people. I belong with *you*. Who is she, Zeb? Tell me now and I'll forget all about this and we can get back to business." She was surprised how calm and in-charge she sounded.

Zebulon's answer was a stinging backhanded blow to her left cheek. She tasted the blood pooling in her mouth. Okay, I gave him his chance. It's not my fault.

She could have read his mind any time during their relationship, but something always made her hang back. Perhaps it was simple fear of what he'd do if he found out. Or maybe she didn't want to know what he really thought about her.

She hoped he wouldn't fight it. She'd never gone into the mind of anyone who knew what was being done to them. His awareness might complicate things and only make it harder on himself.

She was surrounded by memories; some were fresh while others badly faded: Zebulon shaking hands with a local politician, Zebulon eating at a cheap lunch counter outside of Topeka in 1953, Zebulon consummating their marriage, a dim glimpse of breast and nipple as seen by a nursing infant, a pretty girl smiling and placing his trembling hand on the gentle swelling of her bared belly . . . *That one. Follow that one!*

The fool tried to block her attempt to trace the memory to its source. It was a noble gesture, but a vain one.

It had been a near thing, she had to give him that. Just as she accessed the girl's name and address, she felt the pressure building. Zebulon had triggered a massive cerebral hemorrhage. She'd never been "inside" during a blowout and she wasn't eager to find out what would happen should she get caught in the explosion. She had withdrawn halfway when the artery burst, pumping blood into the surrounding brain tissue.

Zebulon's memory banks emptied themselves simultaneously, disgorging the mass of stored conversations, old television shows, bank-account numbers, quotes from the bible, excerpts from Houdini's handbooks and snippets of popular song that comprised Zebulon Wheele's past. A thousand voices, sounding as if they were being replayed on countless tape recorders, each set on different speeds, washed over her. Catherine panicked, terrified of being drowned in the minutiae of her husband's life. As the initial flood of information receded, she realized one by one, the voices were dying out.

Zebulon's memory had bled itself dry. The silence that followed resembled the hiss of blank magnetic tape.

When she regained possession of her physical self, she found Zebulon sprawled on the floor, barely alive. She called Ezra, explaining that Zebulon had suffered "some kind of fit" when his girlfriend called him on the phone and demanded that he divorce Catherine and marry her instead. Ezra was properly shocked and called an ambulance.

Zebulon died in the hospital three days later, never having regained consciousness. Ezra issued a press release citing the televangelist's collapse as the result of too much praying. The death of Mary Beth Mullins, whose car's brakes failed while attempting to merge onto the Interstate, was mentioned briefly on page twelve.

When she looked into the gilt-edged coffin and saw Zebulon's lifeless body, Catherine experienced the giddy mixture of satisfaction and joy she'd known when she'd realized her parents were dead. She was free! Free to shape the ministry in her image. Oh, she'd play the game and be the grief-stricken widow. But once her period of mourning was over, she'd make them forget all about Zebulon Wheele.

Unencumbered by her husband's jealousy, she gave the sheep exactly what they wanted: bigger and better miracles.

The Ultimate Healing was the most daring step ever taken by a television preacher. The legitimate press accused her of bringing the carny into the church, and even her staunchest supporters in the field of checkout counter journalism balked at her psychic surgery stunts.

It didn't matter to her what outsiders did or didn't think about the Ultimate Healing. She made sure to use a ringer and fake blood when professional debunkers were in the audience. As long as the faithful were convinced she was performing first-class miracles and the professional media dismissed her as a hustler, everything was fine.

She picked terminal cases without immediate family or close friends. The ones who were going to die anyway. Who would notice—or even care—if they died shortly after being healed? That simply meant the supplicant's faith had failed and the disease returned. The blame lay with the patient, not the healer.

One or two of her patients actually survived the Ultimate Healing, although most died within a few hours, if not seconds, of being dragged off stage. Already weakened by the ravages of cancer and radiation treatment, most could not withstand the shock of having an unsterilized hand thrust inside their bodies. Then there was the time she'd gone in to remove a tumor and ended up yanking out the guy's gall bladder. But that wasn't her fault. She wasn't a doctor.

The knowledge that Zebulon would never have allowed such an exhibition pleased her. It was too dangerous, too controversial. And most damning of all, it smacked of the geek show.

Step right this way, ladies and gentlemen! Step this way and for the price of twenty-five cents, a mere quarter of a dollar, you can see the Amazing Geek bite the heads off live chickens and snakes! See him put needles in his tongue! Is he man or is he beast? Hurry! Hurry! Hurry!

The Ultimate Healing was tasteless, grotesque, and insulting. The sheep loved it. Within six weeks of the first public demonstration, she'd reclaimed the ten television stations who'd dropped *The Wheeles of God Hour* upon Zeb's death and added seven more.

The only thing ruining her happiness was Zebulon monitoring her sermons. He sat right in the front row, dressed in the powder-blue polyester suit he'd been buried in, his arms folded and legs crossed. The left side of his face drooped, like a mask made from wax and kept too close to an open flame. He looked awful when he smiled. And if that wasn't bad enough, he'd taken to sitting with her family. The members of the congregation seated near the front were blissfully unaware of the ghosts balanced in their laps. Sometimes Zebulon would lean over and say something to Papa, who would nod his head very gingerly, for Mama had done a good job and he was afraid of it coming off. She was glad she couldn't hear what they were talking about.

As annoying as Zebulon's persistent haunting might be, he was only a shadow and she had nothing to fear from him. No, her real problems stemmed from that damned *thing*. She should have known there'd be trouble when she first saw the Brit. What was his name? Chastain.

Just thinking of that leering little bastard was enough to make her uneasy. She'd always imagined she was unique, not counting Zebulon and his paltry gift. Then this swaggering jerk walks in and throws everything out of balance. The irritating part was that while he possessed barely a tenth of her power, he succeeded in outfoxing her.

He sat slumped in the chair opposite her, toying with the paperweight as he spoke.

"Gotta deal f' you, yer holiness. Once-inna-lifetime chance, y'might say. There's this bird I work for—schizzy as hell—says she's Denise Thorne. Yeah, I thought that might snap yer garters."

"Denise Thorne is dead."

"Mebbe. Mebbe not. How are you t' know? Talk to her anytime recent, have you? Y' can fool th' old ladies with that load of bollocks, Wheele, but not me. I know what y' are better'n you do."

She tried to grab him then, reaching out to ensnare him with her mind. To her surprise, he darted away. She made another attempt to trap him, only to have him slip past her again. And again. He seemed to be always just out of reach. She felt like a grizzly bear fishing for minnows. She could overpower him, as she had Zeb, but there was a good chance she'd fuse his synapses and end up with nothing.

"Tsk-tsk! So much horsepower and all y' got is a learner's permit," sneered Chastain. "Now, are y' gonna cut me a deal or are we gonna run 'round Robin Hood's barn again?"

Her cheeks reddened. It was as if she were back at the Hit-the-Cats booth, and she didn't like that at all.

"Hundred thousand American, that's all I'm askin'. Not much f' the whereabouts of a millionaire's long-lost daughter, innit? I'll lead y' right to her. No prob. What y' do with her once y' got her . . . Well, that's yer problem, eh?"

Ezra was against it from the start. He was convinced Chastain was lying. "Forget him, Catherine. He's just out for a quick buck." But she knew he was telling the truth. There was no way she could possibly explain that to Ezra in a way he'd understand, so she didn't try. He didn't like it, but he did as he was told when she ordered him to pay off the Brit. Ezra was right, of, course, but he never got the chance to say "I told you so."

They were sitting in the car, watching as Chastain met the woman at the playground. She couldn't see what was going on too clearly, but it looked to her as if Chastain kissed the woman. The woman staggered backward, clutching her stomach, and Chastain was gone, swallowed by the shadows. Ezra signaled for the man in the second car to join him and they spilled onto the abandoned playground, leaving her to watch from the safety of the Lincoln.

The woman was on one knee, arms wrapped around her gut. The tranquilizer should have knocked her out within seconds, but she was still moving. Ezra was the first one to reach her. He knelt beside her, trying to make identification. It was the last thing he did.

The thing thrust its fingers into his sad brown eyes, puncturing them like overripe grapes, then slammed the flat of her palm into the bridge of his nose, sending slivers of bone and cartilage into his brain. Ezra died instantly. Catherine knew this because she heard his brain shut off as neatly as if someone had pulled the plug on a radio.

The Wheelers were doing their best to keep her contained, although it was clear they wouldn't be able to hold her much longer.

Catherine was in shock. Ezra. Ezra was dead. No, not dead. Murdered. The shock became first grief, then anger. She was startled by the immensity of the hate in her. She had not felt such raw emotion since the night her father raped her. Not since the night Sally came to her and changed her life forever.

She grabbed Sonja Blue and squeezed. The contents of the vampire's mind squirted out like toothpaste. There was too much for her to assimilate fully, but she discovered that this creature had indeed once been Denise Thorne.

There was also a lot of confusing, meaningless garbage about "Pretending people," someone called Sir Morgan, and a lot of conversations in foreign languages. There was also a lot of sexual deviation. She ignored the parts that did not directly pertain to the Thornes.

Blue went into a coma before her memory had the chance to completely empty itself. Catherine had her secured and transported back to the mansion. She had originally planned using psionic interrogation on her, but that strategy was junked the moment Blue regained consciousness; when she wasn't hissing and growling like a rabid animal, she was laughing at the top of her lungs.

When Thorne dismissed the photographs as fakes, she had the videotape made. It was then she made the mistake of putting Wexler in charge.

She shuddered, surprised by the force of her memories. She'd tried to forget the past and banish the phantoms that flickered at the corners of her eyes. The liquor usually helped, but sometimes the shadows refused to be ignored. Like tonight.

Zebulon sat on the edge of the bed, watching her with a horrible, lopsided smile skewed across his face. Her father puttered around the wet bar, pawing bottles with fingers made of smoke. Her mother, a barbecued baby at her breast, studied the array of cosmetics cluttering the vanity table. The rest of the Skaggs children were clustered around their mother, staring dully at their surroundings.

"Go away, damn you," she slurred at her dead husband. "I've made you into a goddamn saint. Ain't that enough?" She hurled the highball glass at Zebulon. It passed through his forehead and smashed against the wall.

Wexler peered out from beneath the bedclothes, eyes white with fear.

There was a knock on the door and a masculine voice. "Mrs. Wheele? It's Gerald, ma'am. You all right in there?"

The room was full of dead people and stank of gin, jism, dried blood and soot. Her head was full of nitroglycerine and Tabasco sauce. She placed her cupped hands against her temples, blinking her eyes.

"It's okay, Gerald. I'm fine. Just fine."

"I'm not sure about this…"

"Look, you're the one bitching about how much you hate being left behind when I go out. If you want to get out of here, you gotta leave my way." Sonja Blue stood with her hands on her hips, scowling at him impatiently.

"Maybe if I tried it one more time . . ."

She sighed and lifted her shoulders in a see-if-I-care-if-you-break-your-neck shrug. "Go ahead. Knock yourself out."

That was exactly what he was afraid he would do. Claude craned his neck, counting the metal rungs leading to the trapdoor set in the ceiling. Thirty. It was the third time he'd counted them, and there were still thirty. He'd hoped that a few would disappear at each recount, but their number refused to decrease.

He grabbed the bottom rung; it was cold to the touch and lightly coated with rust, making it rough against the flesh of his palm. He clutched the second rung with his other hand, using upper-body strength to pull himself along. His right foot groped blindly for purchase on the lower rung he'd just cleared. So far, so good. His head felt like a balloon full of dirty water, and his heart was beating hard enough to shake his ribcage. He could do it. Sure. No prob. All the way to the top. Yeah. He managed two more rungs before his body rebelled.

"Hagerty! Get down from there before you bust your skull."

Sonja's voice cut through the cotton stuffed between his ears, and for one moment he thought he was back in junior-high gym class and Coach Morrison was yelling at him again. Startled, he lowered himself to the floor. His sinuses ached and his shoulders felt as if he'd been attacked with a broom handle.

Sonja Blue positioned herself before the rung ladder. "Hold on tight around my neck, okay?"

"I don't know. Are you sure?"

"Just do it."

Hagerty looped his arms over her shoulders and around her neck. He felt more than a little silly. Here he was, a grown man riding piggyback on a girl four inches shorter and at least a hundred pounds lighter than himself.

Sonja Blue climbed the ladder as if she had a ten-pound sack of potatoes strapped to her back. Claude glanced down at the hardwood floor as it quickly receded beneath his shoes. Vertigo squirted bile through his esophagus and he tightened his grip. Sonja pushed open the trapdoor, and a rush of chill, heavy-industry-tinged air struck Claude in the face. It felt wonderful.

They emerged onto the roof of an old building located in what Claude recognized as the city's warehouse district. It was early evening, judging from the stars overhead, and the area abandoned except for winos and junkies clustered around the down-and-out dives fronting the main traffic artery. Claude collapsed onto the tarpaper covering the roof, staring up at the night sky. His head still ached and his clothes were too thin for the night air, but he didn't care. He'd escaped the monster's lair, if not the monster.

He glanced at Sonja Blue as she peered over the ledge into the alley below. Could she hear what he was thinking all the time? Probably not, or she'd have let him dash his brains out on the floor.

He'd panicked when she first suggested that he hold on to her. Talking to her was one thing, but actual prolonged physical contact . . . He'd rather have a tarantula set loose in his shorts. But it hadn't been *that* bad.

"So what do we do now? Use the fire escape?"

She shook her head. "That's not how I operate. Never know who, or what, might be watching. Never let 'em see where you go to ground. That's rule number one. Besides, there's no fire escape on this rat trap."

"Oh. Then how . . . ?"

"Don't ask. Just hold tight, savvy?"

Claude did as he was told. He was sweating despite the cool air.

She took three steps in the direction of the nearest building and jumped. Claude glimpsed empty space beneath his toes and, below that, a darkened alleyway full of garbage cans and broken bottles. He was jarred loose by the landing impact before his brain had time to register what had happened. He lay sprawled across the roof of the neighboring building, and after a couple of minutes his heart resumed its beating.

"Jesus! You could have at least *warned* me!"

"Told you to hold tight, didn't I?" She helped him to his feet, dusting off his clothes.

"Okay, what now? Do we rappel down the side of the building?"

"You're free to do as you like. You can go home, if that's what you want, but I suspect Wheele's got her zombies watching your place. I can give you enough money to get out of town and start somewhere else. I'll make sure you get away safely."

"What about you?"

She shrugged and smiled without showing her teeth. "I've got payback to attend to."

Yes, I bet you do, he thought. "I think I'll take you up on that offer to get out of town."

"No problem. I need to take care of a little business first, though."

"What kind of business?"

"Gotta go see someone I used to know."

After what had happened to him in the past twenty-four hours, Claude was actually relieved to find himself in one of the worst neighborhoods in town. The menacing shadows and derelict storefronts seemed to exude a folksy charm. His surroundings may have been dangerous, but at least they were normal.

He walked a step or two behind Sonja Blue, who strode down the street with her hands jammed into the pockets of her leather jacket. She looked preoccupied, so he didn't offer any small talk.

Without saying a word, she swerved and headed down a dimly lit alley a platoon of marines would have had second thoughts about entering. Claude hung back for a second, warily eyeing the foul-smelling passage. Sonja did not miss a step, her boot heels measuring out a steady *tap-tap-tap* as she continued on her way. To her this was just another shortcut, nothing to be worried about. Claude hurried after her, breathing through his mouth in an attempt to keep the alley's pungent aroma from overpowering him. It didn't work too well.

It was so dark he nearly stumbled and fell when he collided against her. She lifted a hand for silence and he closed his mouth before he could ask her why she'd stopped. She stood perfectly still, her hands clear of her pockets. She held something in her right hand that Claude couldn't make out. She tilted her head to one side, like a robin listening for earthworms.

Claude felt fear enter his bloodstream. His heart went into overdrive and his ears strained to catch the faintest sound. They weren't alone; he was certain of that, although he'd seen and heard nothing.

There was the sound of an empty bottle rolling across pavement and the scrape of a garbage can being pushed aside. Sonja shifted in the direction the noises originated from. Claude realized she'd placed herself between him and whatever it was in the darkness.

There was a low hissing sound, like the laughter of snakes, before they emerged from the blackness. Claude heard Sonja swear under her breath.

He couldn't see what the problem might be. All that blocked their path were two winos, one black and one white.

The black wino stood a little over six feet tall, although his badly stooped shoulders made his exact height impossible to guess. He was incredibly thin and his head resembled a burnt-out light bulb. He was dressed in filthy castoffs and his feet were bare. His companion was shorter, older, and hairier, with a snarled white mane the color of dirty ivory and a discolored beard that looked like it belonged on a goat.

"Look what we got here, brother," wheezed the stoop-shouldered black, pointing a spidery finger at Claude and Sonja. "We got ourselves a trespasser."

"*Tressssspasssser*," agreed the goaty wino. Claude recognized him as the source of the snake laughter.

"If you wanna come this way, sister"—the stooped Negro smiled, revealing pointed teeth—"you gots to pay a toll. Ain't that right, brother?"

The goat wino grinned, exposing equally sharp fangs. "*Yessss. Toll.*"

"Cute. Since when do your kind work together?" Despite her tone of voice, Sonja did not relax her stance. Claude felt an overpowering need to piss his pants.

The black vampire looked confused. "Don't know what you mean, sister. Old Ned an' me's been together forever. We was partners before. Saw no reason to end such a bee-yoo-ti-ful friendship, eh, Old Ned?" The vampire regarded the bearded revenant with something close to affection.

"*Friennndssss*," echoed Old Ned.

"Don't see how you can kick, sister. By the looks of him, there's more than enough to go 'round."

Claude made a choking sound and took a step backward. Sonja quickly repositioned herself. Old Ned was trying to outflank them. There was the efficient *click!* of a spring-loaded mechanism and Claude saw the glint of twisted silver in her hand.

The stoop-shouldered vampire shook his head sadly. "I was hoping you'd be more friendly, sister. Open to nee-go-she-ay-shun. Guess you'll have to learn to share the hard way."

"*Sisssterrrr.*"

Claude screamed when the goat-faced old man slammed into him, but no sound came out. It was like his worst nightmares made real. He fell amidst a collection of garbage cans and overflowing plastic trash bags. A squealing rat wriggled out from under him. Hagerty's reflexes were the only thing that kept the revenant from burying his fangs in his throat; Claude grabbed Old Ned's thin neck and squeezed as hard as he could. The beast's face was inches from his own. Saliva dripped onto Claude's cheeks and eyelids. The undead bum stank of soured wine, dried feces, and rotten meat. Claude did not want to go through eternity with that stench in his nostrils.

A hand emerged from the darkness and grabbed a fistful of Old Ned's greasy hair, yanking him free of Claude. Hagerty rolled out from under the struggling revenant in time to see the silver blade slice the air.

The body stood upright for a few seconds, the hands clawing at the spurting stump where a head had been, before toppling into the surrounding garbage.

Sonja Blue held the severed head aloft like a demented Diogenes, studying it with mild distaste. Old Ned's eyes flicked back and forth, as if looking for direction from his companion. The mouth continued its ineffectual biting motions for a few more seconds until the brain registered its final death. Claude was reminded of rattlesnakes, how they're capable of delivering a deathblow even after decapitation. Then he blew his lunch all over the alley.

"Damn revenants. Bad as gila monsters," Sonja muttered in the same tone of voice used by homeowners to complain about termites. "Still, that's the first time I've seen 'em work together like that. Revenant and vampire, that is. Pretenders are loners by nature. Unless one of them's a Noble, it's almost unheard of for them to team up. Good thing, too, or the human race would be confined to cattle pens by now." She tossed Old Ned's head, which was beginning to resemble a cross between an overripe cantaloupe and a deflated basketball, into a handy dumpster.

The stoop-shouldered vampire lay sprawled in the garbage, his head twisted at a weird angle. Claude stared at it in sick fascination. "It's still alive," he marveled, staring at the crippled vampire. Its fingers wriggled like the legs of a dying spider.

"So it is." Sonja drove her switchblade into the base of the vampire's neck just as he spoke his final words. Claude could not hear what he said but he could see his lips move.

"I ain't your damn sister," hissed Sonja Blue as she straightened. She aimed a kick toward the dead thing's head, but it had already degenerated into foul-smelling sludge.

Claude leaned against the alley mouth. He was bathed in sweat, his heart felt like it'd been put through a juicer, and his mouth tasted like he'd just gargled with battery acid.

"You okay?"

"Yeah. Sure."

Jacob Thorne was a workaholic. A lot of men at his age and station in life had their vices; some drank too much, others were addicted to various white powders, while still others involved themselves in illicit love affairs with women young enough to be their granddaughters. Thorne's vice was being wrapped up in his work. That's why his household was located atop Thorne Tower.

There were smaller homes salted across three continents, but Thorne never really felt comfortable at the villa on the Côte d'Azur or in the chalet in Colorado. What he liked about the tower penthouse was that he could lock himself in his office and be immersed in the very heart of his empire, concentrating on mergers, takeovers, insider trading and the like while his wife went quietly mad.

Thorne lay in bed, listening to his wife mutter as she slept. She was taking more and more Valium, but it didn't blot out the dreams. Shirley had always been delicate. That was part of what had attracted Thorne to her, forty years ago. She'd been the eldest daughter of a respected banking family, while he was an audacious young upstart, the son of Swedish parents who'd had their name "Americanized" from Thorensen to Thorne by the officials at Ellis Island. It was just like the Hollywood versions of the American Dream said it would be.

Shirley was four years Thorne's senior—which, at the time, was almost as shocking as her choice in husbands—and it was five years before she conceived.

Unhappy with the way his thoughts were going and unable to sleep, Thorne eased himself out of bed and glowered at the digital clock on the night table. Eleven o'clock. *I must be turning into an old man*, he mused sourly. Since he couldn't sleep, he put on his robe and slippers and headed downstairs to his office. Maybe an hour or two of paperwork would take the edge off and allow him to sleep.

Shirley's pregnancy had been difficult, resulting in a dangerously premature baby and the doctor warning that any more attempts might prove fatal. Thorne could still recall Denise's earliest days. He remembered the feeling of frustration when he realized that no matter how much money he had, he was as powerless as some poor shmuck of a charity-ward father.

He didn't sleep the first week of his daughter's life. All of his time had been split between the board room and peering through the plate-glass window at the maternity ward, watching his newborn child in her incubator. She looked so tiny, as pink and fragile as a little bird, that Thorne was overwhelmed by a desire to protect her and make sure nothing bad ever happened to her. He watched the nurses' every move, fearful they might prick his baby while changing her diapers.

When Denise was finally allowed to come home, Thorne scandalized his in-laws by refusing to hire a nurse for their grandchild. For the first six months of his daughter's life he changed diapers, walked the floor, and administered three o'clock feedings, just like any other father would. He was proud of that. So was Shirley.

Thorne cherished those memories, but he resented them as well, for they made the past two decades all the more empty. He had come to grips with Denise's disappearance from his life by submerging himself in his work. His wife, however, did not have that option.

Thorne had watched his wife grow more and more obsessed with attempting to locate their daughter. After the private investigators had run dry, she began frequenting psychics, dowsers, spiritualists, and other sleazy con artists. By the time he decided it was time to step in and try to get professional help, it was too late. The Wheeles had their hooks in her. He'd hoped the faith healer's sudden death would set her free, but he hadn't counted on the widow. She was a thousand times worse than her slime-ball husband ever thought of being.

Thorne opened the door to his private office. He was letting himself get upset. There was no point in worrying about that witch and her threats right now. He smiled to himself as he glimpsed the reassuring outlines of his office, familiar even in the dark. His hand brushed the light plate inside the door and the room jumped out of the shadows.

There was a man sitting in his chair.

Thorne shook his head in order to clear it. The man remained seated in Thorne's green leather chair behind the mahogany desk. The man was large, resembling a football player gone to seed, and his hair was cut short. He looked to be in his late thirties, his blocky chin covered in a dark stubble flecked with gray. He had also been the recipient of a recent beating.

"Who are you and how the *hell* did you get in here?" Thorne stepped into the room, too outraged by the intrusion to be frightened. It was the same instinct that had helped him amass several million dollars over the years. He was suddenly aware of the reek of garbage permeating the room.

"He's with me, Mr. Thorne. I was gambling that you would keep the access code on the private elevators as a sort of keep-the-home-fires-burning gesture."

Thorne turned to see a woman dressed in a black leather jacket and mirrored sunglasses step out from behind the door. He went pale, grabbing the edge of the desk in order to steady himself.

"Oh, God . . . no . . ."

Sonja Blue smiled, revealing her fangs. "Hello, Mr. Thorne."

The big man with the bruised face got up, grasped Thorne by the elbows, and eased him into the vacated chair.

"You better fix Mr. Thorne a brandy and soda, Claude. I think he needs one in a bad way. I'll close the door. I'd hate to have our little reunion spoiled. If I remember correctly, the bar's next to the bookshelf."

Thorne stared at Sonja with open fear and disgust. "She . . . she said you'd never get out."

"Who? You mean Wheele?" Her face was unreadable, but there was something in her voice that made Claude look up from his place behind the bar.

"Why? Why couldn't you stay away? After all this time . . . I used to pray someone could prove you were dead. That way I could get it over with. Grieve and be done with it. That's a horrible thing to pray for, isn't it? Proof of your only child's death? I had my prayer answered, all right." His mouth twisted into a bitter smile. "My daughter's dead."

"Then why did you agree to put me away if I'm not your daughter?"

"She threatened to tell my wife about you. I couldn't allow that."

"But you said I'm *not* your daughter."

Thorne shuddered, refusing to look at her. "No, but you're *hers*. I buried my Denise years ago. My wife's Denise is another story." Thorne let his head drop into his hands. He looked like a tired old man instead of a self-made business tycoon.

Sonja stepped closer, one hand extended toward him. "Father . . ." Her voice contained a hint of Denise.

Thorne snapped back to attention, glaring at her from beneath steel-gray brows. "Don't call me that! *Never* call me that!"

Claude set the brandy and soda on the desk, staring at Thorne in fascination. At first he'd seemed like just another old duffer in his pajamas, but now that the initial shock was wearing off, he was turning into the fabled Jacob Thorne. The old guy was tough as a rhino. Claude was amazed how much alike he and Sonja were.

Thorne's hands trembled but his voice remained steady. "First there was Wheele, threatening to reveal the truth to my wife. Then that degenerate Englishman coming around, hinting that he'd leave the country if I made it worth his while. I didn't believe Wheele at first, naturally. It was just a lot of psychotic hogwash . . . or so I thought. She showed me pictures, but pictures can be faked. Besides, you don't look like Denise. Oh, there's some resemblance, but not enough to convince me. Then she sent me the videotape."

"Do you still have it?"

He nodded wearily. "God only knows why I kept it. It's a hideous, blasphemous thing."

"Could I possibly see it?"

The tape went from magnetic static to picture without any preface. The picture rolled a bit, then automatically straightened itself. The scene resolved itself into a blurred medium long shot of a figure trussed in a straitjacket and a length of chain. As the camera pulled back, it became evident the scene was shot from above. Claude recognized the video-Sonja's prison as a racquetball court. He remembered Elysian Fields' racquetball court for the better-behaved patients.

There was no sound to go along with the picture, but it didn't matter. There was a crude power to the silent, slightly out-of-focus events not unlike the hard-core stag films he'd seen as a teenager in Mike Goddard's garage.

The video-Sonja shrieked and howled soundlessly, slamming herself against the hard white walls. Blood dribbled from her nostrils and the corners of her mouth. She looked drunk. She didn't have her glasses on. Claude realized the graininess of the picture was due to infrared light.

Something fluttered at the corner of the camera's field of vision. A chicken. Someone had thrown a live chicken from the observation deck. It hit the polished wood floor like a bag of suet. The injured fowl flapped about in a feeble attempt to escape the video-Sonja. After she drained the chicken she calmed down. There was a jerky cut, as if the camera had been shut off. The digital readout in the left-hand corner of the screen stated a half-hour had elapsed. This time they threw an alley-wise tomcat into the makeshift geek pit. The video-Sonja ended up with some nasty facial scratches, but it didn't seem to slow her down. An hour later a large dog went sailing off the observation deck. The poor mutt's legs shattered on impact and the video-Sonja's ministrations seemed almost merciful. Two hours after that they threw the wino in.

Claude hadn't expected a human sacrifice. He'd imagined they would continue to work their way through the domestic animal kingdom, hurling innocent sheep, goats, and pigs to their deaths, one after another. He glanced at Sonja Blue as she watched herself murder a man, courtesy of the miracle of videotape.

The wino lay sprawled on the floor of the racquetball court, his legs hopelessly smashed. He looked like every other street person over the age of thirty, with a tangled beard, crooked teeth, and an unwashed face rendered featureless by hardship.

He struggled to raise himself on one elbow. The video-Sonja jumped him like a hungry spider. It was a fierce, bloody transaction, but Claude could not look away. He felt the same uneasy thrill of guilt, excitement, and disgust that had overtaken him when he'd witnessed his first sex act in the Goddards' garage. After the wino's thrashing faded into twitching, the video-Sonja rocked back on her heels and laughed. The camera shut off, leaving the room awash in the hiss of blank tape.

"You aren't my daughter." Thorne's voice was that of a man suffering a deep wound without anesthetic. "You're some kind of freak, an aberration of God and nature. You might have her memories, but you aren't her. You *can't* be her. I won't *let* you be her."

Sonja Blue said nothing. She stared at the blank television screen, her back to Thorne.

"What do you want from me? Money? Do you want money to go away?"

She shook her head and turned to face him. "No, Mr. Thorne, I don't want your money. I want protection for Mr. Hagerty." She gestured to Claude. "He was my keeper while I was incarcerated. Wheele ordered his death under the mistaken belief that he was working for you. As you can see, they almost succeeded. Mr. Hagerty is an innocent bystander and I do not wish to see him harmed."

Thorne glanced at Claude. "What do you expect me to do about it?"

"Tell Wheele to back off or you'll ruin her."

Thorne made a snorting noise.

"You're very good at bluffing, Mr. Thorne. Just pretend she's attempting a takeover. Even if you don't pull it off, it'll give me time to make sure he gets out of town safely."

"What are you going to do?"

Sonja hesitated, uncertain as to whether she could trust him. "Whatever I do—believe me—I'll keep Mrs. Thorne's name out of it."

"Jake? What's going on down here?"

Shirley Thorne stood in the threshold, one hand on the doorknob, the other touching the door frame. She blinked at the strangers standing in her husband's office.

"Shirley, go back to bed. It's nothing." Thorne was trying to sound casual, but his face was that of a man trapped in his worst recurring nightmare.

"What are these people doing here at this time of night?"

"Please, dear, just go back to bed. It's nothing that concerns you."

Sonja stepped back, trying to pull the shadows around herself. The movement attracted Mrs. Thorne's attention. She peered at the girl dressed in denim and black leather, her eyes hazed by tranquilizers. Claude could feel the dread radiating from both father and daughter.

This was the stuff Claude's mother, bless her, had lived for, whether in the form of trashy novels, sudsy afternoon TV shows, or tearjerker movies. Claude bit back a hysterical giggle. He was trapped in an episode of *The Edge of Tomorrow*, directed by Wes Craven.

Mrs. Thorne gave a strangled cry of recognition and rushed to embrace her daughter. She buried her face in Sonja's shoulder, her tears rolling off the leather jacket. Sonja's arms moved to encircle the old woman but halted before they actually touched her shoulders. Claude could see the effort it took to keep from returning her mother's hug.

Claude was painfully aware of Denise's presence permeating the room, like the moan of a tuning fork resonating inside the ear.

"You've come back. Praise the Lord! You've come back to me. Just like she said you would! You've come back. Everyone told me to give up, that you were dead, lost to me, but I never believed them. Never. Never. I knew you weren't dead! I would have felt it if you were really gone. You were always there . . . always."

It was hard, so very hard to deny her. Sonja felt something breaking inside. Her heart was full of shards. She was afraid to speak, afraid that her voice would be replaced by the sound of breaking glass. But she had to speak. There was no way back into the bosom of her family. She'd known that the day she killed Joe Lent. But there had always been the faint hope that she would be forgiven her trespasses and accepted by her family. Now it was time to pull the fantasy out by its roots.

She ached to fall into her mother's arms and weep for the years lost to her, but that was impossible. She knew what she had to do, even though it pained her more than Thorne's denial.

"I'm afraid you're mistaken, Mrs. Thorne."

Shirley Thorne looked into Sonja Blue's eyes, perplexed by the twin reflections of her own face. It was easy to slip into her mind, even though Sonja was repulsed by this most intimate of intrusions.

Sonja dropped through the layers of Shirley Thorne's consciousness, shocked by the other woman's proximity to true insanity. Her mind was an unlanced boil, filled with years of accumulated grief and anguish. At the core of the infection was a human figure.

The nucleus of Shirley Thorne's malaise was Denise. A Denise with features wiped clean of human imperfection or vice. An umbilical cord, as thick and black as a snake, emerged from Denise's belly, fastening her to Mrs. Thorne's unconscious. The Denise of Shirley Thorne's obsession smiled beatifically, glowing like an Orthodox saint, untouched by the corruption it generated.

Left unattended, Shirley Thorne would retreat deeper and deeper into her self-inflicted wound, content to spend the rest of her days in the company of her canonized ghost-child.

Saint Denise stared at the intruder in her realm with the passive eyes of a caged doe. There was no sentience in their depths. Wherever Denise Thorne went when she surrendered her flesh to Sonja Blue, she wasn't gestating in her mother's head. The ghost Denise was a parasite, a cherished memory turned malignant.

Shirley Thorne had spent two decades denying herself the catharsis of mourning the loss of her only child. She'd refused her husband's solution, preferring to embrace hope. But unrewarded faith can curdle, and in time her optimism gave way to desperation and, finally, delusion.

Sonja knew what she had to do, but she was uncertain whether her actions would heal Denise's mother or drive her over the edge.

She was back in her own flesh. A second, perhaps two, of real time had elapsed. "Mrs. Thorne, I'm not your daughter. Your daughter's *dead*." Her words were quiet but firm, just like the push she gave her mother's mind.

She was inside the older woman's head, dressed in black leather and a surgeon's mask. In her hand gleamed a switch-scalpel. The malignant umbilical cord pulsed and writhed and the Denise tumor bobbed lazily like a balloon on the end of its string.

Was this murder? Suicide? Or was it closer to abortion? If so, the mother's life was at stake. There could be no hesitation this time. The scalpel sliced through the fake Denise's lifeline. A look of confusion crossed the clone's blank face as it began to dwindle.

Shirley Thorne stared at the strange woman with mirrors for eyes. She opened her mouth, prepared to deny her daughter's death, but something stopped her. There was a white-hot needle in her head. Something convulsed inside her brain and she thought she heard Denise's voice crying out to her, "*Mommmmmeeeee.*"

For the first time since 1969, she knew her child was dead. With that realization came a rush of relief and an overpowering sense of loss. The emotions clashed and raged inside her like powerful rivers, and she began to cry. The sobs racked her frail body, threatening to knock her to the floor. The girl with the mirror eyes reached out to steady her, but Mrs. Thorne shrank from her touch.

"Don't you touch her!" Thorne was angry and frightened. "Get away from her! You've done enough damage already." He hurried to his wife's side, placing himself between mother and child. Mrs. Thorne clutched his arm, her tears splashing on his hands.

"Jake, Jake, our baby's gone. She's dead, Jake. Denise is dead."

Thorne's sinus cavity ached with unshed tears, but he refused to weep in front of the thing that wore his daughter's skin. "Get out," he hissed. "*Now!*"

Sonja Blue left without looking back, her bruised companion in tow. If she had permitted herself one last look at Denise's parents, she would have seen Thorne reach for the phone.

Claude did not offer any words of sympathy. It was obvious Sonja did not want to talk. Not that he could blame her. He fell into his own private reverie.

He felt increasingly unreal and he wasn't certain if that disturbed him or not. For the better part of two decades his life had revolved around a pattern and, in time, the pattern had come to describe his life.

Due to his work he'd found himself increasingly on the outside of normal existence. He worked when others slept and slept when most people were at work. He spent his waking hours either isolated or in the presence of lunatics. He had few friends and even fewer lovers. At the age of thirty-eight he could talk of leaving everything he owned and everyone he knew without real regret. There was nothing to tie him to the city except his job, and now he didn't even have that.

Funny, only three days ago he was just another slob, trapped in a dead-end job with nothing to his credit except a high-school diploma and a library card. Now he was privy to secrets theologians would kill for, conspiring and conspired against, and permitted the frankest of looks at the private lives of the rich and famous. It was enough to make his head spin. Or was that the cognac? He'd helped himself to a quick, appreciative swig from Thorne's stock. He doubted any of the principals at the family reunion had noticed or cared.

Maybe this was a dream, after all. The mixture of horror, melodrama, and insanity seemed appropriate to fantasy. But if it *was* a dream, it was a particularly vivid one. He could even smell the exhaust fumes, hot as dragon's breath, from the dark sedan that was headed toward them.

She'd been too preoccupied to see the danger until it was almost on her. She was thinking of Thorne and how he'd looked like a scared old man when the dark sedan jumped the curb and headed right for her.

She planted her right hand on the hood of the car, vaulting onto its roof before she had time to realize what she'd done. Her landing was not smooth and she tumbled off the roof, bashing her left shoulder as she bounced off the trunk.

Where was Hagerty?

She got to her feet, scanning the pavement, fearful that his benign bulk might be wedged under the front wheels of the sedan. No, the orderly had leapt clear of the vehicle, although not as gracefully as she had. Hagerty sat half in the gutter, looking somewhat dazed. His nose was bleeding again. For some reason that scared her.

The doors on the sedan opened, disgorging lookalike young men outfitted in suits, ties, and sunglasses. Hagerty began to laugh. He didn't offer any resistance when two men thrust their guns in his face and pulled him toward the car.

Claude was flattered. All this fuss over an ex-jock gone to middle-aged flab and male-pattern baldness! Who'd a' thunk it?

"Stay away from him! Keep your hands to yourself!" The Wheelers paused in their abduction, their fear made obvious by their body language if not their faces. The Other wanted to break bones and rupture soft tissues. Sonja felt the familiar surge of adrenaline that signaled the loss of her self-control. She stepped toward the knot of faceless men; she could almost taste their blood on her lips.

The bullets punched holes in her abdomen, their hollow heads exploding on impact and sending shrapnel through her guts. She'd been hurt hundreds of times before, but not like this. *Never* like this. She collapsed face-first on the street, her torso a mass of blood and exposed intestine. She caught the scent of ruptured bowel and it took her a moment to recognize the stink as being her own.

In all the previous woundings the pain had been sharp but brief. After all, what was pain but the animal flesh reacting out of instinct? But the agony she now felt was unrelenting and quadrupled with every breath, like sunlight reflected in a house of mirrors. Her spinal cord must have been damaged by one of the dum-dum fragments.

The spinal cord—that flexible cable of nerves and tissues—was the vampire's Achilles' heel. Once damaged it could never be regenerated—the same for the brain perched atop it in its box of bone. Sever a vampire's spinal cord and it died. Crush it and the creature was paralyzed and soon died of starvation. It was one of the few physical frailties they shared with their prey.

The car sped off, Claude in the backseat. She found some irony in the fact that she was sprawled in the gutter, exiting the world as she had first entered it, two decades past. It was as if the past twenty years had been the dream of a dying girl. She laughed, but all that came out of her mouth was a lungful of dark blood frothed with oxygen.

As she died, she began to hallucinate.

Or maybe not.

Ghilardi bent over her, his face pinched with concern. Sonja recognized him by his aura more than his physical appearance. He'd been dead for several years and his spirit was hardly the type to confine itself to the structures of aged flesh. He shimmered bluish-white, like the sky on a bright summer's day, and his blurred features were younger than those she'd known. But then, no one ever pictures themself as being old.

"Sonja?"

She'd expected his voice to be as ephemeral as his form, but it was the same as it'd ever been. There was no static on the line. He wasn't talking long-distance. That meant she was close. Closer than she'd ever been before, even in the London gutter.

"I've so much to tell you, Sonja! I was such a fool about so many things! The flesh deluded me, misled me. Everyone finds that out, once they're rid of it. Most do, that is. Some never surrender the illusions of the flesh and refuse to free themselves of its limitations. But I had it all wrong. The *Aegrisomnia* isn't a key to lost powers—I mean, it *is* a key, but not to the doors of human perception. It was written by a Pretender *for* Pretenders. It was intended for Pretender changelings who were ignorant of their birthright and thought they were humans—the ultimate pretense! I had some Pretender blood in me; not much, but enough to be sensitive to the Real World. It was easier for me to claim my powers were inherent in all humans rather than to contemplate an ogre or an incubus in the family tree."

This was all very interesting, but Sonja could not see why her mentor had intruded on her last moments with such late news.

"There's so much to learn and forget once you're free of the business of living. But, you can't die, Sonja. Not *yet*. Much depends on you."

Wheele? Was she that dangerous?

Ghilardi caught her thought and dismissed it. "Wheele is nothing. A fluke. The bastard product of a backwoods incubus. A Pretender unaware she is pretending and armed with more power than she knows what to do with. No, grander and far more horrible things await you."

"Death has made you oblique, old man," she whispered, but Ghilardi was gone. In his place was Chaz.

Unlike Ghilardi, who had problems regaining human form, Chaz's apparition was a perfect replica of his physical self, right down to the collar buttons. The only flaw in the illusion was that he happened to be composed of violet fog instead of flesh.

Chaz leaned forward, studying her with the detached interest he'd give an ant farm. A ghostly French-cut dangled from his lips, phantom smoke curling about and through his head. Chaz and the cigarette smoke shared the same consistency.

"Bummer, innit?" His lips pulled back into a mocking smile. "Spend six months in a loony bin and not three days out when—hey, presto!—yer lying in th' gutter with yer guts in yer hands. Yeah, yer knackered awright. But don't worry about bein' alone, pet. Me an' Joe—you *do* remember Joe, dontcha? *Sure* y'do! —me an' him's waitin' for you, luv. We want t' show you a good time, eh? Joe's been waitin' longer'n me, so he's got seniority. Kinda like a shop steward. But I can wait. I got time, right, luv?" He reached out with insubstantial fingers to caress her. Moth wings brushed against her bloodied cheek.

"Get away from her, hyena!" It was Ghilaldi's voice. "Vile, idiot thing! Wasted in life, useless in death."

Chaz's body dispersed like a cloud caught in a high wind, and Ghilardi's oscillating blueness was back.

"Sonja, I've brought you some help. Sonja?"

Her eyesight had dwindled to monochrome tunnel vision. She felt like she was peering at a Sony Watchman through a cardboard tube, but she recognized the smiling bag lady bent over her.

I'm hallucinating. None of this is real. She hadn't been certain until the appearance of the golden-eyed hag. It was all an illusion, a dream before dying.

The *seraph* trilled crystalline bird song and thrust a gleaming hand into Sonja's guts and there was no more contemplating the nature of reality and illusion.

The *maître d's* scorn was palpable. The very idea that she would set foot in his restaurant outfitted in jeans and a leather jacket filled him with cold contempt.

"Mademoiselle has been waiting for you," he said stiffly. "Please follow me." The head waiter turned his back on her with military precision and marched into the main dining room. Sonja followed, staring at the pristine tablecloths and untouched place settings of fine china and expensive crystal. Although the room seemed to be deserted, she could hear the low murmur of polite conversation going on around her.

The *maître d'* led her to a table located directly under a large crystal chandelier, which swayed and jingled to itself. Denise Thorne sat at the table, dressed in a paisley miniskirt, white midcalf go-go boots, a fringed buckskin vest, and a shapeless, wide-brimmed hat. The *maître d'* did not seem to think *her* wardrobe inappropriate.

"Thank you, André." Denise smiled, and the waiter retired with a formal bow. Denise turned her attention to her guest. "Please, won't you sit down?"

"Am I dead?"

"What makes you think I could answer that question?"

"Because *you're* dead."

"So you keep insisting. But you wear my flesh and have my memories."

"But I'm not you. I'm not Denise."

"So who are you, then? A ghost? A reincarnated soul? A demon?"

"I . . . I don't know."

"But you know you aren't me. How can you be so sure?"

"Because you're there and I'm here."

"Very scientific."

"Okay! So I don't know who I am, or even what. Does it really matter anymore? Your father denies me and your mother thinks you're dead."

"They're your parents, too."

Sonja shook her head. "My father was a rapist. My mother was a London gutter."

"And the Other? Is it your Siamese twin or an unwelcome lodger? Or is it you?"

"Look, I've been through this already. Maybe things aren't as clear-cut as Ghilardi made them out to be. I've known that since Pangloss tried to bribe me into joining forces with him. But I'm not the Other and I'm not Denise Thorne."

"You saw what the Other was like when it was fully ascendant, when your personality refused to function. Was that the Other you're familiar with?"

"Look, what are you trying to get me to admit to? That I'm a figment of Denise Thorne's imagination? That the Other is my id and not a separate entity? Okay, I'll admit those are possibilities, but I don't know if it's *true*. Maybe I'm a synthesis of Denise and Morgan's egos. Hell, I don't even know if you're Denise."

"That's right. You don't." Denise lifted a wineglass to her lips. A drop of wine fell from its rim, staining the tablecloth bright red.

Sonja pounced, digging her fingers into Denise's placid face. The skin came away with a thick, syrupy sound and Sonja stared at the woman smiling at her.

"Time to unmask," said the woman with mirrored eyes. "No more pretending."

"Hey, Moe! Gotta fresh'un for ya!"

Brock looked up from his egg-salad sandwich as the attendant, a grinning black man, trundled another gurney into the morgue's basement.

"Great. Just great. Can't a guy finish his break without being interrupted by a corpse?"

"Hey, you knew th' job was dangerous when you took it," chided the attendant. He thrust a clipboard at Brock. "You wanna sign for this mama?"

Moe Brock quickly scribbled his initials and the corresponding time of arrival while trying to juggle the uneaten portion of his sandwich and a cup of coffee. "A woman, huh?"

"Yeah. Real looker, too. If you like 'em ventilated. The ME said he'd be in to give her a checkup within an hour. Catch ya later, Moe."

"Yeah. See ya." Brock took a quick swallow from his thermos and scanned the ME's street report: unidentified Caucasian female, age approximately twenty-five. Great, another shooting.

"C'mon, honey," he sighed. "Let's get you situated. It's not your fault you screwed up my break, right?"

The morgue dated back before the Depression and showed its age. The walls were covered in white porcelain tiles, except for the patches where squares had been pried away by bored municipal employees, exposing the fossilized epoxy. What wasn't tile was stainless steel. The place echoed like Mammoth Cave, amplifying the squeaking of the gurney's wheels to an unpleasant degree.

Brock maneuvered the gurney into the small, well-lit autopsy room located off the storage facilities. A large stainless-steel table, complete with drains and a microphone dangling from an overhead boom, dominated the available space.

He swiftly transferred his charge to the autopsy table and began the morbidly intimate act of undressing a dead stranger. Every article of clothing had to be tagged, bagged and recorded in case further examination was required by the forensic boys. Once that was taken care of, it was up to the medical examiner to continue the stripping.

The ME would crack her skull and lay bare the folds and creases of her brain, open her ribcage like a venetian blind, juggle her liver and lights, and explore the cold cradle of her womb for signs of violation or stillborn offspring. Then, and only then, would she be handed back to Brock. After her secrets had been revealed he would deftly mend the wounds made by murderer and coroner alike, so her loved ones would be able to identify her.

They called him the Tailor. Never to his face, but he knew that's what they called him. He didn't mind. He'd inherited his dexterity with needle and thread from his maternal grandfather, who'd spent his life working in the Garment District. Let them call him whatever they liked. He was good at his job. The last guy they had doing it left the poor bastards looking like escapees from a Frankenstein movie.

He glanced at the corpse's face. Yeah, she was a looker, all right. At least she'd missed getting a slug in the skull. God, he hated those. Three bullets at close to point-blank range. Whoever did it ruined a perfectly good leather jacket, not to mention the woman inside it. He hoped he could finish before the rigor mortis set in. Funny thing though, she still had her sunglasses on.

The jacket slid off easily enough, and he saw the flesh of her inner arms. Junkie. That explained it. Dope deal gone wrong. He folded the jacket carefully. He'd had one just like it, back in college, and it'd taken him years to break it in just right.

He reached for the mirrored sunglasses that covered the dead woman's eyes. One of the lenses was cracked but still intact. He wondered what color her eyes were.

The body twitched, but it didn't surprise Brock. In the ten years he'd spent prepping and stitching the dead, he'd seen plenty of twitching cadavers. Some jerked like poorly manipulated marionettes. He'd even seen one sit up. It was just the delayed response of the muscles, like the dead frogs and dry-cell batteries back in high-school biology class.

The dead woman's cold hand clamped around his right wrist. Dark lights, like those left by flashbulbs, swam before his eyes. He watched dumbly as the cadaver's abdomen hitched sharply. Once. Twice. For some reason he saw himself sitting behind the wheel of his old Chevy, cursing the motor. The dead woman coughed and a lungful of black blood gushed forth. Brock felt his egg-salad sandwich struggling to freedom.

He tried to pull away, but the corpse wouldn't let go. So he screamed. It echoed and re-echoed in his ears. The dead woman relinquished her hold in favor of sitting up and Moe Brock fled through the swinging doors of the morgue.

Sonja Blue sat up on the autopsy table, her hands laced gingerly over her stomach. She wasn't sure what the *seraph* had done to her, but it'd worked. And not too soon, either. She shuddered at the thought of regaining consciousness as the coroner's electric bone-saw bit into her skull.

Miraculous resurrection or not, she felt like shit. Her head was full of burning water the color of midnight. Another coughing spasm shook her as she slid off the table. The room tilted under her feet.

No! Not now! Not here! People will be down here in a few minutes.

She caught sight of her folded jacket and groaned when she saw the bullet holes. *Oh, well, maybe if I use some more electrician's tape . . .*

She staggered out of the morgue and headed down the corridor leading to the loading dock where the mortuaries came to pick up the dearly departed. Luckily she'd come to in that particular morgue before and was familiar with the layout, so there wasn't any problem escaping.

She was vaguely aware of a terrible pain in her gut, but that no longer mattered. What mattered was the anger. The anger fed on the pain, creating a hatred crystalline in its purity. The rage in her unfurled like an exotic, night-blooming orchid. And there was power in the hate.

She felt its siren call, beckoning her to relinquish control and surrender to its acid embrace. In the past she'd always panicked, disturbed by the visions it conjured, and refuted its source. She'd allowed it to run riot, and when it was sated, she'd blamed the Other for its excesses. Now, for the first time since she'd been remade in Sir Morgan's image, she did not deny herself the pleasure of exulting in her fury.

She embraced the hate as part of her, as natural as breathing or pissing. She felt the power as it coursed through her, teasing her with serpent tongues and electric sparks. She looked down at her hands and saw they were sheathed in a roiling red-black plasma.

She moved through the night streets, unseen but not unfelt. Her passage was marked by a shock wave that affected those around her like skiffs caught in the wake of a battle cruiser.

A mother slapped her child, then slapped it harder when it began to cry.

A small boy pinched his infant sister hard enough to raise a bruise on her defenseless flesh.

A bored housewife glanced at the cutlery rack, then back at her husband, sprawled before the blaring television set.

A thin young man with horn-rims and hair cut so close his scalp gleamed through the stubble pulled down the shade in his bedroom before opening the dresser drawer where the two deer rifles, five handguns and five hundred rounds of ammo were stashed.

Wrapped in each other's arms, amid tangled sheets and sweaty afterglow, two lovers began to quarrel.

The family dog growled, its ears laid flat against its skull, then drew the blood from the master's hand.

Sonja Blue was aware of her handiwork on a level alien to humans. She was with each of them, in some fashion, when they reacted to her goad.

A dozen outbursts occurred with every step she took. Some reacted with petty tirades. Others were far more brutal. She did not create the resentment and frustration locked inside these incidental strangers; she merely permitted its expression. Pangloss had been right: the seeds of self-destruction lurked within every mind she touched. Humans hungered for extinction, be it their own or their enemies'. She felt herself growing stronger with every outbreak, as she incorporated their rage into her own.

Part of her was repulsed by the careless sowing of discord and struggled to make itself heard over the bloodlust singing in her veins. She moved through the city, touching off a thousand domestic quarrels, barroom brawls, backroom altercations and rapes. She heard the police sirens and the strident squawking of ambulances as they responded to the epidemic of shootings and stabbings. Good. That would give her the cover she needed. She nimbly dodged a police car, its lights flashing and siren cranked to full volume, as it rounded the corner.

She laughed, and it seemed as if the sky trembled.

"Claude? Claude? Claude?"

Although distorted by echo, the name sounded familiar. Maybe it was his. He tried to open his eyes and see who was calling, but the lids were epoxied shut. Who'd want to do a dumb thing like that? He moved to rub the glue from his eyes, but his arms refused to respond properly. He felt as if he were moving underwater.

"Claude?"

The lassitude began to seep away, to be replaced by a sense of well-being that was almost frightening. When he tried to remember why he was happy, his head began to swell and his eyeballs throbbed in their sockets.

Why think? Just accept.

The words felt good in his head, even if they weren't his own. Seemed like good advice. Why fight it? He settled back in the comfortable leather armchair, determined to follow the not-voice's suggestion. He turned his attention to his surroundings. He was in a sumptuously appointed apartment, dressed in a quilted smoking jacket. He tried to bring the room and its furnishings into sharper focus, but a lancet of pain jabbed his frontal lobes.

Just accept, warned the friendly not-voice.

"I'm so glad everything's been taken care of, aren't you? Now we can be alone."

Someone was speaking to him. A woman. No, not a woman, a girl. But where was she? He was wary of looking around, fearful that the pain would return.

Denise was sitting on the bed. Claude couldn't remember seeing her there before. She looked just like she had in his dream. She was smiling timidly, her cheeks flushed.

"My parents are so happy you found me. My father will repay you handsomely." She smiled at him and the room flickered. Denise was dressed in a long, flowing gown with a golden diadem perched atop her head. "Half a kingdom is a just reward for the return of a lost princess." The diadem disappeared, although the gown stayed. It was virgin white, her cleavage frothy with lace and satin ribbons. Claude ached to touch it.

Denise left the bed and came to Claude. He couldn't move or talk or think. All he could do was stare at the beautiful creature nesting in his lap. The dress rearranged itself into a bridal gown, complete with veil. Claude brushed his fingers against lace and mother-of-pearl buttons. Real. It was all real.

Of course it's real. Just accept.

But what about Sonja Blue? She's Sonja Blue, isn't she?

The Denise on his lap shuddered. "I'm so glad you got rid of that nasty woman. The one who went around saying she was me. As if that wasn't the silliest thing anyone ever heard of! Why, she didn't even look like me!" Denise leaned forward and kissed his cheek, causing him to forget he hadn't mentioned Sonja Blue out loud.

It had been a long time since he'd last had sex. He was uncomfortably aware of how hard his cock was getting. He was afraid of insulting Denise by prodding her. But she was so close, so warm. He inhaled, savoring her scent. He was surprised by the fragrance of tea rose that clung to her. His aunt smelled of roses. It was hardly the perfume he associated with a blushing nymphet princess.

Denise's flesh became transparent, revealing the skull underneath the skin. The virgin expanse of the bridal gown was mottled with fungus, as if it'd been underground for a long time. The lidless eyes goggled at him from their bared orbits.

The scream wouldn't come out; it sat in his chest like a dead weight.

"What's wrong, Claude? Were you thinking about that horrible woman?" Denise was once again wrapped in flesh and unsoiled satin. "You know how it affects you, and when you're upset, I'm upset. You don't want to see me upset, do you?"

"No . . . no, of course not."

"Very well, then. I don't want you to think about that horrible woman anymore, understand?"

He nodded, the skull face with its peeled-grape eyes already fading from his memory.

The bridal gown was gone. In its place was a sheer white negligée. Although the exact details of her body were obscured by the chiffon, Claude could tell she was nude underneath it. His breathing was ragged and his brow slick with sweat. His fingers trembled as he stroked her hair.

He'd given up wanting things a long time ago. Life had cheated him of everything he'd ever hoped for; athletic scholarship, professional football career, a decent job. There was no point in wishing for things he'd never have. All it led to was frustration and disappointment. He wanted Denise. He'd wanted her from the moment he saw her in his dream, but that was impossible. Denise was a shadow. His desire for her made as much sense as that old movie he saw, where the cop fell in love with a portrait of a murdered woman.

The not-voice was right. There could be no room for doubt. So what if Denise Thorne didn't really exist? And even if she did, she'd be closer to thirty-five than seventeen. Big deal. She was real and alive and young *right now,* and that was all that mattered. For some reason he'd been granted his heart's desire, and he'd be a fool if he let it go to waste.

He stood up, cradling Denise in his arms. She pillowed her head on his shoulder, the soft fragrance of her hair all around him. He was pleasantly surprised by the strength in his limbs. There was no more throbbing in his head or aching muscles, as if his decision had been rewarded by the erasure of pain.

Denise was like a drug, insinuating herself into his bloodstream with every breath. He felt strangely invigorated, as if every cell were supercharged. He wanted to lose himself in her flesh and never return to reality.

They lay side-by-side atop the mattress. Claude was hesitant at first, but the way she wiggled against him dispelled his fear of offending her. Denise teased him with quick, birdlike kisses until his breath came in gasps and his heartbeat matched the throbbing in his crotch.

They were naked but he had no memory of undressing. Not that it bothered him. He'd always hated that part, with its gradual unveiling of physical imperfections. Denise's naked body seemed to give off a warm, diffuse glow that kept him from paying true attention to the details of her flesh, just like the pinup back in his locker.

He entered her, holding his breath lest she break. He needn't have worried. She gasped and moved her hips to meet him, clutching at his buttocks with sharp fingernails. Denise wriggled under him like a wild thing, hissing and moaning with every stroke.

He was afraid he'd erupt upon insertion—it had been a long time—but after the first few thrusts he relaxed, confident he would go the distance.

Denise clung to him, her legs wrapped around his hips. Her cries and whispers devolved into moans and shuddering gasps that seemed, at times, to come from someone else. Claude ignored it. He was riding a sleek dolphin, his arms and legs wrapped around its madly gyrating form as it porpoised through the waves. It was frightening and exhilarating and he never wanted it to end. He felt the urgency that heralds orgasm and strove to contain it. He didn't want the ride to end. He opened his eyes, hungry for the sight of Denise's face.

She didn't have eyes anymore. Lozenges of mirrored glass returned Claude's stare. Her long, blond hair writhed like a sea anemone as it rearranged itself.

"No!"

Too late. The darkness was already staining her hair the color of bibles. She smiled, revealing her fangs, but that didn't scare him. What scared him was the fact he was still hard. He should have lost his erection the moment he realized what was under him; it should have deflated like a toy balloon, but it was still stiff. He tried to push himself off her, but Sonja pulled him back down.

"This is what you wanted all along, wasn't it?" she leered. She moved her hips against his. They were Siamese twins, joined at the groin by a traitorous piece of meat.

"Kiss me, Claude. Kiss me . . ." She laced her arms around his neck and tried to drag his face toward her waiting mouth. Her fangs were the color of aged ivory. Claude couldn't decide whether he was going to vomit or orgasm.

Sonja looked genuinely surprised when he clamped his hands around her throat. His fingers tightened their hold as he brutally thrust himself between her legs. She struggled under him as he strove to squeeze life from her lungs while injecting it into her womb. Her legs flailed and her fingernails sliced into his face, but he refused to stop. He wondered if her head would come off in his hands.

Trick! Trick! Should have known! It was too good to be real! Bitch! Trying to turn me into a fucking Renfield. I'll kill you for this.

Sonja Blue's face disappeared as if someone had changed the channels on a television set. Claude stared at the naked, middle-aged woman thrashing beneath him. Despite the smeared makeup, crooked wig and bulging eyes, she looked familiar.

Perplexed, Claude loosened his grip on her throat. Before he had time to understand what the hell was going on, he was seized by his own orgasm. He didn't feel it when she reached inside his skull and squeezed his brain.

Catherine Wheele experienced a moment of sheer claustrophobic terror when the dead man collapsed on top of her.

She felt as if she were buried alive under the corpse's bulk, the smell of sweat and jism smothering her senses. She wriggled free, an ululating whine escaping her lips.

Her lungs were full of broken glass and razor blades. She touched her throat gingerly—it was already the size and coloration of a ripe eggplant. She stared at Claude's body. *I should have killed him the minute I saw him. That's what Ezra would have done. But, no, I had to try to make him one of my own. Just in case Thorne got any bright ideas about getting rid of me.*

There was no way she could hurt him enough for what he'd done to her. No one, but *no one* treated her like that! She opened her mouth and tried to curse the dead man beside her, but there was only pain and an incoherent gargling.

Her hands flew to her throat, prodding the swollen flesh with shaking fingers. No! He couldn't have! She began to tremble. Her eyes filled with tears. *Nononono . . .* Her fear gave way to rage and she threw herself on Claude's rapidly cooling body, pummeling it until she raised post-mortem bruises. Exhausted, she lay sprawled on the rumpled bed, her vision swimming with tears, as the last of Claude's seed trickled down her thigh.

What had gone wrong? She'd provided the appropriate scenario, the proper stimulation and illusion. So what went wrong? She'd been in control, just like always. . .

But that wasn't completely true, was it?

How did you like it, Kathy-Mae? Did you enjoy your first orgasm?

She clamped her hands over her ears. She refused to open her eyes. She recognized the voice and was fearful of what might be sitting on the corner of her bed, watching her. She prayed it would go away.

But I can't go away, Kathy-Mae. I'm always here. I'm always with you, like I said I would.

Why are you here? Why now, after all these years?

Things are moving. Changing. I came to warn you. You will be having visitors. In fact, one of them is already at the gate.

Catherine knew she was gone before she opened her eyes. Or was she? Sally was right, though. She could feel her visitor approaching. It was time to receive her guest.

Sonja Blue stood outside the gates of Catherine Wheele's mansion, studying the brightly lit driveway and the phalanx of armed guards patrolling the green space around the house. Either Wheele was a practicing paranoid or she was expected.

She slipped over the top of the wall, oblivious to the pieces of broken bottle embedded in the mortar. Such precautions were good for deterring paparazzi and other celebrity-watchers, but not someone back from the dead.

Wheele chose her sanctum well. The mansion was located in an exclusive suburb situated beyond the zone of shopping malls and fast-food strips that separated the city from its satellite communities. A crushed shell drive, flanked by crepe myrtles, curved toward the front of the house. During the day the estate could pass for yet another stronghold of privilege. But at night . . . Well, that was a different matter. The manicured lawn shimmered in the light from the floods mounted in the trees, turning the identical guards into sharply defined silhouettes.

What should it be? Full frontal assault or a sneak approach? What the hell . . . Why waste time on subtlety?

The driveway crunched beneath her boots. *C'mon, bitch, let me see you try to stop me this time. C'mon, whatcha waitin' for, an engraved invitation?*

The floodlights sputtered and flickered like cheap Christmas lights. She could feel the rage-joy creeping along her scalp, sending sparks from her fingertips. No lights. The darkness boiling in her belly was the antithesis of sight and sound and life. Light would not be tolerated in her presence.

She scented the dog before she saw it. Seventy pounds of German shepherd bounded out of the shrubbery, aimed for her throat. She caught it in midair, holding it by the scruff of its neck like she would a pup. Its death was swift.

"Shaitan? Shaitan, what is it, boy?"

The Wheeler stood on the edge of the light, peering into the darkness, his Uzi at ready. He glanced about uneasily when the floods began to stutter.

"Shaitan? Answer me, boy!"

The dog's corpse struck the Wheeler full in the face, knocking him to the ground. The short, staccato burst from his Uzi shredded the bushes and shot out one of the faltering spotlights mounted in a nearby crepe myrtle.

The dazed Wheeler pushed the carcass off his chest. His nose was bleeding and he could taste blood at the back of his throat. Dogs were barking and he could hear the others running in his direction. Someone was bending over him. He looked up and saw twin reflections of his bloodied face. God, he looked stupid.

They found him dangling from the smooth, twisted branches of a crape myrtle; his entrails spilled and looped into a hangman's noose. Some of the guards—the ones yet to undergo Heart's Desire conditioning—decided that it was time to desert when they saw him hanging from the tree like a depraved Christmas ornament. Bilking old ladies of their life savings and roughing up investigative journalists was one thing. This was something else *entirely*. They seemed honestly surprised when their fellow Wheelers opened fire, splashing their insides all over the front lawn.

The dogs began to howl and snarl, straining on their leashes and snapping at one another's flanks. One of the animals, a Doberman, sniffed at the splattered remains of the disloyal guards. Another dog, a German shepherd, nosed the red mess; the Doberman sank his fangs into the other dog's shoulder. Within seconds the dogs were engaged in a fierce melee, tearing at one another's throats and testicles.

When one of the Wheelers made the mistake of trying to drag his dog free of the tangle and lost three fingers, the others opened fire on the animals, raking them with their automatic weapons. The growls of combat became yelps as the hounds forgot about fighting among themselves and tried to flee the barrage.

When the smoke cleared, there were four dead German shepherds and three dead Dobermans on the lawn. A fourth Dobie—the one who'd started the fight—was still alive, although a bullet was lodged in its spine. The animal lay among its kennel mates, whining piteously as it tried to get back on its feet. One of the Wheelers finished it off with a short burst from his Uzi.

The four Wheelers stood and stared at the collection of dead men and animals heaped about them. The lights flickered, dimmed, flared briefly, then went out.

"We have to get back to the house. We're useless out here without the lights."

"What about Dennings?" whispered the one with the maimed hand, his face pale from shock.

The others looked to their eviscerated partner dangling from the crepe myrtle.

"Shouldn't we, you know, cut him down or something?"

"Fuck that. Dennings's not going anywhere."

"Yeah, but—"

"But what?"

"Where's his gun?"

The Uzi fire ripped through them as if they were plastic bags full of foam rubber and strawberry jelly. Sonja marveled at the chaos chattering away in her hands. *No wonder they're so fond of these things.* She kept firing until the clip jammed, then tossed the gun away. The site resembled an abattoir more than an exclusive suburban front lawn.

The porch light flared, doubling its intensity the moment she touched the steps. There was a sharp *pop!* and a shower of frosted glass fell from above.

She passed a large mirror set in a gaudy mock-rococo frame. Blank-eyed baby-fat cherubs smiled at her amid a welter of gilt grapevines. She paused to stare at her reflection.

She was Shiva. She was Kali. She was all that is dark and terrible in nature, adored and scorned, worshipped and reviled. She was sheathed in a transparent caul of darkness the color of a fresh bruise. The caul rippled and roiled like a jellyfish and, while she watched, extruded a tendril that groped blindly in the air as if scenting prey. She knew what it was seeking, and the knowledge neither thrilled nor dismayed her.

She felt no guilt or remorse; the evil that radiated from her wasn't the evil incarnate conjured forth by centuries of theologians in an attempt to shift the blame. It was human evil, nothing more. Granted, it had been recycled and refined until it was the psychic equivalent of rocket fuel, but its source was mortal, not diabolic.

Nobles could live for years on such stored power before requiring a recharge. But Sonja was an unfinished vessel. She couldn't properly synthesize the emotions she drained from others. She was in danger of overloading and spontaneously combusting. She had to release the charge before that happened. But no matter how she did it, it would still prove dangerous.

She remembered the rumors of how the Nazi camps, the Stalinist purges, and the Khmer Rouge re-education farms were the side effects of similar blow-offs. Nothing happens in the Real World that is not mirrored in the half-life of human existence, and part of her was still unwilling to unleash evil on the innocent.

She extended her fangs and grimaced at the mirror. *That's better. There's no point in pretending anymore, right? Where are you, bitch? Come out and fight face to face, like a real monster.*

(I'm in the study. Third door on your left.)

Sonja started, the mirror and its reflection forgotten. The voice had been loud and clear, as if Wheele had been at her elbow. So she was ready, huh? Good. She felt like a Viking berserker, stoned on bloodshed and the inevitability of death. She noticed that she was sweating heavily and that her hands trembled. Fire on the outside and fire on the inside. It would be so simple to surrender to the anger that frothed and foamed in her and charge into battle, screaming like a hell-bound soul . . .

She had to be careful and use her brain. The last time she'd surrendered to mindless savagery it'd come close to costing her what sanity she had left. Still, the temptation was strong. The power filled her until she felt like a balloon made out of skin, stretched to capacity. What would happen to her—and those around her—should she explode?

The lights were off in the study, although it made little difference to her. It might have been high noon with the drapes open.

Catherine Wheele sat perched on the edge of the huge oak desk that dominated the room. She was dressed in a silver lamé pantsuit with a pink cravat knotted around her neck. Her aura shimmered like heat rising from the sidewalk on a summer's day. The hate that emanated from her was nearly enough to make Sonja swoon.

(You've caused me no end of trouble. I should have killed you right away, like Thorne suggested.)

Sonja flinched. She had to be careful and keep herself screened. Wheele had been inside her head and knew how to twist the knife for maximum effect. They were within easy striking distance of each other, not that it mattered. The attack, when it came, would not be on a physical level.

"Why didn't you? Kill me, that is. Why keep me around? Was it just simple greed?"

Wheele looked uncomfortable and plucked absently at the scarf knotted under her chin.

"Or was it something else? Was it because we have something in common?"

Wheele stiffened, her eyes slicing into Sonja like scalpels. Her voice detonated in Sonja's head. (Shut up! Silence, Abomination!)

Sonja clutched her head, her vision momentarily dimmed by the thunder inside her skull. *If she does that again, my brains are going to leak out my ears, vampire or not. But, what the hell . . .*

"Yeah, not all the monkeys are in the zoo, are they? And maybe all the monsters aren't locked up, safe and sound."

Another bolt of white-hot pain surged through her and she narrowly missed biting her tongue in two.

"I'm not drugged and disoriented this time, Wheele. You've got power—I'll admit that—but you don't have knowledge." She smiled bitterly, hearing an echo of Pangloss's infernal wisdom. "What have you chosen to do with your abilities? You bilk sick and deluded humans into giving you their money and—if you're careless—their lives. How pathetic! It's like using a laser to engrave postcards."

Wheele did not move to repudiate her harangue, but her thoughts bristled with anger and embarrassment.

"Why don't you speak?" she asked, exposing her teeth. She grinned even wider at the sight of Wheele's blanched face. "And where's Hagerty? The orderly your zombies snatched. Where is he?"

Wheele's answering smile was unpleasant.

(Why, he's right here. . . waiting for you.)

She gestured to the oversized swivel chair behind the desk. Sonja touched the chair, causing it to turn toward her. She knew what was waiting for her. She did not want to see, but she could not bring herself to look away. Wheele's voice became white noise.

(Too much . . . bastard . . . crushed larynx . . . easy to reach inside his head and *squeeeeze* the aneurysm. It burst like an overripe tomato. Did him a favor, really. It could have ruptured anytime, anywhere; he could have been driving a car when it happened, could have ended up crashing into a school bus or something . . .)

Claude was sprawled nude in the chair. His flesh possessed a bluish tinge, the blood having settled in his buttocks and legs. He looked horribly vulnerable, his face slackened and his privates shriveled by death.

Sonja closed his eyes, her fingers lingering on the cool surface of his brow.

(He watched over you and you tried to return the favor. But you failed.)

Sonja jerked her head in Wheele's direction. Wheele's face was replaced by a lump of shimmering white light that seemed to grow with every heartbeat. Sonja felt her own energy coalesce itself into a protective hood like that of a cobra.

Long, snakelike tendrils emerged from the force field surrounding Catherine Wheele. She resembled a Gorgon transfixing her prey. The creepers hovered in the air for a second, then snapped like whips at Sonja's head, sinking their barbs into the bruise-colored glow.

The castle was very old. It sat on top of a foreboding mountaintop, looking down into a cheerless ravine, at the bottom of which wound a gray ribbon of cold alpine water. It was storming around the castle, its dark corridors erratically lit by sheets of lightning. All the rooms were full of heavy, ornate furniture covered with sheets. The huge portraits on the walls were coated with dust three inches thick. Cobwebs hung from every corner like tattered mosquito netting, fluttering lazily in the breeze.

The vampire killer stood in the main hall, holding the carpetbag that contained the tools of her trade. The peasant coach driver had deposited her at the foot of the road leading to the castle, then driven away as fast as he could, leaving her to walk the rest of the way. Now it was twilight. Soon it would be dark. She had to find the monster and stake it in its lair before it was too late. Hundreds had suffered the beast's leprous touch. The time had come to put an end to its unholy reign of terror.

The vampire killer made her way to the dungeons, where legend had it the family crypts were located. The lightning seared the darkening sky, throwing everything into stark shadow. She made her way down the winding stair, one hand holding aloft a kerosene lantern, the other gripping her bag.

The dungeons were dark and smelled of mold and damp earth. She could hear the rats as they scurried away from the lamplight. Clusters of bats, hanging from the stone arches like bananas, chittered and squeaked as she passed.

She came to an imposing wrought-iron gate, locked and bound with heavy chain. Beyond it lay the ancestral vaults, where the monster slumbered during the day and from which it traveled each night to sate its unnatural lusts and spread its loathsome contagion among the weak and the innocent. Setting aside the lamp, she opened her carpetbag and produced a mallet and chisel. She worked the chisel's point into the lock and began hammering. After the fifth stroke the lock broke and the gates swung inward on rusty hinges.

There wasn't much time left. The vampire killer had to hurry if she was going to catch the beast asleep in its coffin. The burial vault was a huge subterranean room with numerous stone sarcophagi scattered throughout. Which one was the vampire's resting place? And how could she lift the heavy marble lid in time? She fought the panic blossoming inside her as she moved from grave to grave, lantern held high.

There! There it was! The only sarcophagus missing its sealing slab. The light from her lantern reflected off the dark, highly polished wood of the casket. There was an emblem, made of gold, fastened to the top of the coffin. It showed a large bat, wings unfurled and jaws agape, clutching a woman and a man in its taloned feet. The vampire killer was uncertain whether the tiny humans were terrified or ecstatic.

She shook herself free of the languor the golden bat seemed to radiate. Clutching a silver crucifix, a wooden stake and her trusty mallet, the vampire killer threw back the lid of the casket, steeling herself for the evil that lay within.

"*Sur-prisssse!*" cried the vampire, popping up from its coffin like a grinning jack-in-the-box, slamming a pie into the vampire killer's face.

The vampire killer stumbled backward, her vision obscured by pie crust and Boston crème filling. She clawed at the muck clogging her nostrils and eyes, sputtering her rage.

"You must *really* think I'm stupid," laughed Sonja Blue as she climbed out of the casket. "Did you really think I'd be taken in with these third-rate illusions?" She dug her fingers into the surface of the sarcophagus. It broke off in her hand with a dry crackling sound and she shoved it under Wheele's nose. It was Styrofoam spray-painted to resemble marble. "And look at this." She waved a fistful of gauzy cobweb in her face. "Spun sugar!"

Sonja snatched up Wheele's carpetbag, scattering its contents across the dungeon floor. "I can't believe you were actually inside my head and didn't learn a damned thing!" She pointed at the garlic, rosary, and flask of holy water, shaking her head in amazement. "Ghilardi was right: you *are* a fuck-up."

She grabbed Wheele by the collar, jerking her to her feet. "You picked the wrong woman to fuck with, preacher. You let something out that should *never* have been free."

Wheele stared at the sweat pouring from the vampire's brow. She looked like a woman in the grips of malarial fever, radiating heat like an old-fashioned stove.

Let it go, the Other whispered. *Set me free. It's the right thing to do. Can't you feel it?*

She *could* feel it; that was what worried her. The overload was affecting her dream self as well as her physical form. She was racked by alternating waves of freezing cold and boiling heat. She thought she could smell circuits burning, deep in her head.

Set me, free. Set me free or we both die.

"No."

There was a noise, like a hundred angry voices shouting, and the villagers burst into the crypt, holding aloft burning torches and waving pitchforks and scythes in a menacing manner.

"Kill the vampire!"

"Death to the monster!"

The vampire dropped the vampire killer, hissing her anger at the intrusion. She made to escape, but the village priest moved to block her path, holding aloft the crucifix from the church. The vampire shrank from the upraised cross, lifting her arms to shield herself from its glory.

"Catch it!"

"Kill it!"

"Murderer! Fiend!"

Rough hands grabbed the snarling, impotent vampire, pinning her to the wall. The ruddy faces parted to allow the vampire killer access.

"Permit me." The vampire killer held aloft a sword. As the peasants looked on, the sword's blade miraculously burst into blue flame. The villagers gasped in awe, but did not lessen their hold on the captive vampire.

The vampire hissed, thrashing wildly in an attempt to free herself, but it was no use.

Wheele placed the tip of the burning sword above the vampire's heart and pushed the blade home.

The vampire screamed, arching her back as the sword pierced her heart. Wheele wrapped both hands around the hilt of the sword and pushed it in deeper, until the vampire's body was transfixed by the blade. Blood seeped from the corner of the vampire's eyes. The vampire was laughing.

"Oh, puh-leeze, Miz Wheele, don't strike me with that terrible swift sword." The voice was and wasn't Sonja Blue's.

"Now you've done it," sighed the vampire, wrenching the sword from her chest. The torch-bearing peasants wavered, then winked out like holograms. "Now you've *really* done it."

Catherine Wheele was once more in her own body, although she couldn't remember disengaging. Blue must have been responsible for jettisoning her. She hadn't expected the vampire to be so strong. She'd planned to spear Blue's unprotected psyche as easily as she would gig a frog. For the first time in her life, Wheele was facing an adversary as powerful as herself.

Blue was the center of an energy field that wobbled and warped about her like a malignant soap bubble. Catherine's eyes were focused on Blue—her arms now upraised, as if in ecstatic communion with the darkness she generated.

She knew she should try to flee, but she couldn't move. She watched in dumb fascination as Sonja Blue's head expanded until it assumed the proportions of a Macy's Parade balloon. The sunglasses that shielded her mutated eyes dissolved, revealing bottomless pits and the purplish-black nebulae that swirled in their depths. Blue-green sparks danced from the vampire's fingertips, tracing alien designs in the ozone-heavy air.

Catherine Wheele experienced a response to the vampire's evil that went beyond the sex urge. For one brief moment, the doors of Catherine Wheele's perception were thrown open. The Pretender in her emerged from its hiding place. The part of herself that considered itself Catherine Wheele cringed at the sight of its demonic counterpart. The Pretender was smooth-bodied, its skin the color of cinnamon. It had two pairs of breasts, one above the other, with tiny eyes, like those of mice, in place of nipples. Despite its monstrous otherness, the Pretender exuded a horrible familiarity, and she felt an urge to name the beast, but her larynx could no longer form words.

Catherine wrenched herself free of the vision before she could see the thing writhing in the folds of the succubus's labia. Blue still stood in the middle of the bubble, her eyes rolled back and a beatific smile on her face.

(To hell with this. I'm going to blow her fucking head off.)

Catherine opened the top drawer of her desk, careful not to brush against Claude's cold flesh. The Luger was there, primed and ready. The gun had originally belonged to Zebulon. While working the carny it had become something of a necessity. Later on, he used it as proof of his stint in the army ("Took it off a dead Kraut") and his support of All-American values whenever the NRA came around. Catherine was glad she'd ignored Ezra's pleas to dispose of it.

She flicked off the safety and aimed at Sonja's head. She wasn't sure what killed vampires, but *nothing* could survive having its brains splattered across the room.

The pistol kicked in her hand and she saw the bullet emerging from the barrel of the gun. Everything seemed to be going much too slow; it was as if she'd fired while underwater.

She saw the nose of the bullet touch the skin of the bubble surrounding her enemy. She saw the skin dimple slightly, then bend slowly inward. She had a vision of herself lighting a match while sticking her head inside a gas oven.

Wexler knew it was time to abandon ship when he heard the machine guns on the front lawn. He didn't have to look out the window to know the score.

His body ached and his head felt like it was full of bar-room sawdust. He passed and repassed the vanity table's mirror as he got dressed, each time trying not to look at what she'd done to him.

The grimace disappeared after the first hour, but the facial tics that skewed his features into a death's-head grin occurred every ten minutes. He glimpsed the raw scratches left by her nails crisscrossing his back, shoulders and the flat of his belly. His dick was swollen and red, but sexual arousal had nothing to do with it. His penis hadn't felt so maltreated since the day in sixth grade, he'd jerked off twelve times in a row.

How long had she been in control? Hours? Days? The fact that she'd used him for her puppeteer experiment was reason enough to chuck it all. To hell with Elysian Fields! He'd welcome being shunned by his peers if it meant he'd be safe from that painted *thing*.

He found himself experiencing a delayed memory, mercifully blurred and missing its soundtrack. He watched himself service Wheele as if he were a spectator at a cheesy live-sex show, only there was no sense of excitement. His prick was hard—as rigid as it'd ever been—but there was no pleasure involved.

Wexler nearly retched on the shame flooding him. He'd been turned into a living dildo. He struggled into his pants, relieved to find his keys still in the pockets. His BMW was parked on the turnaround in front of the house. If he were lucky, he might escape while the two horrors fought it out downstairs, just like in the old monster movies he'd watched as a child.

He'd empty his bank account and take the first plane out of the country—it didn't matter where: Rangoon, Mexico City, Düsseldorf, even a malaria-ridden pesthole would be preferable to another night in Catherine Wheele's arms.

He eased down the heavily carpeted stairway, his Gucci shoes in one hand and the keys to his car in the other. Everything was so quiet. No, wait! He thought he heard the murmur of a woman's voice coming from the study, although he didn't recognize the speaker.

Wexler's testicles tried to crawl up into his belly, and his face twisted itself into a grotesque parody of a leer. The effect was devastating, transforming one of the country's leading popular psychologists into the stereotypical dirty old man—wink-wink, nudge-nudge. He'd have to lay low, anyway, until the facial tics went away. He doubted he'd sell many books looking like a refugee from an old Batman comic, even on *Donahue*.

The grass was wet with dew and other things, but he couldn't afford to be squeamish. He hurried toward his car. His luck had held out, after all. He wanted to laugh, but was afraid it'd set off another spasm.

Made it. I made it. Home free.

The shock wave slammed into him like a fist, knocking him to the ground.

He was in the middle of a firestorm whose flames did not burn flesh and bone but seared the mind. He felt something reach into him with knitting-needle fingers, exposing the soft, wiggling things at the bottom of his soul. The something had vermilion eyes and a gaping mouth outlined in blood.

There was a brief spasm of pain in his chest that mirrored that in his head. Wexler dropped alongside his BMW, felled by an exploding ventricle.

Wexler was the first, but not the only, victim of the blast to die of acute cardiac arrest that morning.

Coroners and emergency-room personnel claim that the hours between two and five in the morning are when most humans decide to enter or depart this world.

After a hard day shuffling papers and wending their way through the barbed wire of office politics, the victims go to bed, and during deepest sleep, where the dreams are never recalled, their hearts malfunction. Some wake up long enough to know what's happening to them; others don't. It's a perfectly natural phenomenon.

When the authorities got together with their files and maps in an attempt to discern a pattern in the madness and death that marked that night, their data resembled the concentric circles that mark an atomic bomb blast.

Two miles out: Dogs howled like lost things while neighborhood cats cried like abused babies. Children awoke in tears, screaming that a "red-eyed woman" hovered over their beds.

One mile out: Four epileptics suffered grand-mal seizures, including one previously undiagnosed case. Mrs. Darren McClintock, a widow and chronic insomniac, claimed she saw the outline of a woman, doused in blood, standing on her back patio.

Half-mile out: Nine recorded cardiac arrests were phoned in, four of them instantly fatal. Three of the attacks involved individuals not known to be suffering heart ailments. The surviving patients, when interviewed, complained of a vivid nightmare involving a "woman with red-glass eyes."

Three blocks out: Two suicides reported, both involving victims described as "perfectly normal" by family and friends. Mr. Jackson Marx, age thirty-eight, got out of bed without waking his wife, then retired to his study, where he blew the top of his head off with a handgun he'd purchased the year before as a precaution against burglars. Cynthia Anne "Cissy" Fife, age eighteen, was last seen watching the *Late Late Show* in her room. Her exact time of death is uncertain. She was found by her parents at eight the next morning. She used her manicuring kit to open her veins while in the tub.

One block out: Noel Landry, age thirty-four, fell asleep in front of the television at eleven p.m. His wife, Elizabeth, knowing he'd wake up on his own accord once the station went off the air, retired for the night. Landry woke as expected but took the shotgun from the hall closet with him when he went upstairs. He shot his wife and their two children (ages six and four) before placing the barrel in his mouth.

Ground zero . . .

She'd been unsure as to what would happen when the charge was purged, but Sonja never expected *this*.

Catherine Wheele stood with her arms splayed outward, like a small child playing Frankenstein. A greenish material seeped from the televangelist's nostrils, mouth, eyes, and fingertips. The muck possessed a faint luminescence, like a cheap glow-in-the-dark Halloween mask. Sonja recognized the viscous glop as ectoplasm, although in quantities unprecedented in the annals of paranormal history. Wheele literally dripped the stuff, like one of those grotesque toy monsters that squirt slime from every possible orifice when squeezed.

The ectoplasm writhed and bubbled, sculpted by invisible hands into humanoid shape. Sonja stepped back, wary of the phantoms emerging from the goo.

There was a ragged, hawk-faced man in overalls and a woman with hollows where her eyes should have been. The woman held a half-formed infant to her breast. An amorphous clump of slack-faced, empty- eyed children—joined like paper dolls—drifted in the phantom mother's wake.

There were ghostly senior citizens, walkers growing out of their hands, and cancer victims that could almost pass for living, save for the luster of their skin.

The entourage was dominated by the spectral image of a tall, well-groomed man with the manners of a fox. His three-piece suit merged with his flesh and his hands sprouted growths that resembled a bible and a microphone. Sonja recognized the man as being Zebulon Wheele, Catherine's late husband.

The final figure to emerge from the supernatural plasma was massive. Sonja belatedly recognized Claude's blurred features. She moved deeper into shadow, uncomfortable with the idea of brushing against the dead man.

There was a weird quiet, like the hush in the eye of a hurricane. The room was bathed in the strange greenish light given off by the assembled ghosts. Their odor was a cloying mixture of woodsmoke, burned pork, white lightning, and decaying roses.

Wheele blinked as if she'd emerged from a deep sleep. She seemed baffled by the witch light permeating the room. When she saw the blurred faces of those surrounding her, her sanity disintegrated.

The Claude-thing grabbed her, pinning her arms. She emerged from her state of shock, struggling fiercely to free herself, but it was no good. All she did was unseat her wig.

A weird chuttering—like the sound of high-speed helicopter blades—emerged from the mouths of the dead. They were laughing.

Zebulon Wheele separated himself from the others crowding around his widow. The dead evangelist gestured broadly, pointing to his wife. His lips moved, voicing a warped imitation of human speech. He sounded like a badly out-of-synch foreign film.

Sonja wasn't adept enough—or dead enough—to understand what he was saying, but she got the drift. So did Wheele, judging from the look on her face.

As if to drive his point home, the shade of Zebulon Wheele thrust his bible hand into Catherine's face and disappeared, absorbed through the pores in her skin.

The faith healer's body convulsed, then went limp. The Claude-thing let her drop. The other ghosts crowded around the fallen televangelist, watching as she twitched and shuddered on the floor.

Catherine Wheele lifted her head and grinned at the dead. It was Catherine's mouth, but not her smile. Her gaze fell on Sonja, but it was not Catherine looking at her. Wheele was wobbly on her feet, suddenly unfamiliar with high heels. She moved like a drunkard, her eyes and lips twitching like a poorly operated ventriloquist's dummy. Zebulon had been dead little over a year. That's not very long, as the dead estimate time, but it was enough to forget the complexities of flesh.

His fellow dead pressed against Catherine Wheele, their faces expectant. The eagerness in their expressions made her skin crawl.

Catherine Wheele's mouth opened and from her ruined larynx came a sound that might have been a word.

"Tak."

She gestured with a perfectly manicured hand, the fingers writhing.

"Taik."

The hand became a claw.

"Take," gargled the almost voice. The claw disappeared into Catherine Wheele's abdomen.

The hand reemerged a second later, slick with blood and clutching a length of pink intestine.

"Take," growled Zebulon. "This is my body."

Pale hands closed on the proffered intestine, stringing like a ghastly party streamer. The warped corpse laughter swelled as the Skaggs children grabbed their sister's entrails and began to twirl around her as if in a perverse May dance.

Wheele's hands dug deep into the wonders of her flesh, offering up the choicest morsels to the wraiths clustered around her.

Papa Skaggs snatched at his daughter's liver, his radiant fingers probing the cirrhosis scars. Mama Skaggs, having received her child's kidneys, unleashed a pungent shower of blood and renal fluid on the Persian carpet.

Claude was made a present of her uterus, while George Belwether received a lung. Mrs. Barker, who'd thrown away her insulin at Catherine's behest, was presented with a bladder. Mr. Winkler, who'd poured his nitroglycerine tablets down the drain, ended up with a matching set of breasts. And still they thronged about her, eager to participate in communion. Sonja watched as Catherine Wheele dispensed chunks of her body like an indulgent grandmother handing out Halloween candy.

When the last of the phantoms had received its due, Wheele turned and stared at Sonja with empty sockets, the eyes having been parceled out long ago. She stood there, waiting for Sonja to come and take her pound of flesh. Sonja wondered how much of the faith healer was actually left inside the shell that stood before her. Surely there wasn't much: Zebulon had been doling out fistfuls of gray matter at the end. She looked at the army of ghosts as they milled about the room, each fondling its own souvenir. She shook her head and stepped toward the door. Her desire for revenge had disappeared, leaving a heaviness in the pit of her stomach.

Wheele resembled a hideous scarecrow robbed of its stuffing. Her skin hung like an emptied sack. Zebulon's essence oozed from the empty sockets like a cheapjack jinn attired in otherworldly polyester. He hovered near the ceiling, scowling at what remained of his wife.

The hollow woman tottered, bereft of the supernatural energy that had sustained the illusion of life. She raised scarlet fingers to her blind face, the lower jaw dropping in a parody of a scream. There was no sound since she no longer possessed larynx or lungs.

How much did he leave? Just enough to know what had been done to her, that's all.

Catherine Wheele collapsed like a dynamited building, toppling into herself. The ghosts flickered, their faces dripping as they began to melt. Sonja Blue watched as Zebulon Wheele, Claude and the Skaggs clan ran together like candle wax. Within seconds the room was ankle-deep in viridescent muck. The ectoplasm's phosphorescence was already waning, and within an hour the stuff would be indistinguishable from fungus.

Sonja stared at the carcass sprawled amid its own viscera. Wheele's body was unmarked, except for the mutilation to the head. The medical examiner was going to have a hell of a time explaining this one as suicide.

Wexler lay on his back in the grass, one hand clutching the embroidered polo player over his heart. His feet were bare and a pair of shoes lay in the grass alongside him, the expensive leather ruined by the dew. His face was pulled into a crude parody of the classical Greek comedy mask. He reminded Sonja of the nameless hobo thrown into the racquetball court.

She shifted her burden as she bent to retrieve the keys to the BMW. Wexler refused to let go. She brought her boot heel down on his hand. The sound of breaking fingers brought a smile to her face.

She had to hurry. The cops would be there soon. She glanced over her shoulder at the mansion. She could detect a glimmer of the fire in the downstairs windows.

She unlocked the trunk, placing Claude's body inside. She'd made an improvised shroud from one of the drapes in the study. She'd used the other to start the fire.

It would be better, in the long run, that no questions be asked as to the exact nature of Wheele's demise. Mysterious deaths were one thing, inexplicable deaths another.

Sonja paused once more before sliding behind the wheel of Wexler's car. It was almost dawn and the morning air was redolent with the smell of death.

✳

The TV anchorman, his hair styled and face unmarred by frown lines or crow's feet, smiled into camera number one.

"... and congratulations to the zoo's newest proud parents!"

The smile dimmed, but did not fully disappear, and the anchorman lowered his voice to indicate the next item was serious.

"The city's police and fire departments continue to be baffled by what is being called Mad Night. Early this morning, during the hours between midnight and dawn, the city and its surrounding suburbs were plagued by an unprecedented number of violent domestic disturbances, suicide attempts, rapes, street fights, and outbreaks of arson. At least fifteen people are known dead and forty-five reported injured during the early-morning chaos.

"In a related news item, authorities are investigating what is being described as a 'Guyana-like spectacle' at the estate of controversial televangelist Catherine Wheele. The carnage was discovered early this morning when the city fire department responded to a three-alarm fire at Wheele's exclusive Jonquil Lane address. Details are as yet unclear, but Mrs. Wheele is believed to have perished in the blaze. Also listed among the dead is noted pop psychologist and lecturer Dr. Adam Wexler, author of the best-selling *Sharing, Caring and Swearing*.

"Well, so how's the weekend shaping up, Skip?"

"Looks like a doozy, Fred, with almost no chance of rain."

EPILOGUE

Children begin by loving their parents. After
a time they judge them. Rarely, if ever, do
they forgive them.
—Oscar Wilde

Sonja Blue stood among the monuments and watched them put Claude Hagerty in the ground.

It was drizzling and the rain served to muffle the words spoken over the casket. The coffin rested above the open grave on a machine that would lower the loved one into the cavity with the press of a button. Besides the sad-faced minister reciting the burial prayer, the only other mourners were an elderly woman Sonja guessed was an aunt and a couple of former co-workers.

Sonja quietly studied the old woman clutching a damp bouquet of Kleenex. She kept shredding and reshredding them as she stared at her nephew's casket.

Would his aunt appreciate the fact that she'd climbed the fire escape to Claude's apartment, all the way to the fifth floor, his corpse slung over her shoulder? That she'd tucked him in bed? No, probably not. She turned the collar up on her jacket and squared her shoulders against the rain.

Perhaps she'd done him a greater disservice in death than she had in life. If she'd left him among the smoking ruins of Wheele's mansion, at least he'd have had a decent crowd for his send-off. Atrocity victims are always popular. But that would have led to questions about exactly what a lowly orderly was doing at the home of a famous religious leader, and Sonja could not allow that.

"Ms. Blue?"

She'd been so involved in her thoughts she didn't hear him until he was at her elbow. She turned a bit too swiftly, and glared at the little man in the dark suit. A taller, younger man in chauffeur's livery stood behind him, holding an umbrella.

The little man in the dark suit faltered, his eye contact sliding across her polished lenses. He coughed into his fist.

"Ahem, Ms. Blue, my name is Ottershaw. I represent the interests of my employer,

Mr. Jacob Thorne. I have been instructed by Mr. Thorne to give this to you"—he produced a business envelope from his breast pocket— "and to inform you that, while he greatly appreciates the efforts you have taken on his behalf, he hopes you understand that he wishes to never see you again."

Ottershaw handed her the envelope and, having relayed his message, turned and walked toward a limo parked on the narrow road that wound through the cemetery, the chauffeur following him.

Sonja slit the seal on the envelope with her switchblade. It contained a cashier's check drawn on the family bank. She stared at the zeroes for a while, then at the limousine.

The windows were tinted black, but she could make out two figures huddled on the backseat. Ottershaw . . . and Thorne.

He's as guilty as Wheele. He told her to kill you. And you know he's the one who told Wheele where you were you were after you left his apartment. He probably even ordered Claude's death.

"Yeah, I know that."

Is that it? Are you going to stand here and let him get away with it?

The chauffeur started the car and the limousine pulled away, Thorne's profile a darker blur behind the glass.

Claude's funeral was over and none of the mourners stuck around to see him lowered into eternity. A cemetery worker operating a small earth-mover scooped fresh dirt into the hole.

Sonja stuffed the envelope into the pocket of her jacket and began walking toward the gates of the graveyard, threading her way through the field of the dead.

"What do you expect me to do?" she asked the Other. "He's our father."

Artist Bios

DAN HENDERSON. Dan Henderson's work has been seen primarily in the realm of "fine art" (he has a master's degree in drawing). He confesses, however, that his first love lies in the rich history of illustration and its potential for immediate and unavoidable evocation. Henderson has taught art at The American College in London, England and is currently a faculty member at American Intercontinental University.

MATT HOWARTH. Although Matt Howarth is best known as the creator of "Those Annoying Post Bros.", his work has appeared in the most unlikely places, illustrating Philip K. Dick to "Teenage Mutant Ninja Turtles" to his "Sonic Curiosity" music review comic strips. Now, he's illustrating Nancy Collins Who knows where he'll pop up next? Check www.matthowarth.com to find outmore.

KELLY JONES. Kelly Jones has been a leading comic book artist for over ten years. Specializing in the macabre and unexpected, his work has included such titles as DC's *Sandman*, *Batman* & *Deadman*, as well as the creator-owned *The Hammer* mini-series for Dark Horse.

PAUL MAVRIDES. Paul Mavrides' comics, paintings, graphics, performances and writings encompass a disturbing, if humorous, catalog of the social pathologies and shortcomings of human civilization. He is best known for bludgeon-like proselytizing on behalf of J.R. "Bob" Dobbs' SubGenius Foundation, his work with Gilbert Shelton on the Fabulous Furry Freak Brothers comic book series, and caustic black velvet paintings depicting various modern social and political disasters. His artworks have been shown in New York, Paris, Los Angeles, Berlin, and San Francisco. He recently served as Art Director and CG animator on a theatrical documentary film, GRASS, a history of American marijuana prohibition.

JEFF PITTARELLI. Jeff has been painting for nearly 20 years in the realm of Horror, Sci-Fi and Fantasy. His work was recently featured in THE CROW: SHATTERED LIVES AND BROKEN DREAMS an anthology in which Jeff illustrated a short story by Nancy Collins called "Variations on a Theme". His fondness for Bass Ale and Jamaican Blue Mountain Coffee only matches his strange collection of things in jars. To view the latest creations from The Illustrator of the Unreal, go to www.pittarelli.com.

HARRY S. ROBINS. Harry S. Robins (1950-) is an illustrator and internationally known comic book artist. He is also by turns a writer of plays, poetry and fiction, an actor, a public performer, a radio broadcaster and a Deacon in the Church of the SubGenius. His voice characterizations may be heard in the controversial and ultra-violent computer game, Half-Life, which in 1998 won the award for Game of the Year. Robins has lived in San Francisco since 1976.

STAN SHAW. Stan Shaw has been illustrating for various oddball clients all over the country. They include, The Village Voice, Esquire, Slate, Starbucks, Nintendo, Rhino Records, Microsoft, REI, BET, P.O.V., ABCNEWS.com, Amazing Stories and Willamette Week. This year so far he's done four Y2K illustrations. Stan was the artist on the official Sunglasses After Dark comic book adaptation from Verotik Publications (1995-1997).